By Dean Murray

Bound

Dean Murray

Published by Fir'shan Publishing

ISBN 978-1-9393631-8-3

www.FirshanPublishing.com

First Edition

For Cameron

If not for your friendship growing up I would have turned out much worse than I actually did.

Chapter 1

Alec Graves
Graves Estate
Sanctuary, Utah

It was exactly the wrong thing to say. I knew it as soon as the words hit the air. Jasmin probably knew it even before she opened her mouth, but that didn't stop her from saying it.

"Oh, yeah? Well, better a second-rate wolf than a third-rate hybrid who exists solely to serve as Brandon's whipping boy."

It was exactly the opening that Vincent had been looking for. He'd been riding Jasmin for days trying to get enough of a rise out of her to justify putting her in her place, but she'd been unusually calm—at least right up until that point.

Jasmin and I had slipped out to nearly the outer reaches of the estate in an effort to get away from the constant dominance games that were an inherent part of pack life. We'd found a quiet spot out by the mountain that overlooked Graves Manor from the north and hunkered down to do some homework.

Once upon a time just getting away from the house would have been enough to guarantee ourselves some privacy, but ever since Brandon had manifested his full hybrid ability Kaleb, my father—although I didn't like to think of him as such—had been giving him and his lackeys a much greater run of the estate.

Vincent backhanded Jasmin into a scrubby tree with enough force that she would have at the very least had a concussion if she'd been merely human. As it was she still hit hard enough to see stars, and her knees buckled as soon as her feet touched the ground, but she still managed to glare up at him from the ground.

"I'd tell you what I really think of you, you illiterate piece of crap, but I'd have to use words bigger than two syllables, which you wouldn't understand. Not even your own mother could put up with you long enough to teach you basic manners."

If Jasmin's first comment had been the spark that started a fire, this was pouring gas on the flame. Vincent had the incident he'd been angling for, but her comment must have actually upset him. Rather than playing things cool and using the opportunity to abuse her without actually triggering a full challenge, instead he screamed and shifted.

Jasmin had to be at least a little unsteady on her feet, but she likewise changed forms in an explosion of clothing that left fragments of material fluttering in a circle around her. As Vincent stalked towards Jasmin in his hulking hybrid form my pulse sped up.

A hybrid has a head, two arms and two legs, but that's about where the resemblance to a human being ends. Humans are tool users, hybrids are six-foot plus tall mountains of muscle and fur that were designed with only one purpose in mind.

Everything from the backwards-articulating knees, to the talons on their feet and the eight-inch semi-retractable claws at the end of each finger, spoke to the ability of a hybrid to explode into motion without warning and rend flesh as though it was nothing more than wet paper.

Jasmin hadn't ever manifested a third shape. She was a wolf now, sleek, fast, and deadly in her own way, but she wasn't a match for Vincent, not today, not as shaken up as she was after being thrown into a tree like that. There were things that were even bigger and nastier than a hybrid, but even if one of them had been close at hand it would have been just as likely to kill Jasmin as help her face down Vincent.

I knew Vincent wasn't going to be satisfied with just roughing Jasmin up. He might even be far enough gone to kill her despite the hot water that it would get him into with Kaleb. It was one of those times where nearly every part of me was screaming that it was time to panic, but I'd learned that these kinds of situations are usually when it's most important to take a second and calmly analyze my options.

The breeze played across my face and I took a deep breath, reveling for the briefest of moments in the smell of cedar trees and sage. There were a thousand other scents, some of them only just detectible to me in this form, but it was the cedar and sagebrush that formed the bulwark upon which all of the other scents rested.

I could hear Vincent's heavy stride and Jasmin's lighter, four-footed steps, but I tried to put that out of my mind as I let my eyes play over the landscape. The estate was situated around one of the area's only artesian wells, which meant it was a relatively unique pocket of green in the otherwise dull brown and red southern Utah landscape. Zion National Park was just visible off in the distance and it had its share of foliage as well, but between here and there was little more than rocks, dust, and dying plant life.

I looked back at Jasmin and Vincent and suddenly knew how to stop him. "If you attack Jasmin, then I'll kill you, Vincent."

I'd been half afraid that he was too far gone to register my words, but he pulled up as though he'd run into something.

"That's the prerogative of a pack alpha, Alec. If you're creating your own little pack then there's no need for me to stomp Jasmin into the ground because your dad will rip both of you into little pieces."

"I'm not saying that you can't challenge her, I'm just saying that once you are done fighting her I'll challenge you myself."

It was risky. Custom usually provided both parties to a challenge fight with a few days of immunity from dominance fights so long as they didn't get in people's faces over stupid stuff. We didn't have much in the way of hard-and-fast rules, but we shape shifters tended to treasure the few we had. They were the only thing keeping us from devolving into the savage animals whose forms we assumed.

"You've got an overinflated sense of your own lethality, Alec. Even if you manage to beat me using such an underhanded tactic, you'll still lose your own traditional period of immunity. There won't be anything stopping Nathanial and Simon from ripping you apart once you're done fighting me. You'll have people lining up to take you down."

My heartbeat had slowed back down. It was debatable whether or not Vincent was close enough to hear my pulse, but I found myself hoping he could. When you're up against people with superhuman senses it becomes very difficult to bluff. I'd found that it was just best not to even try. Instead I always tried to make sure that whomever I was up against understood exactly what I was prepared to do.

"I can take you down, and you know it, Vincent. I came out on top in both of our last fights and Jasmin is bound to do at least some damage to you no matter how badly you beat her in the end. It's not a question of *if* I'll kill you, it's just a question of what happens after you're gone. You may be right that Nathanial and Simon will jump in afterwards, but that's not going to make any difference to you, not once you're dead."

"Your dad has forbidden the pack from killing each other. He'll stick you in a box somewhere for a week while he decides whether or not to execute you."

"You can't have it both ways, Vincent. Either your friends are going to kill me or they aren't. I don't think you understand what I'm telling you. I don't particularly care how I go at this point, I just want to make sure that I stop you from hurting Jasmin before I go down."

"Maybe I should just kill you now and then I can do whatever the hell I want to Jasmin after you're gone."

"What about Kaleb?"

"Brandon will keep him off of my back. Your dad's not going to risk pissing Brandon off, not for you, not when you still haven't manifested that power that Mallory is so excited ab—."

BOUND

The transformation ripped through me in a flash as Vincent sprang at me.

Vincent had been talking to try and catch me by surprise, but I'd been expecting as much. I spent nearly every waking hour trying to keep my beast, the violent urges that separated me from a normal human, caged up, but I'd loosened the metaphysical chains on him as soon as I'd decided on this course of action.

I hadn't manifested one of the unique powers that made some hybrids even more deadly than the norm, but I was still a hybrid and I was slightly bigger and stronger than Vincent now.

Vincent came in low and fast, but I knew it was a trap. With another hybrid I might have gone for it and tried to latch onto his back so that I had a killing hold, but Vincent was fast enough that it was almost impossible to use that particular opening against him.

Instead of going high and trying to dodge to the side I dropped down even lower and dug my talons and the claws on my left hand into the dirt. With so many anchor points to the ground I was capable of generating a lot of force, but even so I knew it wouldn't be enough to let me straight-arm him away. Not even the awesome strength of a hybrid was equal to redirecting the force of two NFL linebackers at full run.

If Vincent was thinking clearly he would know that I was setting up to do something impossible, but I was counting on the fact that

Vincent rarely thought things through in the middle of a fight.

I had only a split second between when I got myself set and when Vincent hit me and I did my very best to sell the idea that I was about to meet brute force with brute force.

Vincent came in moving even faster than I'd realized, but by then it was too late. I threw myself forward as hard as I could at the same time that the claws on my right arm sank into the front of his chest. The tendons and muscles in my arm screamed in pain, but my hybrid body didn't feel pain the same way that my human one did. I knew that I'd just pulled a whole host of muscles up and down my arm and shoulder, but the pain was a distant thing that served only to inform rather than distract.

It was a very close thing, but I managed to get low enough and hold my arm straight enough that I redirected most of the energy of his attack upwards. The entire technique was tricky, but assuming that you were strong enough to keep your arm straight, then the most difficult part was figuring just exactly how much momentum to generate when you threw yourself forward at your opponent. Too much and you canceled each other out leaving the two of you more or less motionless but you at a disadvantage because your off hand was still out of position. Too little and you'd get bowled over and pinned to the ground under several hundred pounds of wickedly-clawed hybrid.

Things seemed to balance on the edge of a knife and then his momentum carried us backwards. I tried to convert the fall into a roll, but his right hand slashed downwards towards my head at the last second, and writhing out of the way of his attack forced me out of position.

Rather than me ending up on top it almost looked like I'd failed completely, but as we crashed into the ground I heard a meaty thud and Vincent relaxed his grip on me momentarily.

I shoved him off of me and rolled to my feet at the same time as he picked himself up off of the ground. Out of the corner of my eye I could see the rock he'd banged his head on, but there wasn't time to dwell on the sheer dumb luck that had saved me. Vincent still had an edge of grogginess to his movements so I charged in, raking the claws on my much-abused right arm across the outside of his leg.

My blow struck true and cut deep, but it was all I could do to dodge his follow-up strike to my head. The unsteadiness from hitting his head wasn't entirely feigned or he wouldn't have missed me, but it was obvious that he wasn't as far gone as he'd wanted me to think.

Neither of us seemed to have any fancy tricks left, so the fight moved into the brutal, sudden savagery of a normal hybrid matchup. I hadn't been lying when I'd said that I'd beaten him in both of our last two matchups, but those had been close fights and it was still too soon to tell who had the upper hand this time.

His next blow came at me too fast for me to completely dodge and hot trickles of blood started making their way down my chest as he tore a set of furrows in my flesh that were more than a foot long. Vincent was smiling now, his bestial lips pulled back to reveal long fangs. Nathanial and Simon had transformed into wolves and were yipping in excitement, but I'd sunk the talons on my left foot several inches into his leg as I'd tried to get away from his last attack.

It looked like he was following his usual route and trying to bleed me out, but it took a lot to bleed out even a normal hybrid and although I hadn't manifested a power yet I still wasn't just a normal hybrid.

I charged forward with a sudden change in direction that Vincent wasn't entirely ready for, and raked my talons across his leg again in return for a shallow slice on the outside of my left arm. His blow was hard enough to nearly knock me into the boulder he was trying to drive me towards, but the bones that ran along the outside of the arm served their intended purpose and protected the muscles and veins that otherwise would have been shredded by the attack.

Vincent's next blow had even more force behind it, but he'd incorrectly assumed that I'd continue working his leg. Instead of dodging away or just trying to deflect the blow, I stepped inside of the attack and sank my talons eight inches into the left side of his chest. Collapsing a single lobe in one of his lungs wouldn't be enough to put him down immediately, but another strike or two like that and he'd start feeling the need to finish the fight up quickly before I just ran him into the ground.

It still wasn't any kind of guarantee that I'd win, but I was starting to set things up for the kind of sudden upset that had allowed me to beat him the last two times.

I deflected the next two attacks away so that they hit the rock he was so busy trying to back me into and sent a shower of sparks skittering away. Nathanial and Simon had quieted back down when I'd landed that blow to Vincent's chest, but they were vocally happy again now that it seemed as though Vincent had regained the initiative.

I caught flashes of movement out of the corner of my eye as Jasmin positioned herself to jump into the fight if either of the other two interfered, but most of my attention was on Vincent as he stepped forward to launch another attack. His left foot was forward this time, which was exactly the kind of opportunity I'd been waiting for. I pushed off against the rock behind me, and hit Vincent head-on with as much momentum as I could muster.

The collision had only a fraction of the forces that had been involved in the one at the start of the fight, but he wasn't expecting it this time, and his right leg was the one that I'd been savaging every chance I got. It was just too much for him, and I rode him down as he fell backwards to the ground.

Just taking him to the ground would have been a point in my favor, but I managed to immobilize both of his arms and I sank my fangs into the muscle alongside his neck so that he couldn't get his fangs into me.

That was all just a sideshow though. It was an important sideshow, but the real action was the way that I'd managed to sink the talons on my feet into both of his legs. If I could keep his arms out of commission for long enough then I'd shred his legs to the point that they were all but useless.

It was like trying to ride out an earthquake. The last time we'd fought I'd been slightly stronger than Vincent, but it was starting to look like my advantage there had evaporated over the last few weeks. Vincent was fighting smart now, using short, explosive movements that strained my ability to hold onto him to the very limit. I couldn't hope to control the situation anymore, all I could do was try to stay on top so that he couldn't reposition and kill me.

I was moderately successful for another couple of seconds and then Vincent broke his left arm free of my grasp and sank it into my side only a couple of inches from where he'd already wounded me. Part of my lung collapsed at the same time that a spray of hot liquid leaked down onto my left arm and hand which I'd stuck into Vincent's side only a split second after he'd stabbed me.

In theory I was still winning simply by the fact that he'd taken twice as much damage to his lungs as I had, but this was turning into the kind of slow-motion demolition derby that had always seemed to end up favoring Vincent in the past. I needed to break free, but as I moved to try and disengage Vincent locked his claws around my ribs and made a fist.

The pain as the two ribs he had ahold of started to fracture was still muted, but I had to fight the urge to panic. I tried to push away, but that was all that Vincent needed to free his right hand and now I was in even more serious trouble.

He had better positioning by virtue of the fact that his arms were on the inside. I could tear the outside of his arms into ribbons, but that wouldn't let me get to anything vital and my efforts to attack him anywhere else were being made ineffective as he moved his arms to deflect the worst of my blows away.

I tried again to push away from him, but his right arm was buried in my chest now too, and the pain was rising to the level of excruciating. I had to be getting close to bleeding out, I simply didn't have any more time, so I took the only route left open to me.

I let go of the hold I had on his neck with my fangs and stopped pulling away from Vincent.

Instead of resisting his efforts to pull me closer, I added my strength to his and slammed my forehead down against his face with every ounce of force I could muster.

The shock of the impact made Vincent loosen his grip and I rolled off of him just in time to block another slash that was aimed at my already-mangled chest.

As I desperately backed away in an attempt to give myself enough room to avoid another clinch, I saw what was probably going to be my last opportunity. Vincent's footwork had continued to deteriorate as a result of the damage I'd inflicted on his legs.

I dropped my arms slightly as though trying to provide extra protection over the places on my body where he'd already done so much damage, and that was all the opening he needed. He sprang forward in an attempt to close and finish the fight off. It was a masterful display of the raw aggression that usually won Vincent fights, but he was a fraction of a second slower than normal and I used that fact to step off to the side, grabbing his arm and using it to pull him off balance so that the force of his spring threw him headfirst into the boulder just behind me.

Vincent hit hard enough that I half expected him to have a broken neck, but I couldn't afford to just wait and see how badly he'd been hurt. I jumped on his back, pinning him to the ground as I stuck my talons in to his legs so that I could control them.

I savaged his sides and back, digging until I'd managed to open up several of the veins that were closer to the surface, and then realized that it was time to make my choice. I'd been serious about my willingness to kill him if he attacked Jasmin, but that didn't necessarily mean that I had to kill him now. There was a lot to be said for getting rid of him once and for all. Vincent was the kind of scum who reveled in other people's misery and the world would be better off with him gone, but there were other considerations.

Kaleb factored in there in a major way. He'd forbidden fights to the death years ago and he'd consistently come down in a spectacular manner on anyone who broke that rule. There was a chance that he'd let me live because of the potential for future power that I represented, but there was no guarantee and if he did kill me then I'd be leaving behind people who currently depended on me for protection.

I knew that the allure of oblivion was a siren call that needed to be resisted, but despite that knowledge I still found myself digging my claws deeper into Vincent as he tried to buck me off. He had his arms underneath him now and he was struggling furiously, but there was a reason that hybrids worked so hard during fights to deny their opponents access to their backs.

I already controlled his legs by virtue of the steel-like talons sunk into the muscles he was trying to contract, but now I repositioned the rest of my body, sinking my fangs deep into the muscle of his left shoulder as my right arm snaked around and latched onto his right arm.

I didn't have to control his arms, all I had to do was just impede his efforts for a few short seconds while I used my left arm to end him. The possibilities were many. I could go for the heart or the neck, or even bleed him out by opening the veins that ran along the inside of his left arm.

The temptation was so strong that I sank the tips of my claws into his arm. I was half convinced that I should just do it, and then I got hit by a figurative wrecking ball and the question of whether or not to kill Vincent was entirely out of my hands. I rolled to my feet and faced off against Brandon, who must have arrived on the scene during the very end of my fight with Vincent.

"What's your dad going to think when I tell him that you were going to kill Vincent?"

"Nothing, because you don't have any proof that I was about to kill him."

I took in the rest of my surroundings as Brandon shook his head mockingly. James and Jessica had arrived too and, unlike Brandon, they hadn't shifted forms yet, but it was obvious that they were only a step away from rushing to my defense if I needed them.

"Alec, you can't really think that you'll get away with lying to your father."

"I'm not lying. I hadn't decided whether or not to kill Vincent yet, and everything I did up to this point was nothing more or less than you'd expect out of a dominant who was trying to discourage a rival from contesting their supremacy in the future."

Brandon gave me a considering look. He could tell that I was telling the truth, but it was obvious to me that he was weighing the odds. Jasmin and Jessica would counter Simon and Nathanial, two wolves to two wolves. Vincent was out of the picture and in fact needed some first aid or he was going to bleed to death sometime in the next few minutes, which just left Brandon, James and me. James was a hybrid too, but like me, he hadn't manifested any kind of special ability, so he wasn't any more of a match for Brandon's unnatural speed and strength than I was. At least not by himself.

Together James and I might have had a shot at beating Brandon, but there was no way to know for sure without actually fighting for real and if that happened, Kaleb would kill both of us for breaking his laws.

It was a moot point anyways. I was barely able to stand, let alone fight. I wouldn't be any kind of significant help for James and that meant that Brandon had the upper hand just like usual. He and his lackeys could kill us if they really wanted to, but unless they could goad us into starting the conflict then that would just mean that *they* would be the ones who Kaleb would make an example of.

It was a complicated, frustrating dance, but despite consistent rumors otherwise, it was all the two of us had been able to do for years now. We hated each other's guts, but as long as neither side messed up and did something to bring Kaleb down on the other side, there wasn't much we could do other than just insult each other.

"Maybe you're not lying, but that doesn't necessarily mean that you're going to get off scot free this time. I think it's time your dad really understood how much trouble you're causing inside of his pack."

I managed to keep my surprise off of my face, but I could tell by the way his grin widened that I hadn't managed to control all of the indications of my emotional state. I'd expected our two groups to posture a little more and then go our separate ways, but instead he was choosing to escalate things in a way he'd never done before.

It looked like I was about to find out whether or not the rumors were true. I was about to see just how much Kaleb was prepared to give Brandon in order to keep him happy.

Chapter 2

Alec Graves
Graves Estate
Sanctuary, Utah

Brandon ordered Simon and Nathanial into human form so that they could tie scraps of cloth around the worst of Vincent's wounds. As much as I would have liked to just stand there and glare at Brandon the entire time, I knew that I wasn't a whole lot better off than Vincent was.

After a fight where we'd almost died, my beast was subdued enough that it was a small matter to push it back into a corner of my mind so that my form shrank back down. Changing back to human form kick started the healing process and stopped some of the bleeding, but I had a lot less blood to lose in this shape, so Jess started ripping long strips of cloth off of her shirt as I walked back to her, James and Jasmin.

As Jessica's shirt was quickly turned into bandages, the black, stretchy fabric of her ha'bit became visible, which made me look down to make sure that my ha'bit had survived the fight more or less intact enough to cover the important parts.

The ha'bits allowed us to switch forms without worrying about the complications that would have been part and parcel of dealing with casual nudity inside of the pack. They were one of Kaleb's inventions, one of the few good things he'd done for the pack back before he'd thrown in with the Coun'hij, the shape shifter ruling body.

Jasmin changed out of her wolf form with a cool rush of power and then joined us. "James, give me your shirt so I can help Jess."

"It figures. Rachel just bought this one for me and now it's going to be turned into sixty-dollar bandages."

Jasmin shook her head at him as she accepted the shirt from him. "It's not like Rachel won't buy you another next week."

"Yeah, I guess you're right there."

Brandon had shifted into his hybrid form to tear me off of Vincent, but unlike everyone else, he didn't shift back to human form once the immediate chance of confrontation had passed. It was always possible that he'd worn too many different shapes today and was risking a painful set of muscle cramps as a result, but I was pretty sure that Brandon just enjoyed being a hybrid, enjoyed lording over the rest of us that he was nearly untouchable in single combat.

Brandon waved for Simon and Nathanial to pick Vincent up, despite the fact that it would have been much easier for his hybrid body to carry Vincent's bulk, and then we started towards the house. It wasn't until we were nearly home that I realized that there was probably a secondary reason that Brandon had chosen not to resume his normal shape.

With the ever-improving march of technology, it was harder and harder to keep the existence of shape shifters like us a secret from the world at large. Kaleb hadn't gone quite so far as forbidding everyone from wearing anything other than our human shapes outside in broad daylight, but the message had been clear. Short of some kind of dominance fight that arose too quickly for it to be moved inside to the caverns under the manor house, we were all expected to present unremarkable, human faces to the outside world.

Brandon had taken to breaking that guideline on a regular basis lately, but I was pretty sure that he was doing so today as a way of making the point that Kaleb valued him a lot more than me. It wasn't a particularly welcome reminder, which was of course exactly why he was doing it.

As we neared the house I tried to determine whether or not anybody was watching us approach. The house looked just like it always did, a massive block of stone and glass. Most of the manor was a single story, the natural result of building such a large structure back before air conditioning had been invented, but even the single-story sections were nearly as tall as a normal two-story house. The vaulted ceilings meant that during more peaceful times it was possible to open up the windows during the night and cool the house down enough that even July summers in Sanctuary were still bearable.

Kaleb had paid to have air conditioning units installed and piped into a number of key rooms sometime before I'd even been born, but by and large they were redundant. Sometimes the gray rock exterior walls managed to look inviting, but this wasn't one of those times. For all of the luxury and comfort contained inside of the manor house, it wasn't really a home. It was more a prison than anything else.

Mallory met us at the entrance to the suite of rooms that Kaleb used as his command center for all things pack-related. As usual she was dressed in dark colors—jeans, a utilitarian top, and a leather jacket. Mallory didn't need piercings and tattoos to look like she could have belonged to some kind of outlaw motorcycle gang.

"Shift back into something less ominous, Brandon. You're scratching up the stonework on the floor."

"What if I don't want to shift back?"

Mallory looked up at Brandon with a bored expression on her face. "Then you're an even bigger idiot than I thought. You've recently asked for a rather large boon from Kaleb, and I expect you're probably here to try and get Alec into trouble with his father. Do you really think that now is the best time to be trying to flex your muscles?"

Brandon bent down until his huge, hybrid face was only inches from Mallory's human features and when he talked it was in a low growl that humans wouldn't have been able to hear.

"I'll play nice right now, but you'd be smart to stop mouthing off to me. You're no match for me and sooner or later things are going to change around here."

Mallory was either a much better bluffer than anyone else I knew, or she really wasn't bothered by Brandon's threat. He was right, in a dominance fight Mallory couldn't hope to beat him. She was a hybrid, and she'd been around long enough to have the skills that came from dozens, if not hundreds, of challenge matches, but while she had manifested a power, it wasn't one that directly improved her odds if she came to blows with Brandon. With anyone else I would have figured that they were just an incredible liar, but Mallory was closer to my dad than any of his other advisors, so it was possible that she knew something that Brandon should be worried about.

I watched as Brandon followed the same trail of logic and I suppressed a small flash of satisfaction at Brandon's frown as he shifted back to human form. It would have been more satisfying if I'd thought that Mallory was a possible ally, that she wouldn't stick a knife into my back just as casually as she'd stick one into Brandon.

Mallory looked us all over and then grunted at Nathanial and Simon. "You two get Vincent to whoever is on medical duty. By the look of him he's going to be down for a couple of days at least, but at least go see if someone can get him back on his feet in time for his rotation down to the border."

Nathanial and Simon nodded unhappily and then headed down the corridor, at which point Mallory made a shooing gesture at James, Jasmin and Jessica. "It's not like we need any extra witnesses or anything. Go find something useful to do or barring that, at least get out of my sight."

Mallory watched until our respective friends had disappeared and then motioned with her head back towards the rooms she'd just exited. "Whoever was on duty saw the eight of you coming this direction fifteen minutes ago so Kaleb is expecting the two of you. He said to have both of you sent to his office."

I filed the information away and nodded. If she'd told us that he wanted one or both of us incarcerated until the next regularly scheduled public audience then it would have been a definite sign that we were headed towards big trouble. Anytime punishment was dished out in a public venue it was because Kaleb wanted to make an example of the offender. That wasn't to say that he didn't occasionally dish out spectacular beatings, literal or otherwise, in private, just that at least in private there was a *chance* that you weren't going to end up bleeding and wishing you were dead.

I waited a second to verify that Mallory wasn't planning on accompanying us in and then started towards Kaleb's office with Brandon only a couple of steps behind me. I didn't make it very far before Mallory stuck her head back into the foyer. "I'm well aware that you've been ducking me for the last few days, Alec. If I didn't have somewhere I needed to be, I'd be sitting you down right now for our session. Don't think that you can keep avoiding me forever."

Kaleb was leaning back in his chair waiting for us as we stepped into his office. I would have said he looked like a successful businessman in his slacks and dark blue polo, but there was something hard behind his eyes, harder than could be explained by just cutthroat business dealings. "Sit down so we can talk like civilized people."

The chairs were leather which meant that it would be relatively easy to clean my blood off of them once I was gone. I sat down and attempted to give off an air of unconcern. Brandon on the other hand looked like he was trying to come up with a way to remain standing or at least to make sitting down appear as though it had been his idea all along.

"I said sit down, Brandon. Trust me, you don't want to turn this into a pissing match."

Brandon frowned again and then nodded and sat down. I hoped that I was managing to keep my astonishment off of my face. Brandon was usually more of a smooth operator than this. Whatever he'd asked Kaleb for must be something he needed pretty badly in order to be so far off of his game.

Kaleb seemed content to wait for one of us to initiate the conversation, but I'd decided on the way down that I'd be best off acting as though I'd done nothing wrong. I hadn't technically violated any of the pack's rules, unwritten or otherwise, so I wouldn't be served by spouting off a bunch of justifications before Brandon had even had a chance to start making his case.

Brandon took a couple of seconds to gather himself and then launched into his accusations. "It's become apparent to me that Alec is directly working against you. He seems to be trying to create a splinter faction inside of the pack, probably in the hopes that he can set himself up as some kind of tin god out in the middle of nowhere."

I revised my estimates of Brandon's ability to lie upwards slightly. He'd put in plenty of qualifiers to cover himself, but I still would have expected his heart rate at least to go up slightly given that he knew I wasn't actually trying to tear the pack apart. Kaleb leaned back and gave Brandon an appraising look.

"I think that I just heard a whole lot of supposition, none of which justifies me taking time out of my day to see the two of you."

Brandon leaned forward with a smile on his face. "This piece isn't supposition, it's fact. Alec interfered with a dominance challenge between Jasmin and Vincent, which is the kind of thing that has always been the domain of pack alphas, not a second- or third-tier hybrid who happens to be your son."

"Interesting. Given that Vincent seems to have come off second best in that fight it would appear that the pack's 'second- and third-tier' hybrids are much more dangerous than I realized. Maybe I should be looking to have the pack expand its territory and spend more time down at the border killing those damn cats if the pack's pool of talent really runs so deep."

Some of my anxiety evaporated. I wasn't entirely out of the woods, but it appeared that whatever hold Brandon might have over Kaleb wasn't sufficient for the older hybrid to just roll over and give him whatever he wanted.

"Well, Alec. What do you have to say for yourself? Brandon's accusation, for all that he's more than likely elaborating on the truth, is a serious one."

"I've done nothing to splinter the pack apart." Mostly because it was already coming apart at the seams. "Furthermore, I in no way acted outside bounds of the position in the pack that my skills have won for me. Vincent lost our last several matches and I found that I didn't like his manner today, it wasn't properly respectful towards one who is clearly his better, so I informed him that I planned on challenging him." All of that had been inferred, even if it hadn't been explicitly stated.

"After he'd already challenged Jasmin!" Brandon's outburst was yet another sign that this meeting wasn't going the way he expected it to.

"I gave him a choice, it was entirely his decision to put off his dispute with Jasmin until after he'd dealt with me."

Kaleb gave me a dark look. "You're walking a very fine line there, Alec, but you're right, technically you've done nothing I can censor you for."

Brandon opened his mouth to protest, but Kaleb kept talking. "You've had your chance to file your complaint, Brandon. Your unhappiness has been noted. You can get out of my office now."

I would have just beaten a relieved retreat, but Brandon stood up and let loose a flash of power that made my skin tingle.

"I'm not some nobody to just be dismissed from your presence like that, Kaleb. My unhappiness can have very long-term ramifications for you and everyone else in the pack."

The natural response for any shape shifter when faced with the kind of metaphysical wind that was lashing out from Brandon was to counter with a surge of energy from our own beasts, but Kaleb was too controlled for that.

"You are a valuable member of this pack, Brandon, but don't think that I've failed to notice the way that you've been politicking lately. If anyone is trying to set themselves up with a power bloc it's you. You're unquestionably the best fighter in the pack, but that doesn't mean that you're irreplaceable, and it doesn't mean that I can't have you put down if you get too far above yourself."

Brandon laughed the threat away. "You just said it yourself. You don't have anyone else in the pack who can beat me. The only reason that you're still running the show around here is that I haven't decided to take over."

"No, I still run the show around here because you're too inexperienced to run things yet and you know it. I'm the pack alpha, which means I can kick you out of the pack at any time with the most threadbare of pretexts. If that happens it's the entire pack against you and while you're really quite good, you can't take on the entire pack at once, not by yourself."

"I wouldn't be by myself. There are people in the pack who would support me over you if it came to that."

"Sure there are, but for the most part they are just a bunch of wet-behind-the-ears kids without much real combat experience. Mallory and I are keeping a very close eye on where the wind is blowing and you're still a very, very long way away from having a chance of pulling off some kind of coup d'état."

"I don't have to overthrow you, I could always just take my people and leave."

Kaleb shook his head. "Let me give you a free bit of advice about these kinds of things. You never get all of the people you think you're going to get. There is always a larger contingent than you think who are happy to talk big, but when it actually comes to striking out, leaving home and going off to establish a brand-new pack they end up chickening out. You don't have anywhere near enough people to actually create a viable pack that would have a chance of holding its territory."

I'd expected Kaleb's remarks to put Brandon even further on his back foot, but if anything he seemed more confident than before.

"It's only a matter of time. Eventually I'll have enough, and then I'll either take this place over, or I'll take my people and leave. Eventually you won't be able to stop me."

Kaleb sighed. "This is the last freebie, kid. There isn't anywhere you can go where you'll be safe if you piss me off. I run the Coun'hij. Do you really think that there is a single pack anywhere in North America that would raise even the slightest fuss if I had your entire pack destroyed? If you continue to work with me I can make it very worth your while, but if you cross me I'll bury you."

Brandon was actually speechless for the first time I'd seen in months. It took nearly a full minute before he shook off the shock. I suspected that he was smart enough to read between the lines and understand that Kaleb was threatening to unleash Puppeteer on him if necessary. Brandon was good, but Puppeteer would swarm him under without even breaking a sweat.

"I understand your position. Does that mean that you're refusing my request from the other day?"

"No, I haven't decided with regards to that yet. I meant it when I said that you'd be rewarded if you work with me, and I understand that on some level rewarding your people is the same as rewarding you, but I'm not entirely sure about this particular reward. There are obviously some…complications with that sort of thing. You're going to have to be patient for a time still."

Brandon shot one last parting comment back over his shoulder as he left. "My patience isn't infinite."

"I'm well aware of that fact."

I started to stand to follow Brandon, but Kaleb waved me back down into my seat and then watched the closed-circuit monitor to verify that Brandon left the suite rather than staying to eavesdrop.

"Close the door, Alec."

While I saw to the door, Kaleb turned on the white noise generator that had sat on his desk for as long as I could remember. I hated the crackle and hum that it created, but it was a necessary evil in a house full of shape shifters if you really wanted privacy.

"What you did today was reckless and I want to be clear that a repeat will be punished very severely."

I opened my mouth to protest but Kaleb talked right over me. "I had someone debrief Simon and Nathanial while they were waiting to see if Vincent would be okay. The report hit my monitor before Brandon left. The long and short of it seems to be that Jasmin shot her mouth off and you got involved rather than just letting her deal with the consequences of her actions."

"Vincent has been riding her for days. She can hardly be blamed for losing her temper."

"Yes, she can. She's got the heart of a fighter, but this isn't the first time that she's written checks with her mouth that she can't cash. If this were a single incident I might have a different view of things, but it's not and she's not going to learn any different if you shield her from the consequences of her actions."

"What exactly is she supposed to learn, Dad? That Vincent is an ass and she just has to put up with whatever he decides to inflict on her?"

I'd meant to just use his name like always, but somehow it had just slipped out. It wasn't like I thought it would buy me anything.

"That's exactly what she needs to learn. It's not fair, but it's the way life works. The pack needs aggressive, strong fighters, and Vincent pulls as much or more time down on the border than anyone else we've got."

"So just because Vincent is a better killer Jasmin has to suffer?"

"Yes, not to put too fine a point on it. I'm fighting a war, Alec, and that means that I need soldiers. Jasmin probably would have adjusted to her lot in life years ago if you'd just let things follow their natural order. Instead, you've covered for her time and time again and the result is that she's constantly getting in over her head and you're getting involved in fights that you can't win."

"I beat Vincent just fine."

"No, Alec, you got lucky. I can see that just by looking at you, but even without the obvious evidence of how close you came to losing, I could still have predicted that Vincent was too much of a handful for you now. He's been in combat at least fifty percent of the time for the last six months. This is the longest stretch of time that he's been back in Sanctuary at once and the only reason he's stayed this long is because I ordered him to take some time off."

"So send him back out there. It's not like anyone around here will miss him."

"No. Vincent needs some downtime. Even the most aggressive warrior will eventually burn out if he's in a hot zone for too long. Besides, things work best when the two of you are kept far apart and it's past time for you to spend some time out on the frontlines yourself. I've tried to give you time to manifest a power out of all that potential that Mallory is convinced that you have, but I can't wait any longer. The cats have pushed back up above the Mexican border and I need more bodies down there."

Kaleb rubbed his eyes and then took in the damage to my chest with another wave. "The other packs have noticed that I've kept you and some of your friends out of the fighting longer than is normal and some of them are starting to complain. The truth is though that even if the war wasn't going against us I'd still be sending you down there. You need more experience. You need to toughen up or the next time Vincent will come out on top and there's no guarantee that he'll be satisfied with just putting you in a bed for a few days."

"If he did that you'd be forced to kill him."

"Don't be so sure of that, Alec. You're creating a lot of resentment in the pack with the way you're acting lately. You're trying to swing above your weight class and everyone knows it. Only the fact that you're my son has kept some of the old guard from putting you in your place before now."

My beast surged up in a flare of power. It wasn't the full heat of a transformation, but it was close. I knew that I wasn't a match for Kaleb, but we'd never actually fought so my beast didn't share my certainty and it didn't like the way that Kaleb had just called us weak.

"This isn't about your friends from back in the day, Kaleb, this is about the fact that you would let Brandon protect Vincent despite yelling at me for protecting Jasmin."

"You still don't get it, Alec. Brandon is becoming a force in this pack. I wasn't lying earlier when I said that I could still deal with him if I had to, but I don't want to resort to calling on Puppeteer to wipe out a third of the pack. I *need* the people he's so busy trying to splinter away from me. Things with the rest of the Coun'hij are balanced on a razor's edge right now. I'm holding onto control of the Coun'hij by a margin that is so slim that you'd have to be directly involved with our meetings to appreciate it. If I lose control of the Coun'hij things will get a lot worse."

"Yeah, a lot worse for you."

"No, a lot worse for this entire pack, and a lot worse for the rest of the shape shifters out there. Puppeteer likes to exercise his control over the werewolves and he's not particularly picky about who he uses when he feels like it's time for an object lesson. I know you've never been involved in any real fighting, but try to imagine for just a second what the estate would look like if two dozen werewolves came through on a rampage. Your mother, your sister, everyone who wasn't fast enough to get out before the house was surrounded, would be killed."

"Even if you lost control of the Coun'hij, Puppeteer wouldn't dare attack us like that. We're the largest pack in all of North America. The rest of the packs would band together and destroy the Coun'hij if they tried anything like that."

"Don't be so sure, Alec. Nobody banded together when the Coun'hij took down the monarchy however many thousands of years ago. There have been plenty of other packs that Puppeteer has wanted to take a hardline position with recently. Jaclyn and her people down in Arizona have been especially difficult lately, and while Jaclyn's power makes her more than a match for any normal hybrid, her pack wouldn't have a prayer even against just a dozen werewolves. I'm the only thing holding him in check right now."

Kaleb suddenly looked tired and a part of me wanted to forget all of the times he'd screwed me over during my life and not be quite such a jerk towards him. It was a tempting prospect to imagine that we could still be one big happy family, but experience had shown me that Kaleb always had some kind of ulterior motive when he was acting the most reasonable.

"The truth is that our pack has simply gotten too big, Alec. We're ten percent bigger than the Chicago pack now and given all of the kids running around here we'll probably see as many as two dozen more shape shifters join our ranks in the next four or five years."

"So let Brandon split off. He'll take most of the undesirables with him and life will get a lot easier."

"Undesirable to you maybe, but Vincent and the others are some of our most promising young fighters. I need them, I need every person we've got if I'm going to keep control of the Coun'hij. You're at least partially right, the sheer size of our pack serves as an incredible deterrent for everyone from the dispossessed all the way up to guys like Puppeteer. I'm going to eventually have to let the pack fragment into smaller units, but that needs to happen in the right way and at the right time. I've got to hold things together until the pack can split into three parts rather than just two."

Kaleb pointed at the door that Brandon had used to leave and then pointed at me. "I'm hoping that Brandon will take part of the pack and that you will do the same. If we split the pack three ways then you'll be able to help me make sure that Brandon doesn't get out of control. It will get rid of a lot of the internal pressure that we're experiencing right now, but as long as the two of you base your packs somewhere close then it goes a long way towards preserving the deterrent that we've built up right now."

It was the best bait that Kaleb could have possibly trolled out in front of me and he knew it. I'd wanted a way out for years now, but this represented something even better—a way out not just for me, but for the people who were important to me as well.

"That's right, son. That's the reason that I haven't made any kind of fuss about the way that you're starting to create your own little power bloc. Ultimately that's exactly what I want you to do. I would have let Brandon split off already but I'm trying to hold things together for long enough that your power can manifest and give you the most important tool you'll need as a pack alpha."

It was a tempting vision of the future, but I knew it was nothing more than a mirage. I tried to conceal my disbelief behind a well-worn bitterness regarding my situation. "It appears that you're going to be waiting for a long time. Maybe it's time to start developing some contingency plans."

"Your power will manifest eventually, Mallory is sure of it. She's never seen someone with your sheer level of potential fail to manifest a power and she's seen a lot of hybrids come and go, both inside the pack and outside of it, in the last few decades. Don't lose heart, Alec. This is bigger than just you or me. There are a lot of people, more than you can imagine, depending on us getting this right."

Chapter 3

Alec Graves
Graves Estate
Sanctuary, Utah

I left Kaleb's office wobbly on my feet from blood loss and mentally and emotionally exhausted. Part of me wanted to just go curl up on my bed and sleep off the worst of my injuries, but I knew that would only solve my physical problems, so I headed the other direction, away from my bedroom, towards one of the few sources of solace that I still had.

My mother's suite of rooms occupied nearly one whole side of the wing that housed them. Built during a happier time, back before Kaleb had been able to wrangle himself a spot on the Coun'hij due to the sheer size of his pack, Mom's rooms hinted at what Kaleb might have been if he hadn't decided to pursue power at any and all cost.

It took more than five minutes to cross the length and breadth of the house, but the journey was worth it. I knocked on her door and then at her invitation I entered into what felt like an entirely different world. Most of the house seemed to consist of dozens of long halls with no natural light, but Mother's rooms were liberally sprinkled with windows that allowed plenty of light in regardless of the hour or season.

The masterpiece of the entire suite was the receiving area in its center which was a giant solarium that contained dozens of plants, an exquisite grand piano, and half a dozen simple chairs scattered into different corners of the room. Some of the tension seeped out of me as my mother and my sister Rachel looked up at me and smiled.

Mother was dressed in a light cotton dress that looked like it belonged on a runway in Paris. "Come sit down, Alec, you look like you've had a rough day."

As I made my way around the greenery that seemed draped on every horizontal surface, Rachel jumped to her feet.

"Can I get you something to eat or drink, Alec? You probably need to build back up your reserves after being in another fight."

"Thanks, Rachel, the usual would be great."

"Right, one baby elephant, raw, coming right up."

I rolled my eyes at her as she left, started to sit down, and then stopped as I realized I'd get

Mom's chair bloody if I did that. Mother turned the fountain at the center of the room to full strength and then motioned at the chair again.

"Please, Alec. Sit down. The chair can be cleaned up later, but you look like you're carrying the weight of the world on your shoulders. What happened today?"

The fountain served very nearly the same purpose as Kaleb's white noise generator, but was much more pleasant than the hissing and pops that the small boxes produced.

"Vincent has been baiting Jasmin for days now. She's done a decent job of keeping her cool until today. She said something that really pissed him off and he was pretty much ready to rip her head off, so I intervened."

An uninformed viewer might be forgiven for thinking my mother frail, but while her body was indeed slender to the point of almost being unhealthy, there was something in her eyes that gave lie to that appearance of weakness. Mother would never go toe to toe with someone like Vincent, not given that she was *only* human, but there was a strength of will to her that exceeded anything I'd ever seen out of anyone else.

"I can't fault your loyalty to your friends, Jasmin especially, but you risk so much each time you put yourself between one of them and Vincent or the others. If your father decides that you're getting above yourself the consequences may be profound."

"I know. I've already been to see Kaleb. I got off on a technicality, but I think he mostly went easy on me because he started to expose a little bit of his master plan to me today. He's hoping that I'll manifest an ability soon, and that it will be strong and useful enough that he'll be able to set me up as a counterweight to Brandon."

I almost missed the fine tremble in her hands as first she and then I mentioned Kaleb. Someone else probably would have thought that there wasn't anything wrong, but I'd had years to learn the subtle signs. She was still occasionally able to maintain her composure enough that I didn't notice what it cost her to talk about him, but today wasn't one of those days.

Mother noticed my stare and shrugged away my concern. "It's not as though we can avoid talking about him. I actually relish the withdrawal symptoms. It means that I've succeeded in staying away from him for longer than I thought possible at one point."

Of all the things I hated Kaleb for, addicting my mother to his touch was at the very top of the list. All shape shifters gave off an energy that provided a subtle high for the humans who came into contact with their skin, but the effect was magnified for the most powerful hybrids and Kaleb was one of the most powerful shape shifters currently living.

"Why do you let him re-addict you?"

She sighed and then looked towards the door that led to the kitchen where I could just hear Rachel pulling together a light snack for us.

"I wish I could give you an answer and feel like it was the full truth, but I'm not sure *I* really know. I keep telling myself that I stay because of you and Rachel, that I stay because of the innocents that are born into the pack every month, that I'm doing all of this because, although Kaleb has a terrible hold over me, I also have a different kind of hold over him. I'm doing good by being here. I wrangle concessions out of him that make life better for the weakest members of the pack, but there is a tiny part of me that whispers late at night that I don't leave because I don't want to, because his hold over me is stronger even than I want to admit."

It was a rare moment of vulnerability for my mother and I didn't know how to respond, but she shook off the brooding air that had come over her while she'd been talking and smiled at me as Rachel walked back into the room.

"Sorry, Alec. I'm afraid that we're fresh out of baby elephants in there, but I did round up some cheese and crackers."

"Thanks, Rach. That sounds perfect."

Rachel set the large silver tray down on the low table that our chairs were arranged around and then frowned.

"You guys have paused like you were having a conversation that I'm not allowed to participate in."

I saw a flash of alarm in Mother's eyes, but lying to Rachel was a simple matter compared to dealing with other shape shifters.

"It wasn't anything big, Rach. I was just telling Mom about my latest run-in with Dad."

There was an innocence to Rachel that usually made me refer to Kaleb as our father in her presence. At fifteen she was more than old enough to understand all of the ways in which he didn't deserve the familial title, but she still held out some kind of childlike hope that we'd find some kind of justification for the worst of what he did and that would in turn allow us to be one big happy family again.

"How did things go?"

I shrugged, unwilling to disillusion her further. "About like normal. He told me that I'm not measuring up and threatened to punish me if I can't get my act together."

Rachel frowned, but Mother had pulled herself together enough to defuse the situation. "Rachel, dear, why don't you go to my bedroom and grab the bags from our last trip down to Vegas. I've been thinking about that black cashmere sweater we bought. I think we should give it to Jasmin, but let's see what Alec thinks before we actually wrap it up."

Rachel rolled her eyes at us. "I know that you're just trying to lose me so that you can go back to talking about stuff you don't want me to know, but I'll go as long as you agree to take me shopping again next week."

Mother smiled. "I should know better by now than to try to pull the wool over your eyes, my darling. It's a deal. Will Las Vegas suit or do you want to range further afield than that?"

Rachel shrugged. "I'll think about that and get back to you tomorrow." A second later she'd disappeared into the hall that led towards Mother's bedroom.

"I'm glad that your conversation with your father went okay, Alec. How did you feel about his offer to set you up as a pack leader?"

"It was tempting, but the more I think about it the more I realize that you can't be set up as a pack leader. It's the kind of thing that you have to earn yourself or you'll always be looking to whoever installed you as alpha in the first place to secure your position."

Mother's smile and nod was like a ray of sunshine. "I think you're absolutely right there, and I think that you would find that the arrangement your father has in mind is less about you helping put the brakes on Brandon and more about you and Brandon occupying each other so that he can remain in ultimate control with the minimum amount of effort possible."

I picked some crackers up off of the tray and nodded as I chewed. She watched me for several seconds before frowning.

"There is something else bothering you."

"Yeah, I guess there is. Kaleb said that he is working for a greater good again. What if Rachel is right, what if there is just some kind of misunderstanding that's making us view his actions in the worst possible light?"

"I...well, I think that it reflects well upon you and Rachel that you both want to believe the best of your father. I'm not going to tell you that he's completely evil, but you've had enough interaction with him to know at least some of the things that he's capable of. The only caution I can give you is that in the more than twenty years that I've known him I've found myself wanting to trust him again and again, but each time that happened he used my trust to further some goal of his own at my expense. Be careful, Alec."

I swallowed past a lump in my throat. "You're right. He as much as said that I should have let Vincent kill Jasmin today rather than putting myself at risk like that."

I could hear Rachel making her way back to us, so I let the subject drop. Rachel reappeared a few seconds later with the black sweater that Mother had sent her for, and a black, long-sleeved t-shirt for me which I slipped over my head with relief.

I wasn't anywhere near as powerful as Kaleb, but there were times when I was pretty sure it was all that Mother could do to stop herself from brushing up against my skin regardless. Now that my arm was safe to touch, Mother reached over and patted it.

"Alec, there's something else bothering you still. What is it?"

Rachel frowned. "Does this mean I have to leave again?"

I shook my head. I hadn't realized it until it had been pointed out to me, but my mother was right. There was something else bothering me.

"No, Rach, you can stay. It's not any kind of big deal, I just had that dream again."

"The one with the blonde girl?"

"Yeah, the one with the blonde girl."

"Did the two of you talk this time? If you're having the same dream, of the same person, this frequently then it's significant."

I snorted. "It's just a dream, Mother. My power hasn't activated yet, so there's nothing significant there. I didn't talk to her in the dream because she's not a real person."

"Alec, you live in a world that most people would tell you was impossible, a world where people shift into wolves and hybrids and go off to do battle against werewolves. Just because you can't explain it doesn't mean it's not important or any less real for having occurred entirely inside of your own mind. What do you remember? Was there anything new at all this time?"

"I don't think so. It was pretty much the same as always. I watched her from a distance and then she disappeared. The only thing odd about it is how she made me feel. It was like I was supposed to be with her, like she was important, but in a way that I knew I wouldn't remember when I woke up."

"Did she feel familiar?"

"I think so. She felt like someone I'd known for years. It was like she was an anchor I could latch onto and feel really safe for the first time since I was a kid."

Mother patted my arm again. "I think that these dreams are significant, but I don't know how exactly. For now I think you should write down everything you remember of them when you wake up and keep an eye out for the girl in case you run into her in real life. You never know..."

Whatever else she'd been about to say was cut off by a knock on her door. Donovan, our butler, stepped inside the room a half second later.

"I'm sorry to interrupt, my lady, but I'm afraid that I must announce a visitor. Your husband is on his way."

The tremor was back in Mother's hands as she picked up a large bottle of perfume and sprayed it into the air, but she kept her composure admirably. "Thank you, Donovan."

I was already standing by the time that Mother turned back to Rachel and me.

"The two of you should leave now. You can take the garden exit."

I helped a greatly subdued Rachel to her feet and then followed her out of the solarium. We threaded our way towards the west garden door, but some impulse made me stop short of the exit.

"Go ahead, Rachel. I'll be along in a couple of minutes."

"Alec..."

"It's fine, Kaleb probably hasn't arrived yet and I need to tell Mother one last thing."

Rachel didn't have the advantages of one of the moonborn, the shape shifters, but she seemed to know that I was lying regardless. She shot me an unhappy look and then opened the garden door and disappeared behind one of the tall hedges that were liberally sprinkled throughout the garden.

I crept back towards the solarium, stopping with enough doors between Mother and I that I could just barely make out her heartbeat. With the fountain positioned as it was in the middle of the solarium it would tend to push the sounds of her and Kaleb's voices towards me at the same time that it muffled and prevented the sound of my heartbeat from making it to Kaleb. I'd noticed months ago that everyone in the pack seemed to assume that once a white noise generator was activated they were safe from being overheard, but it actually mattered quite a bit where the noise generator was positioned.

I didn't have to wait very long before Kaleb arrived.

"I was right, you did have visitors. You never spray that damn perfume unless you've had someone here within a few hours of my visit."

Kaleb took a deep breath. "Alec and Rachel. I suppose that shouldn't come as any surprise.

Rachel hardly leaves your side and Alec usually comes running to you after every time we meet."

"You're guessing, just like always. You know that I've sprinkled scents from nearly all of the pack into that perfume mixture. I don't know why you bother trying to ascertain who I'm entertaining, you know I won't confirm or deny any of the names that you throw out there."

"I *guess*, as you call it, because I want you to know how ineffective your little efforts at subterfuge really are."

"No, you guess because you want to see my reaction each time. You continue to hope that I'll give something away on one of your visits. You know I won't do anything of the kind."

"You're a magnificent woman, Samantha. Few humans are so adept at concealing their thoughts and feelings from the moonborn, but your control over yourself isn't perfect. You let things slip still, not as much as I might like, but much, much more than you realize."

"What do you want, Kaleb?"

"I've honored your wishes. I allowed Donovan to announce me well in advance of my arrival, I gave you time to send our children scurrying to safety, and I entered through the designated door, leaving all of your other bolt-holes unwatched. I've complied with all of your little rules and in return I'd like to spend some *quality* time together with my wife."

"I have some demands that will need to be met before that can take place."

"Of course you do. Not surprisingly I have a few demands of my own. Shall we let the games begin?"

The tremble from before had made it into my mother's voice now.

"You're a complete monster, Kaleb."

"Of course I am. Just be glad that I've never decided to put your willpower to the test, my love. I've considered doing so a thousand times, but I have a feeling that in the end you'd break and if that were to happen, then you'd be so much less fun than you are now."

"You greatly overestimate your charms, Kaleb. You're welcome to try to break me any time. My willpower is equal to anything you can bring yourself to visit on me. The mere fact that you've waited so long to try is plenty of evidence to the fact that you know you'd fail, that you'd finally free me of the last hold you have over me. You just can't bring yourself to destroy one of the few remaining spots of decency in your life."

"That's an interesting theory, my dear, but the truth is that I'm simply reluctant to risk permanently damaging you. I rather suspect that I would have to look far and wide in order to find another woman able to fight the skin addiction, the Ja'tell bond so well. I've taken other lovers over the years and I can honestly say that once they are addicted most of the sport is gone. You on the other hand provide me an unending source of fun."

It sounded like she threw something at him, but he must have caught it because he was laughing as he set it down.

"It's been quite a while since you've gotten that riled up so quickly. The withdrawal effects must be especially bad this time around. You know, the mere fact that you've stayed around for so many years is the best evidence of all that you can't bring yourself to let go of your shameful little addiction. You'd have left years ago if you'd had the willpower required to truly kick the habit."

"No, Kaleb, it isn't your touch that keeps me here, it's the thought of what you'd do to the few remaining decent people in this pack if I weren't here to negotiate concessions from you. If I thought that I could take them all with me and disappear to someplace where you'd never find me, I'd do so in a heartbeat."

"There's your first mistake. There is no place where you could go that I couldn't find you."

I turned and crept back towards the garden door. I'd heard enough. If I'd had any doubts about the fact that my father, that Kaleb, presented a different face to Rachel than he did to my mother or others, they were settled.

I no longer had any questions where Kaleb was concerned. If only it was as easy to solve the riddle of my recurring dream. I had a lot of other things that I knew should be more important, but the question that kept surfacing inside my mind was *who was she?*

Chapter 4

Alec Graves
Lambert – St. Louis International Airport
St. Louis, Missouri

I actually hadn't flown much considering that our family owned two private jets. A lot of the pack liked to claim that it was the tithe from the pack that supported some of the more extravagant trappings of wealth that Kaleb indulged in, but I had it on good authority from Donovan that the tithe was an almost insignificant percentage of the income that my father had him managing.

Our family had been in positions of power for centuries and they'd been gifted with a large number of able financial managers during that time. The actual origins of the family's wealth had been lost in the mists of time, but I suspected that it had a lot to do with the tithe, in some form or another, which had been paid by early members of the pack and the monarchy to my ancient ancestors.

My father claimed to be working towards some greater good, but I suspected that more than anything else he just wanted to see himself restored as the ultimate power over our people. A lot of the expenditures that Kaleb made were absolutely done to maintain the kind of opulence that went with ultimate power. I didn't agree with that on a number of levels, but the planes had actually been a good purchase, one which I supported entirely—not that my approval meant anything.

Neither of the planes were the kind of hangar queens that only rarely made it up into the air. Both planes were worked and worked hard. Other than the occasional shopping trip for Mom and Rachel, nearly all of the rest of the usage came down to operations like the one that we were currently on.

Kaleb had apparently been serious when he'd said that he was going to start sending my friends and me into the field. He'd called us all into his office yesterday and told us that we were being deployed to St. Louis today.

Jasmin had actually been excited at the prospect of getting out of the manor house and seeing some action. Jess had been doing her best to hide just how scared she was, while James was obviously worried about his mother. Addison had long been one of my mother's most staunch supporters inside of the pack.

Back when my parents had first gotten married Addison's support, contrasted against the grudging acceptance nearly everyone else had displayed, had garnered no small amount of favor with Kaleb. As the years had gone by and Mother had become further and further estranged from Kaleb, Addison had become more and more tormented by the rest of the pack.

Mother had done her best to protect Addison, and Kaleb had agreed to forbid the rest of the pack from challenging Addison to any kind of dominance fight, but that hadn't stopped some of his people from tormenting her in a thousand smaller ways.

James had been a fierce protector of his mother for as long as I could remember. Back even before he'd manifested the ability to change to a wolf, he'd still gotten in the face of anyone who harassed his mother when he was around. It had earned him far more than his fair share of beatings over the years, but things had just escalated once he could shift. A wolf was almost never a match for a hybrid, so his aggressive defense of his mother had meant that he had taken a lot more damage from the few hybrids who'd still had it out for his mother after so many years.

Jasmin and I had both been worried that James would end up dead before he hit sixteen, but his relentless refusal to back down where his mother was concerned, combined with his complete disinterest in fighting for almost any other cause, had earned him a kind of grudging acceptance from the hybrids that he tangled with.

They all knew that they could wipe the floor with him at any time, but after a while they'd stopped doing the things that caused him to get in their faces. That would have been a tremendous win for a young wolf, but he also tore into any and every wolf he even suspected was tormenting his mother.

He was too young and inexperienced to win very many of even those fights, but they were always much closer affairs and his opponents quickly realized that it was a lot easier to just avoid a fight with James than it was to continue to tangle with him and risk getting beaten and losing their current position inside of the pack dominance hierarchy.

It was an admirable display of James' loyalty to his mother, and it was when I'd first realized that dominance inside of the pack wasn't just about who could beat who in a fight, it was also about who was the most passionate about what they were fighting for.

It took a lot of willpower to throw yourself into a fight that you knew you'd probably lose, a fight that might even result in your death, but if you did it often enough, if you were determined enough, then you could effectively swing above your weight class and convince people who were more dangerous than you to back down.

James, Jasmin and I had used that principle to good effect several times over the first year or two after we'd manifested a second form. It had generated some unhappiness inside the pack, but we were careful to only use it defensively, which meant that for the most part the people who were grumbling were the kind of bullies nobody particularly liked in the first place.

Life had been pretty crappy for those first years, but then James and I had manifested the ability to shift into hybrids and things had gotten better. The wolves had pretty much left us alone after that, and even the hybrids mostly didn't bother us unless we were truly out of line. They knew we'd hang together and that as soon as they healed up from fighting one of us, another one would be challenging them.

Life got a lot better for James' mom after that, but he and she both knew just how fragile her newfound peace was. If James were out of the picture, or even if our little coalition lost too many members to back James up, then she'd once again become an easy target.

James had stewed about it for the entire flight out to Missouri, but once we arrived at the airport, the hybrid Kaleb had put in charge of our operation snapped James out of his funk.

Jack had been with the pack since before even Kaleb had taken power. He was a grizzled old hybrid who was partway into his third century and he had a history of raw aggression in dominance fights that had allowed him to carve out a spot towards the top of the food chain a long time ago.

The aggression that had served Jack Senior so well had proved to be his son's undoing. Jack Junior had been killed in a dominance fight only a few months after he'd first turned, and a lot of the fire seemed to have gone out of his dad since then.

As near as I could tell, the posting out to St Louis was a blessing and a curse all wrapped up in one for Jack. Kaleb had used Puppeteer two years ago to shatter the stranglehold that the vampires had on the city. For centuries we wolves had fought a defensive shadow war with the vampires. Our biggest advantage had been that the vampires didn't even know we existed. We'd used our knowledge of them to kill them whenever they ventured outside of the cities that were their natural breeding ground, but the urbanization of America had meant that their reach had continued to grow while we were slowly pushed out of one city after another.

A lot of people had said that Kaleb was courting disaster to attempt an all-out frontal assault on St Louis, but he and Puppeteer had proceeded with their plan despite the disapproval of most of the individual packs.

Puppeteer had used his power to bring scores of werewolves into the city. Werewolves were even bigger than hybrids and seemed to view anything other than another werewolf as their rightful prey. We shape shifters had tried to wipe the werewolves out a couple of times in the past, but the disease that transformed them from thinking people to mindless beasts was an unusual strain of rabies that had an extremely long incubation period.

No matter how drastically we cut back their numbers, they eventually came back and started killing innocents again. The only good thing about werewolves was that they tended to be fairly solitary and they preferred preying on vampires more than humans.

Puppeteer's ascension to the Coun'hij had resulted in a drastically different policy on the part of shape shifters towards werewolves. We weren't allowed to hunt them down and kill them anymore. Instead Puppeteer was cultivating them as elite shock troops that only he could control.

Nobody was exactly sure how Puppeteer's particular gift worked, or what exactly his limits were, but he was able to control individual werewolves completely enough to force them into massive cages which he'd then used to ship them into St Louis. Some of our pack had been stationed along the major routes out of the city, so even those of us back in Sanctuary for the operation had heard firsthand accounts of large semi-trucks, each containing three or four werewolves, being unloaded in the outskirts of the city.

BOUND

Every so often they'd get a call from an untraceable number instructing them to let one of the werewolves out. It was always obvious which werewolf they were supposed to free because it would go from snarling and hissing to quiet and calm. Our people would open the cage up and each time the werewolf would run off into the night under Puppeteer's control.

There were rumors that the werewolves our people had been responsible for had been nothing more than backups. The rumors said that Puppeteer had arrived in town on a large commercial bus the night the operation started and that the bus had been filled to the brim with werewolves that he'd compelled back into human form for the duration of the trip until he could unleash them on the unprepared vampires of the city.

I wasn't sure how much faith to put in those particular rumors. Puppeteer was possibly the most hated member of the Coun'hij. He, if he really was a male, had gone to great lengths to keep his identity a secret. It seemed very unlikely to me that he'd really arrived in town with a bus full of werewolves, but if he had, he wouldn't have allowed anyone to live to spread that particular tale around.

The siege of St Louis had lasted nearly seven nights, but when the dust settled hundreds of vampires were dead and the humans were blissfully unaware of the scope of the battle that had just been waged inside of their city.

For some reason that no one understood, werewolves exercised as much care to remain undetected by humans as both we and the vampires did. They occasionally preyed on humans, either to feed or to replenish their numbers, but that usually only happened when there wasn't a shape shifter or a vampire around to provide a more tempting target.

The only sign of their presence in a particular town was usually the rolling blackouts that they invariably spawned. It didn't manifest when they were in human form, but once a werewolf shifted forms to the bestial, two-legged animal that had spawned so many legends, they served as a kind of energy vortex, grounding out electrical power as well as short-circuiting any abilities that a vampire or a shape shifter might try to use on them.

In a lot of ways werewolves were the ultimate predators. Their superior size and strength meant that on a purely physical level they were more than a match for any single hybrid, and their unique ability to nullify special powers meant that any fight involving a werewolf was fought on an exclusively physical plane.

Once the bulk of the vampires in the city were either dead or disorganized and demoralized, Puppeteer had marched his werewolves back to the empty cages they'd arrived in, and forced them to remain still as our people had locked them back up and loaded them into the trucks that were awaiting them.

Ever since then, Jack had been stationed here in St Louis with a squad of wolves to support him. The wolves scoured the city each day looking for the distinctive old-blood scent trail of vampires. When they tracked a single vampire back to its lair then Jack and the wolves were more than capable of eliminating it, but when they found a nest of vampires he called for backup and Kaleb would reroute a squad through St Louis on their way down to fight the cats on the southern border.

The position meant that Jack was away from all of the things that reminded him of his son, but it also meant that he was out of circulation enough that a good percentage of the up-and-coming hybrids now viewed him as a target that they could take down in order to bring up their own standing in the pack.

The fact that he'd fought several challenge matches against the people Kaleb had sent out to help him was evident in the cautious, almost resigned way that he greeted us as we walked across the scorching hot blacktop the plane had landed on.

"Am I going to have any problems with you lot?"

James and I looked at each other and then I shrugged as a stray breeze teased my nose with the smell of hot rubber and jet fuel. "I'm not particularly interested in fighting you, Jack, and my beast seems remarkably calm right now. If you can avoid lording the fact that you're in charge over us, then it's possible that we can avoid any kind of petty fights."

Jack grunted and then nodded. "Okay then. My boys and girls have found a group of four or five vampires that need to be taken out. The four of you, plus me and the four of my people I can spare means that we should have them outnumbered roughly two to one."

"Roughly?"

James' question could have been interpreted as questioning Jack in some form or fashion, but Jack showed an unusual amount of restraint and just answered the question as though it was nothing more than a request for information.

"Vampires are easy as hell to track because the scent of a vampire is so distinctive, but that signature scent is so strong that it can be hard sometimes to identify individuals. I had my best people scour the area and then added a third again as many vampires as they felt like they could identify. That usually works out to about the right number of vampires, but the system isn't perfect."

"What's the worst-case scenario that we're looking at?"

"Them waiting for us, fully prepared for an attack and outnumbering us two or three to one."

My question apparently hadn't been respectful enough. It had triggered a pulse of power from Jack's beast and a short, almost dismissive, response from him which in turn sent my beast dashing towards the surface, eager to display its own dominance and power.

I didn't want to fight Jack. I wanted to get the operation done and go home, hopefully without anyone on our side getting seriously injured. My beast had other ideas though. *He* wanted to beat Jack and demonstrate conclusively that we were tougher. Increasing our dominance inside of the pack would mean safety for us and our friends, but my beast didn't care about that as much as he did testing himself against a worthy opponent, an opponent who had just questioned his status.

My flare of power triggered an even bigger flash of energy from Jack, which tipped some kind of lever inside of me. What started out as a steady but containable pressure inside of me suddenly crested into a tsunami of power that ripped through me in an unstoppable explosion that could only have one outcome.

I felt the transformation trigger, but I knew now wasn't the time. We were in full view of the public and a dominance fight between Jack and me would just cause Kaleb to come down on me like a ton of bricks.

I'd never stopped a transformation when it was this far along, but this time I had to stop it or the consequences would impact more than just me. The rush of power didn't want to be stopped, it fought me as it looked for an outlet through which to escape.

Molten lead surged up through my core and rebounded off of my will. I'd never realized the full extent of my capabilities before. I'd thought I'd tested myself previously, but now I realized that I hadn't, that I'd always had a safety net, always husbanded reserves of strength for a future time of greater need.

These reserves went up in a flash of heat and fire as I latched onto the forces that were trying to tear my body open and remake it into something more dangerous. I directed my mental hands into that stream of pain and grabbed hold of it in an effort to stop something that I wasn't sure was even possible.

The power seemed to grow even more ferocious as I tried to control it. Heartbeats seemed to pass as hours in my fight to keep control of myself. I almost thought I had the battle won and then suddenly my beast crashed into my defenses, lending his considerable power to the forces trying to shift me.

I lost my grip on part of the power and it streamed through my body once again, but I had managed to funnel it even though I wasn't capable of controlling it. My right hand shifted, taking on the longer proportions and deadly claws of my hybrid form.

Jack took a step back in astonishment as he saw my limited transformation. "I thought you said I wasn't going to have any problems with you."

"I said that I'd try not to get in your face as long as you didn't lord your position of command over me. You didn't exactly make that easy."

My words came out through gritted teeth. The human part of me still didn't want to fight, and the transformation had bled off an appreciable chunk of the energy that my beast had conjured up, but my beast was still pushing for a confrontation, preferably a deadly one so that we'd never have to worry about Jack coming back for a rematch.

"Look, I really don't want to fight you, Alec. If I apologize will that be enough to let you keep control of yourself?"

"I don't know, give it a shot and let's see where things go."

My response was too curt. It was the kind of response that generally led to an escalating pattern of posturing, but Jack just held his hands up in a calming manner.

"I'm very sorry that I took your question the wrong way. Let's just finish this briefing so that we can go beat on the vampires rather than on each other."

It wasn't a great apology as things went, but the mere fact that he was making it told my beast that Jack didn't want to fight us. There could be a lot of reasons for his reluctance to embrace a dominance challenge right now, some of which might not have anything to do with fear of us, but I'd just done something I'd never done before and my beast was prepared to be magnanimous given just how likely it was that my display of a partial transformation had intimidated Jack.

The pressure inside of me reduced to the point where my hand was able to shrink back down to its normal size and shape.

"It looks like that did the trick. Thank you for the apology. You were saying?"

I could tell by the set of his jaw that Jack didn't think that my response was conciliatory enough, but he let it stand.

"In answer to your question earlier, I don't know for sure how bad things might get. Our entire operation here has been designed to keep our presence, our very existence, secret from the bloodsuckers. We've been hoping that they'd key into the werewolves as the only threat that they are facing and that they'd attribute our ongoing reduction of their numbers to more werewolf kills or else to infighting between various factions among the vampires."

"You're not confident that you've been entirely successful though?"

Jack shook his head. "There's no way to be completely confident, not given the fact that some of the vampires still alive in the city are undoubtedly powerful mentalists. The odds that one of them will happen to scan the minds of one of our people rather than one of the humans is incredibly small, but if we operate in close proximity to the vampires like this for long enough it becomes just a matter of when rather than if."

Now wasn't the time to be questioning the policies that Kaleb and the Coun'hij had settled on, but I couldn't help myself.

"Once they figure out that there are more supernatural threats out there than just the werewolves, how likely do you think it is that the information will spread?"

Jack shrugged. "It's impossible to say. Inside the city it will probably spread pretty quickly. The different vampire elders and factions may not be on good terms, but an external threat like that always goes a long way towards making people set aside their differences. Their only real difficulty will be in making contact with each other. We've kept them from developing the kind of social hubs that they had in the city before, and I expect that the different factions don't have each other on speed dial or anything."

"What about the odds of it spreading to other cities?"

Jack looked as unhappy as I felt. "I just don't know, Alec. I would expect that there is much less in the way of information flow between cities, but what information flow there is won't have been as disrupted by our operation here."

"So really it's only a matter of time before the vampires know about our existence and we're actively hunted by them."

Jack nodded, seemingly unwilling to put his assent in words. I let my statement hang in the air for a few seconds. It was a chilling prospect for any shape shifter to consider. We tended to live for three to four times as long as humans, but our fertility rate and resulting population growth was commensurately lower. That meant that a war was especially devastating to our population base as we had a hard time replacing individuals in a short period of time. The Sanctuary pack seemed to be an exception to that iron-clad rule, but nobody seemed to know exactly what was going on there.

Vampires on the other hand were a parasitic organism that could grow at almost exponential rates as long as their host population held out. One vampire could conceivably infest multiple humans per day who could in turn each infect additional people. There was a limit to how fast the vampire population could increase without becoming common knowledge to the humans, but apart from that, or them running out of people to feed on, there was realistically no top end on how many vampires we could find throwing themselves at us if they decided to try to wipe out our entire race.

We'd always relied on secrecy to shield us while we tried to wear down the vampires' numbers, but Kaleb and Puppeteer had said that it was only a matter of when rather than if the vampires would discover us, and they'd thrown millennia of tradition to the wind.

There might have even been some justification behind their position that we needed to strike now while Puppeteer could field armies of werewolves on our behalf, except for the fact that our race was also prosecuting a war against our cousins who lived in South and Central America. It was very much feeling like we'd put ourselves into a two-front war that we couldn't possibly win.

Jack seemed to be waiting for me to give him permission to proceed. It took me a little aback until I realized that it was the natural effect of what had just transpired. We hadn't had a dominance challenge, but his words and actions had established me as at least somewhat dominant to him. It probably wasn't even something that he realized he was doing, but on an instinctual level he was going to defer to me at least slightly.

I'd had it happen with those my age or younger, but it was a heady thing to have someone of Jack's age and experience deferring to me. I took a deep breath and reminded myself that being dominant didn't equate to being qualified to lead.

"Please proceed, Jack. You're the expert and the four of us are simply here to assist you."

He shook himself slightly and I got the idea that he'd just realized that he was deferring to me and he didn't particularly like that he'd been doing so.

"The plan is to try to lure or drive the vampires out of their den. It doesn't do us any good to outnumber them if we can only send a fraction of our people up against them at any given time. I can do a full briefing once we're back to the hotel that we're currently using as our base of operations, but I think you're all going to like this."

Like it indeed. The plan involved using explosives and small, hopefully contained, fires to drive the vampires into a large, empty warehouse. I would have said that it was reckless, but Jack seemed confident that his people could keep the blaze from getting out of control and that the fight would be long over by the time the police and firefighters arrived.

Pseudo-dominant to him or not, it wasn't my place to second-guess his plan, so I nodded in all of the right places and a few hours later found myself sitting with James in a dusty corner of the ambush warehouse as the sun went down.

"How long have you been holding out on us, Alec?"

"What are you talking about?"

"Being able to shift just your hands like that is a big deal."

"I haven't been holding out on you. I didn't know I could do that until just this afternoon. I'm not even sure that I could repeat it."

"Well, once we're back home you should spend some time figuring out how to do it and then we should start telling everyone. That's going to be a huge deterrent for guys like Vincent."

I shook my head. "I'll see if I can replicate it, but this needs to stay quiet."

James looked at me like I was crazy. "Alec, it's a big deal. Only the most powerful hybrids have that kind of control over their transformation."

"I'm still the same guy Vincent practically hospitalized a little while ago. Maybe you're right and this is a sign of good things to come, but right now it would just be painting a big target on my back. Maybe it would make Vincent back down from the next fight, but it would also bump me up into the territory where Brandon would start fighting me instead of just insulting me all of the time. I'm not ready to go up to the next weight class yet. I'm planning on trying to get Jack off by himself before we go and asking him to keep it quiet too."

"You're sure you don't feel any different?"

"Not even a little bit."

James looked disappointed. It seemed like everyone had something riding on whether or not I managed to finally manifest an ability that would make me a force within our pack and the wider world. Sometimes I wished that I could tell everyone to go away. I already had enough to worry about just trying to keep James, Jessica and Jasmin safe, not to mention our families.

It wasn't like I didn't have help, but in some indefinable way I knew that I was the lynchpin to it all. With me it all hung together more or less well enough to keep everyone alive and in one piece. Without me it would just be a matter of time before our entire wobbly house of cards came down.

Further conversation was cut off by the sound of an explosion. The building muffled it, but to shape shifter ears it was still loud enough to serve as a signal that we were about to be up against company. James and I spread out slightly to give each other room to work. I looked back to confirm the position of the exit that we were guarding and then as I felt a surge of energy from James, I also loosed the chains on my beast.

The roar of power from my beast was greater than I remembered it being. It was like I'd satisfied my beast that it could take the kid gloves off and it was responding by doing exactly that. My transformation ripped through my body, lengthening bones and bulking up muscles at the same time that claws formed on the end of each finger.

Despite my words to James earlier I did in fact feel a little different. My skin felt tight and there was an extra measure of restless energy bouncing around inside of me. I opened my mouth to tell James that maybe I'd been wrong, but the sound of running feet stopped me before the words could form.

The vampires came pouring through the door on the far end of the warehouse and there were more of them than we'd been expecting. I counted seven emaciated, dirty figures led by an eighth, a huge man who was nearly as big as Brandon in his human shape.

The leader already had a pair of smallish hand axes out and the two vampires at the back of the pack were armed with swords, but as the vampires saw us the other five of them pulled out a motley assortment of weapons that ranged from short swords and knives to lengths of chain.

Based on the sheer amount of noise still coming from behind the vampires Jack was making sure to move slowly and give the vampires plenty of time to get out into the center of the warehouse before arriving on scene.

"We may only have seconds before the ones from behind us catch up. Spread out and swarm these two under."

The siege of the city was obviously having an impact on the vampires. Other than the leader and one or two others, this group all moved with an obvious exhaustion, but as they got close to us and massive amounts of adrenaline dumped into their systems they started moving more quickly.

Jack had doubtless heard the leader giving orders because the cacophony of sound from the other end of the building had stopped and only half a second later Jack and the others appeared behind the vampires.

The vampires compressed back towards a wall as wolves came streaming around the other side of the open space so that they could support James and me. Jessica and Jasmin were closest to us which was reassuring on several levels. I liked the idea of having them close enough that I could support them if things started going badly for one of them, and I was more comfortable with the idea of having them backing me up than Jack's people, even if Jack's wolves were the more experienced fighters.

"Spread out and try to use our advantage in numbers."

Jack's voice was barely recognizable as a consequence of the changes that being in hybrid form put onto his vocal cords, but his people moved forward without any hesitation. I stepped forward, James and the others at my flanks, and suddenly the room was engulfed in combat.

The leader took a swing at me with the axe in his right hand, but it was nothing more than a feint. I dodged backwards and then tried to slash his arm with my claws before he could recover, but he was superhuman fast.

His offhand flicked his axe forward and knocked my claws wide a split second before the weapon in his right hand licked back out and nicked the top of my left arm.

I knew it was just the opening stages of the fight, that we were just feeling each other out still, but so far he was proving to be the better fighter. It wasn't a realization designed to fill me with confidence.

I caught snatches of the fight around me as I backpedaled to get out of range of his next attack. James was up against a skeletal-looking woman with a huge two-handed sword and a look of intense concentration on her face while Jasmin and Jess were squared off against what looked like a kid our age who was stabbing at them with a pair of short swords.

My guy slashed at me with a complicated double attack that I couldn't follow and only barely managed to knock aside with the back side of my claws, and then someone screamed and I saw one of Jack's wolves burst into flame. She hit the ground and rolled in an effort to put the fire out, but it continued to burn despite her best efforts.

Jack swore and picked his opponent up, spinning once before throwing the struggling man into the vampire who was responsible for the fire.

"Quit screwing around and just commit. You're fighting their kind of fight instead of our kind of fight!"

He was right. Facing off against people who were armed instead of against hybrids or wolves had thrown us all off of our game, but Jasmin was the first to recover. I saw her take advantage of an opening and throw herself at her opponent, jaws finding his throat as Jess grabbed hold of his right arm, slowing it just long enough for Jasmin to plant her legs and start whipping her vampire back and forth.

James was trying to create an opportunity to get in close to the girl he was fighting, but she seemed to be anticipating every move he made. He was already bleeding from half a dozen slashes to his arms and legs, but even more concerning was the spot where she'd stabbed him in the chest. It had obviously missed his heart, but he was clearly outmatched.

My vampire attacked again, burying one of his axes in the muscle of my left arm before spinning away and grabbing another axe from his belt.

I couldn't see enough of the rest of the fight from where I was standing to tell whether or not Jack's people were holding their own, but our little corner wasn't going well. Jasmin was still trying to kill the vampire she had latched onto. He'd dropped one of his swords and Jess had ahold of his arm again to prevent him from stabbing Jasmin with his other weapon, but he was proving remarkably hard to finish off.

It was only a matter of time before Jasmin and Jessica succeeded in killing the vampire they'd been fighting, but there was no telling how much longer James was going to last and that was even assuming that they didn't get wrapped up in a fight with one of the other vampires.

My opponent looked like he was experiencing some of the same kind of frustrations I was feeling. I hadn't succeeded in marking him yet, but it was obvious that he'd expected to beat me already and be on to his second or third opponent.

He needed to connect with a blow to my neck or chest if he was going to end our fight quickly and so far all I'd given up was strikes that were only slightly more than flesh wounds.

He attacked again, but this time his hands were slightly out of position. There was a very high likelihood that the opening was something he'd left there on purpose in an effort to draw me out, but I couldn't afford to pass it up, not if I was going to help James and the girls.

I took the opportunity, but I took it the same way that I would have attacked another hybrid. My left hand shot forward claws seeking for his chest, but at the same time I charged forward with all of my considerable weight bearing down on him as my right foot came up so that I could sink talons into his stomach and carry him to the ground.

Against an off-balance hybrid it was a devastating attack. Against a vampire who couldn't weigh much over two hundred and thirty pounds or so, it was practically guaranteed to be successful. It was just a question of how much damage he'd do to me as I killed him.

Only suddenly it wasn't a foregone conclusion like I'd thought it was. My left hand hit *something* a few inches in front of his chest, something hard and unyielding where my eyes were telling me that nothing existed. I'd been leading with my left arm and while bringing my left arm to a complete halt wasn't sufficient to completely arrest my forward momentum, it was definitely enough to slow me down. It felt like the barrier hadn't been intended to stop as much force as I'd generated. Rather than a plate of steel, it now felt like a block of wood. I could feel my claws catch on imperfections in the surface as my talons sank into my opponent's flesh.

He'd set himself and was trying to bring his axes back around to take advantage of the edge that his telekinetic shield had bought him, but the combination of my talons in his belly and the force of me slamming into him, even slower than I'd intended to, was enough to knock him off balance and break his concentration.

As his head slammed into the warehouse's hard concrete floor his shield disintegrated and my claws tore into his chest. Mindful of just how hard of a time Jasmin was having putting her vampire down, I put my other hand through his heart and then rolled back to my feet.

Jasmin and Jess were still working their fallen vampire over, so I sprang at James' opponent. I was coming in from the side and slightly behind her, so there was no way for her to have seen me, but somehow she still started around, almost managing to bring her sword up fast enough to impale me through the heart. I managed to slap the blade aside at the last second, claws screeching against steel, and then I was within arm's length of her.

She blocked my first strike with her hilt in a masterful display of swordsmanship, but James grabbed both of her arms in his claws and a second later she was dead despite all the advantages that her hardy vampire constitution gave her.

In the end the pyromancer vampire started another of Jack's wolves on fire, but Jasmin ripped his throat out before the blaze managed to really get burning hot. I visually checked the vampires over as I walked towards Jack, confirming that none of them were a threat anymore.

"What next?"

Jack looked at me and shook his head. "We need to get the wounded into the vans and start first aid on them. I'll start dousing the vampires in oil and we'll torch them before we go."

"Where is the oil? I'll go grab it."

Jack grabbed my arm, his lethal claws gently stopping me from turning away without breaking the skin.

"You need to get into the van with the rest of the wounded. We don't have much time and I'm not eager to have to carry you there if you pass out and don't shift down to your normal form."

"What do you mean? I'm fine."

Jack pointed at my right side and I looked down to see that my first opponent, although off balance and disoriented, had still managed to sink both of his axes into my side before I killed him. I made it four more steps before my knees started to buckle. I passed out about the same time as I hit the floor.

Chapter 5

Alec Graves
Clean and Tidy Chain Hotel
St. Louis, Missouri

The clock said it was eight a.m. when I woke up in what was obviously a modest hotel room, but there was no way to know for sure how many days I'd been out. I pulled my sheets back and gingerly probed the bandages that had been liberally applied to my side. They didn't hurt, which was a good sign, so I stripped back the corner of the biggest bandage back to verify that the flesh underneath had knit back together.

The wounds had scarred over already and were starting to trade in the pink of recent scars for the white of old scars. Given that Kaleb had wanted us down at the border less than twenty-four hours after we arrived in St. Louis, that was bad news. Normally I'd have said that it would take roughly twenty-four hours to swing that much healing, but that didn't match up with it being morning rather than evening.

The only answer was that I'd been more injured than I'd realized and I'd been down for at least thirty-six hours. I'd heard plenty of the older members of the pack quietly complaining that Kaleb's troop deployments never seemed to include any leeway for injured people, so I already knew that he'd be pissed that we'd missed our scheduled flight down to Arizona.

There wasn't much to do but go find someone and figure out just how much trouble we were in. I pulled some clothes on, grabbed my phone, and walked out into the hall. Our rapid healing was sure nice when it came to getting us back up and mobile after a fight, but it tended to leave muscles sore and subject to cramps, so I gingerly stretched my arms and torso as I walked.

The hotel was a single-story, sprawling structure that was kept clean enough that I was having a hard time picking up scent trails from any of the other shape shifters, so I walked to the front desk and tapped the girl manning it on the shoulder.

She turned around and I nearly gasped in surprise. I'd spent so many weeks and months wondering about the girl from my dreams and here she was. I was at such a loss for words that the silence stretched out into something uncomfortable.

"Can I help you?"

It was like I'd been punched in the gut. The voice wasn't right. It was silly, I couldn't remember my dream girl ever having spoken, but the voice I'd just heard didn't belong to the person I was looking for. That realization caused the rest of the illusion to unravel. This girl looked very much like my blonde, but there were differences. The eyes weren't quite the right shade of blue and her lips were slightly too full.

"Sorry, for a second I thought you were someone else."

The semi-annoyed, startled look was gone from her face. Her expression was much more inviting now.

"I'm pretty sure that we've never met—I think that I'd remember you."

I made it off of the estate so infrequently that it still took me by surprise when a female showed interest in me. Part of me wanted to respond in kind, to get to know her, to pursue the possibility of a relationship, but I refused to be so selfish.

It was impossible for my kind to have a normal, healthy relationship with a human. If I'd had any doubts of that watching my mother and Kaleb for so many years would have cured me of them. Actually, now that I thought about it, the odds were overwhelmingly on the side of the blonde from my dreams being a human as well.

The thought was depressing enough that I didn't manage to keep my feelings entirely off of my face.

"Are you okay? You suddenly look like someone drowned your puppy."

I mustered a smile that I knew from experience was believable for anyone that didn't know me well and shook my head wryly. "I'm sorry, seeing you made me take a stroll back down memory lane, which is always a dangerous thing to do when you've had as rough a week as I've had."

She looked like she was about to ask me more questions but I beat her to the punch.

"I'm in room 139 and I've got a friend who's staying here too, but I don't know which room he's in. His name is Jack Donahue. He's in his late forties and is about my size. He probably comes across as being pretty intense, maybe a little scary from time to time. Have you seen him around?"

I got a bit of an odd look, but she was still smiling. "Jack spends a lot of time out next to the pool. At least I think that's the guy you're looking for. He's the right age and size, I just wouldn't describe him as scary."

"Thanks, I'll go see if I can find him."

It wasn't until I was walking away from the desk that I realized I probably should have asked her where the pool was. I didn't actually need directions as my nose, even in human form, was more than equal to the task of following the smell of chlorine, but it was the small things that helped keep up the appearance of normalcy.

Jack was sitting cross-legged on one of the deck chairs that was positioned only a few feet away from a tiny fountain. He didn't open his eyes, but he no doubt smelled me coming as soon as I stepped into the pool area.

"You're up sooner than I expected, Alec."

"Then I must have been even more injured than I realized. I expected to be back up and moving around way before now."

He opened one eye and arched his eyebrow at me. "You've been out for less than a day. It was just last night that you were injured."

He'd shocked me enough that I dropped down onto the chair next to him hard enough to make it creak in protest.

"I've never come back so quickly from something like that before."

"Yeah, I was planning on asking you about that. How long have you been able to shift just your hand like that?"

"About twenty-four hours."

Jack uncrossed his legs, straightening the loose workout pants he was wearing, and leaned back in his chair. "So what is your next step now that you've joined the select group of hybrids who can partially transform? Are you going to run back to Sanctuary and show it off to anyone who will stand still long enough to see it?"

I shook my head. "I actually was hoping to get a few minutes to talk to you before we left so I could ask you not to spread that particular development around."

Jack pursed his lips. "Frankly that's about the last thing I expected out of Kaleb's son. He's been angling to hand you a pack ever since you turned. You outing the fact that you've got that level of control would make his job a lot easier. You could probably be calling the shots with your own little group before the year is out."

"I don't want to run a pack, at least not on Kaleb's sufferance. Besides, this is nothing more than a parlor trick. It doesn't make me any kind of a better fighter, it just paints a bigger target on my back."

"You're wrong there, Alec. It may not improve your technique any, but you've got a level of support from your beast that most of our kind won't ever experience. It doesn't necessarily mean that you'll develop any kind of special ability or anything, but you're going to find that you hit harder, take more damage, and recover faster than you did before."

He wasn't talking like someone who knew these things secondhand, he was talking like he knew them from personal experience. Suddenly a bunch of seemingly unrelated facts snapped together for me in a way that they never had before.

"You can do it too, can't you?"

Jack nodded, looked around to make sure that we were alone, and then shifted just his right hand in a cool wash of power that was somehow too calm for such a demonstration.

"I've never heard even the slightest rumor that you might be able to do that. How long have you been able to partially shift?"

"Years, decades maybe. You've never heard any rumors to that effect because you're the first person I've ever shown."

My head was spinning. "Why didn't you capitalize on it? There's only what, Kaleb and two other people who can do that out of our entire pack?"

"I was already towards the top of the food chain and I always figured that it would be better to have an ace up my sleeve. A bit, I think, like you're figuring."

I cast back over what had happened right after we'd landed in St. Louis and tried to make sense of everything.

"Why did you back down at the airport? I thought that I just surprised you with my partial transformation and that it shook you up enough that you decided not to mix it up with me."

Jack nodded. "That's actually about right, just not in the way you're thinking. You did surprise me, not just with your new trick there, but the fact that you were trying so hard to keep it from turning into a dominance issue."

"You were trying just as hard."

"I was actually trying a lot harder. I've spent most of my time out here over the last two years trying to master my beast, to calm it down to the point where I don't have to deal with dominance fights every single time your dad sends in a new group of bruisers to help bust up a nest of vampires. You said that your beast was unusually calm when you arrived. I was the reason for that. Usually I can keep things from boiling over, but seeing you there looking so much like your dad made my control shakier than it normally is."

"You hate him, don't you?"

"Of course I do. He's the reason that my son is dead. He didn't kill my son with his own hands but he's kept the pack together for far too long. Having half of the pack deployed out on combat missions to places like here helps, but there's still too much internal pressure. I haven't been back to Sanctuary in a while now, but last time I was there it seemed like the dominance structure was in a constant state of flux."

I nodded. "It hasn't changed at all for the better over the last couple of years. There are just too many bodies there. Nobody has fought everybody, so dominance is mostly done by inference. When you encounter someone it's like you have to sit down and compare notes on who you've both fought and try to figure out who's got the best record."

"Yeah, that's about like I remember. I remember when Kaleb was young. He had a way of talking about the future that made you want to help him bring about the big dreams he had. Turns out that the dreams all just involved him horning into the Coun'hij all along. I blame Kaleb for Jack dying, but I also blame myself."

"How come?"

"I had a pet theory for a lot of years. It was something that Kaleb and I used to talk about late at night after your mom had given up on waiting for us and gone off to bed by herself. I thought that need and natural aggression were a key part of just how powerful any particular wolf could become. It seemed to me like my beast was somehow limiting the amount of power I could access and it wasn't until I really needed that power and demonstrated that I could control it that my beast let me access it."

I almost interrupted to tell him just how similar his experience was to what I'd felt last night, but I hesitated and he kept talking.

"My son, Jack, was my guinea pig. He had a natural aggression that reminded me a lot of myself at that age, but I pushed him to be more. I tried to get him to harness that aggression in the hopes that it would let him be more powerful. I knew that there were risks, but I told myself that it would be okay. I planned on being around to make sure that none of the dominance fights got out of hand."

Jack was silent for several seconds as he relived painful memories. "I figured that I was dominant to nearly everyone other than Kaleb, so I could make sure that nobody really took him to the cleaners. Besides, Kaleb had promised to help keep an eye on him."

The calm mien that had almost seemed to be Jack's trademark was gone now. His fists were knotted up and I could feel power lashing outward as his beast tried to *do* something about the feelings raging through him. The beast dealt with blacks and whites, it didn't know what to do with a problem that it couldn't fight into submission.

"I knew that things were heating up between him and Brandon's contingent, but I was only supposed to be gone for one day, only one day turned into three and Jack shot his mouth off to the wrong person. When I got back and found out that Jack was dead Kaleb refused to tell me who'd done it. To this day I still don't know."

I shook my head at him. "I wish I could tell you, but I don't know either. It happened out on the far end of town. I'm not sure that anyone really knows what happened. I mean other than Brandon's people."

"Yeah. I would have beaten an answer out of Brandon back then, but Kaleb refused to let me challenge any of those kids. He told me that I wasn't thinking clearly, and that he'd kill me himself if I tore into any of them."

I shook my head in astonishment. It wasn't necessarily any worse than some of the other stories I'd heard about how Kaleb had screwed people over, but it was remarkable that Jack's story hadn't been more talked about when it happened.

"I'm surprised that you stayed around."

"I didn't, not really. Your dad kept me deployed down to the border pretty much constantly until I volunteered for this assignment."

"Why did you volunteer to help out here? It's about the worst assignment imaginable. You've got a near-constant stream of hybrids coming through town who are going to want to challenge you to prove their dominance."

Jack shrugged. "It's actually not that bad of a gig. I've gotten pretty good at sidestepping the issue of who's the biggest, baddest wolf on the block, so I can usually avoid fighting the people that Kaleb sends to help. It really comes down to the fact that I can make a difference here. The vampires need stopped."

"You could say the same thing about the cats on the southern border, or maybe even some of the worst of the dispossessed."

"No, I'm not sure you can. I'm tired of killing my own kind. Most of the dispossessed are nothing more than round pegs in square holes. They aren't all that different than me, they just didn't luck into an assignment that let them nominally stay part of the pack while keeping enough independence to not go crazy. As for the cats, I just keep wondering how much of the snake pit down there is directly a result of the monarchy going in and assassinating most of the leadership in South America. Once you create that kind of a power vacuum it's almost guaranteed that you'll end up with a bunch of petty warlords who spend most of their time trying to kill each other."

"Which is exactly what we've got, isn't it?"

"Yeah, pretty much. At least that's what we had until your dad got us started fighting with them again. Now they've got a common enemy and that's done more to unite them than anything else possibly could have."

"It's them or us now. If we can't break them, then they'll eventually come up into our heartland and destroy everyone."

"That's the official party line."

Jack didn't look convinced, but I didn't want to press him on it, at least not considering some of the other questions I wanted to ask. He was astonishingly easy to talk to considering that the question of who was dominant hadn't ever been settled between us, but there was still a distinct chance that things could degenerate into posturing and a fight at any moment.

"Have you thought about really leaving? With your skills and experience, not to mention your insight into how Kaleb's operation works, you could be a real asset to the dispossessed. It's even possible that you could mold a group of them into a proper pack."

"That's kind of a seditious suggestion to be coming from Kaleb's son."

There it was. We'd come to the very end of how far he felt he could trust me. All of the things he'd said so far were either common knowledge or would merit nothing more than a slap on the wrist, but I'd just taken the conversation in a direction that could get somebody killed.

"The truth is that I've thought about leaving a lot myself lately. Mentally I keep coming back to the fact that I have to stay to protect the people I care about, but if it wasn't for them I'd have left a long time ago."

As assurances went it wasn't particularly strong. If I was working with Kaleb in an effort to frame him then it wouldn't matter what I said because I wouldn't be punished for it. It had been the truth though and my respiration and heartbeat hadn't fluttered even a little when I'd been speaking.

It was back on him to decide whether or not he thought I was a good enough liar to lure him into some kind of trap.

"Yeah, kid. I've thought about leaving hundreds of times. My wife and son are both long gone, but I'm staying for the same reason you are. I've got people who depend on me here. My boys and girls out there in the city need a strong, experienced hand holding the reins or eventually they're going to get blindsided and most of them are going to get killed."

It had been a really long time since I'd felt like I had someone who understood the situation

I was in. Mom understood to a degree, but she was working from a position of weakness and probably always would be.

Jack knew what it was to find his choices circumscribed by his loyalty to his friends. I'd found a kind of kindred spirit without even looking for one.

"Are we making the right decision?"

Jack's snort was eloquent. "Hell, kid, I ask myself that question every day and I'm no closer to answering it now than when I first came out here."

"I keep wondering how many people are like you and me, unhappy with the way things are going, but unwilling to stand up and be a target in an attempt to change things."

Jack looked off into the distance and shrugged. "There are lots of people who are unhappy with how things are right now, but that doesn't necessarily mean that they view the world through the same lens as you do. If you could change things, what would you change?"

"I...well, I guess I don't really know. The Coun'hij for one. I don't think that it's right that they've got every single pack in North America under threat of death."

"We're at war, kid. That requires a strong central authority if you're not going to be steamrolled by the other side."

"We're at war because Kaleb and the rest of the Coun'hij put us there."

"Fair point, but how are you going to change that? Are you going to make peace with the vampires? What about the cats down south? Do you really think that they'll agree to stop fighting us now that they've started to win the war?"

There didn't seem to be much else to say. Jack was right. The position we were in was a terrible one, but the Coun'hij pretty much had us backed into a corner. The silence between us stretched out almost for a full minute before Jack sighed.

"I've run through thousands of scenarios over the last couple of years. We can't use the humans to help contain the cats. They are already struggling to deal with just the little bit of violence that leaks over into their area as part of their war on drugs. I was around to see this nation founded and I never even imagined it could become as powerful as it has, but I also never would have guessed that it could fall so far. It's little more than a Third World government teetering on the edge of bankruptcy these days."

I opened my mouth to protest, to defend the country of my birth, but Jack pinned me to my chair with a glare.

"Don't try to tell me otherwise. We've fought our last few wars using other people's money. The humans and this country can't handle another war right now, at least not unless a whole lot of people are willing to get their hands out of their neighbors' pockets. The humans are useless in this fight unless we're prepared to tell them everything that we've been hiding from them for millennia and let them fight informed."

I cleared my throat. "I'm not sure that would be a good idea. We could just as easily end up on the bad guy list from their perspective as the vampires."

"Yeah, I had the same thought. The way I see it, me staying here has the biggest benefit for the largest number of people. It protects my boys and girls and it helps millions of humans who otherwise would be at risk from vampires. It's a crappy decision when it comes to looking out to the interest of my species, but it helps just about everyone else."

"The greatest good for the greatest number. I guess it works out pretty well for ants."

"Yeah, well people aren't ants. Ants don't spend most of their time figuring out how they can screw the system, they're just happy to let the system screw them. It's a terrible way to make decisions and it is one eventually doomed to failure, but it's all I've got right now. What we need is a serious disruption to the status quo."

"Like what?"

"Like somebody manifesting a new power that changes up the playing field, someone who has the guts to stay out of the Coun'hij and who's smart and strong enough to survive when Kaleb and the rest try to kill him as a result."

I pursed my lips and nodded. "It's happened before. Puppeteer to name just one. You could even say with the way that the population of our pack is exploding that it's only a matter of time until we see one or more game-changing abilities manifest."

"You mean assuming that our young hybrids don't get killed off in the fighting before they have a chance to realize their potential? Oh, and assuming that Mallory doesn't have every single hybrid with the potential to manifest a powerful ability already scouted out and wrapped around Kaleb's finger?"

My breath caught. He was right, Mallory and Kaleb were so many steps ahead of me that it wasn't even funny. Everywhere I turned Kaleb had already been there and made contingency plans to make sure that things went down exactly the way he wanted.

Jack looked over and gave me a sad smile. "Don't feel too bad, kid. Like I said, I've been thinking about this for years. If we had a viable standard to rally around then things would be different, but until then I'm just going to do the best I can to keep hunting down vampires while keeping my skin in one piece."

We sat there in silence for several seconds before Jack shrugged and took in the hotel with a broad sweeping gesture.

"For now you should just enjoy the hotel. I bought you guys forty-eight hours. Once we made it back here and I'd seen to the rest of the injured, I called up Kaleb and told him that you and James were both injured. He wanted me to send all four of you back so that he could at least ship the girls down to the front, but I figured that you wouldn't want to get split up like that, so I told him that I needed Jessica and Jasmin here to help me cover the holes left by two of my people getting roasted by that vampire last night."

"I appreciate that, I expect it probably wasn't a very pleasant conversation."

"Yeah, well, I try to avoid talking to Kaleb whenever possible, but I make an exception for worthy causes."

Feeling like an idiot, I asked the question that should have been the first thing out of my mouth when I saw him.

"How is everyone doing? Your two wolves who got burned are going to pull through then?"

"Yeah. I wouldn't be here peacefully meditating if things were looking at all touch and go. They're both drugged to the gills in their rooms sleeping. Their eyes seem to be undamaged and everything else will heal in the next week or two. Your people are all okay too. Jasmin and Jess came through with nothing more than flesh wounds and James should be up and moving around late today or early tomorrow."

His manner implied that I'd already subconsciously realized that everything was okay and that was the reason that I hadn't asked sooner. It was nice of him to give me the benefit of the doubt like that, but I wasn't as convinced.

It felt more to me like I'd just forgotten my friends and his comrades in my rush to pick his brain for information about everything else under the sun.

"I should go check in on James. Which room is he in?"

"The one across from your room, but there's not much point stopping by right now. Like I said, he'll be out for at least another few hours. Your girls will be back to check in sometime around noon. Until then you really should just enjoy the hotel. There's a decent restaurant on the west end and they've got pretty good exercise facilities. Just don't come swimming—I'd like to get back to my meditation without having to listen to a lot of splashing around."

I nodded, but my mind was still caught up in the idea that there might be a much bigger groundswell of dissatisfaction with Kaleb than I'd ever realized.

"Do you know of anyone else who might be equally willing to work against the Coun'hij if they thought that there was a chance to improve things?"

"Kid, you've been out from under your dad's thumb all of what, two or three times in your entire life. Go enjoy some freedom."

"This is important."

"So is getting some downtime. You're going to see some terrible stuff down on the border. One of the first things you learn after being on a combat op or two is that you take every opportunity to decompress you get. You never know how long it will be before you get another chance."

"I saw bad things here."

"Not like what I suspect is going on down there. I wouldn't wish those memories on anyone, but there's not a damn thing you or I, either one, can do to prevent you from going down there."

I opened my mouth to persist, to try to get him to understand that we might not get another chance like this to sit down and plan, but he silenced me with a lash of power that exceeded anything I'd ever felt out of anyone before.

I'd thought that I was capable of producing a tornado of power, but it was nothing compared to what Jack hit me with. It was like trying to compare a ripple to a tidal wave. My beast wanted to send out a wash of power in response, but I forced it back into a corner of my mind and managed, by the slightest of margins, to avoid responding.

It went against every aggressive instinct in my body, but any response I provided would only highlight the fundamental difference in power between the two of us.

"I'm not going to talk about this anymore, kid. If I had a list of people inside my head who were ready to come out in open rebellion against Kaleb and the rest of the Coun'hij, it's not the kind of thing I'd be sharing with you. If you manifest some earth-shattering ability then you can come back to me and we'll talk, but until then we're done here."

My instincts told me to back slowly out of the pool area, but at least part of that was the natural effect of finding out just how much more dominant he was than I'd realized. The raw amount of power that someone's beast had access to didn't directly translate to being a better fighter, but it was a lot like Jack had said earlier. More power, even if it didn't result in manifesting some kind of unique ability, generally meant that you hit faster and harder and that you could take more of a beating before being put down for the count.

All by itself, even if I hadn't liked Jack, that would have been enough to give me pause, but I'd never felt that much power out of anyone else before. Even Kaleb and Brandon hadn't had access to that kind of white-hot torrent. I was pretty sure that it wasn't possible to be that powerful and not have it result in someone manifesting an ability.

"How long have you had an ability?"

"I don't, kid. I'm three centuries old and I've seen and done things that would blow your mind, but all of that power is just useless, flashy power. Like I said before, it helps me hit harder and take more damage, but I'd still go down like a house of cards against someone like Brandon."

"That's why you stay out here. If you slipped up and revealed your power level back in

Sanctuary you'd almost certainly be pushed to challenge Kaleb for the top spot."

"Yeah, that's definitely part of it. Right now Kaleb feels pretty secure. He's more powerful and deadly than all of the older hybrids and the young guys like Brandon are all too inexperienced to have any prayer of holding the pack together if they took him down. If Kaleb knew how I've changed, he'd almost be forced to challenge me. Out here I can lose control occasionally without it immediately being front-page news back in Sanctuary."

Jack rubbed his eyes and then shrugged. "For a while there I thought that Mallory had been wrong. I thought that if I could just tap into my beast powerfully enough that I'd develop an ability, but it never happened. Aggression and need only go so far. They can raise you up higher than you'd be without them, but apparently I'm missing some key piece to my makeup that would allow me to take that final step and be a real player."

"I'll keep your secret. Nobody back home will find out from me."

"Thanks, kid. I'll do the same for you."

I stood up and turned to go, but Jack had one last thing to say.

"I really am sorry that you're going down to the border. I hope I'm wrong about what Kaleb is doing down there, but if I'm not wrong then just remember that it isn't your fault. You have only so many options that will let you live to fight another day."

It was about as cryptic of a warning as was possible, but I could tell that he didn't want to talk anymore and I wasn't about to start a fight with him over it. Even assuming I could beat him, which was doubtful, I'd have to torture him to get more information out of him and that was the last thing I'd do to someone who'd already helped me so much.

I left the pool area and headed to the weight room. Something told me that I was going to need to bulk up if I was going to keep up with Vincent and the rest down on the border.

Chapter 6

Alec Graves
Graves Estate
Sanctuary, Utah

Mallory was waiting for us, for me really, at the airport as the plane landed. I thought about making some kind of wisecrack about there being no need for her to express her thanks quite so profusely, but one look at the expression on her face convinced me to keep my mouth shut. The simple black dress pants and a white blouse she was wearing indicated that she was off to work some kind of 'respectable' business deal for Kaleb, but somehow her attire didn't manage to make her any less menacing.

She wasn't the strongest or toughest hybrid in the pack and it had been ages since she'd been sent down to the border on any kind of active combat op, but Mallory was Kaleb's strong right hand and anyone who really pissed her off seemed to eventually find themselves in dire straits of some kind or another. Sometimes when Kaleb was extremely confident he could win he would challenge the subject of her ire himself, but usually he just paid one or more of the other dominants to beat on the poor soul who'd crossed her.

Ulrich Bishop in the Chicago pack had pretty much written the book on using fiscal incentives to keep a pack in line, but Kaleb had been forced to add a chapter or two of his own in the course of keeping the Sanctuary pack from shattering into half a dozen pieces.

"You're late."

The question wasn't actually directed at anyone in particular, but I was dominant to the other three so I answered.

"The pilot said he encountered stronger than expected winds which slowed us down quite a bit."

Mallory frowned. "I'll have to have a word with him about that. The planes are being scheduled too tightly to allow for this kind of slippage. Between the four of you missing your original transit window and Samantha's little joyride the schedules are all shot to hell."

I nodded and made a non-committal noise as I turned to go, but she pulled me up short by saying my name.

"I told you that you wouldn't be able to continue ducking me forever. Your friends can leave if they want to, but you and I are going to find a quiet room while the crew gets the plane refueled."

I motioned with my head towards the waiting car.

"You three go ahead. Heaven knows we've got little enough time before we've got to ship back out, the last thing you need is to be cooling your heels here waiting for me."

Mallory didn't wait to see if I would follow, she just turned around and headed back into the administrative building that she'd just come out of.

I shrugged at James and the others and followed Mallory inside. The staff inside the building practically fell all over each other in their eagerness to show Mallory to a private conference room. Kaleb was the single biggest patron of the airport. His fuel bill alone probably exceeded the revenues from the next three biggest customers and there were persistent rumors that Kaleb and Mallory were considering increasing the pack's fleet by at least another one or two planes.

It would have been a lot cheaper to fly commercial, but an awful lot of the pack's dominants didn't play very well with civilians. That, combined with the fact that Kaleb frequently needed to move around groups of relatively large people at short notice, meant that most of the pack's travel would probably continue to be via the private planes.

Once everyone else had cleared back out of the conference room, Mallory sat in one of the plush chairs and motioned for me to kneel down in front of her. I could have just as easily sat in a chair while she stood, but she liked to reinforce the fact that I was submissive to her at every turn. Apparently I waited too long to comply because she snapped her fingers at me and gestured again.

"I don't have all day, Alec. The plane will be refueled in the next few minutes, at which point I need to be on my way."

I reminded myself of all of the reasons that I hadn't mouthed off to her earlier and dropped down to my knees, suppressing an internal grimace as she placed her hands on each side of my head and sent a rush of power out.

My beast didn't like it, he responded with a surge of power of his own, but she was too focused on using her ability to notice and take umbrage. I was fairly sure that it was nothing more than my imagination, but I always came away after a session with Mallory feeling cold and clammy inside.

Nearly a minute passed before she released me and sat back in her chair with a considering look on her face.

"You're more powerful now than you were the last time I scanned you. What happened?"

Her statement took me completely by surprise. I'd known that her ability allowed her to see when another hybrid had an ability of their own as well as giving her some very specific information regarding what that ability was able to do, but I'd never known that she was able to sense general changes in the amount of power a given shape shifter possessed.

"I don't have to tell you that. Now that you've confirmed that I still haven't manifested an ability I'm going to go home."

"An increase in power level is useful all by itself, Alec. Surely you can't be as cavalier as you pretend regarding your ongoing inability to realize the potential I saw in you so many years ago when you were born. An ability would allow you to call your own shots, make your own way in the world…protect those you care about."

"Don't mistake my ability to differentiate between the things I can control and the things I can't as apathy."

"Ah, good, some fire finally. You're right, you have not manifested an ability despite the fact that your general power level has gone up noticeably."

I stood, but she waved me back to a seat. "I'm not going to force you to tell me what triggered your increase in power. Mostly I'm not pushing because I already have a pretty good idea. It's not uncommon for the first real dose of combat to trigger a power increase in someone, but you need to find a way to grow your power level even more. A lot rides on it."

I had to force myself not to laugh in her face. "I know that you're a level removed from most of the dominance posturing, but I've been in plenty of combat before now. It's a rare week when I don't end up tangling with someone."

Mallory waved my comment away. "It's not the same. Dominance fights do occasionally end with someone being killed but it's a rarity. Your father's rules help somewhat, but mostly it just comes down to our natural instinct. A beaten foe, one whom our beast is sure is inferior to us, is more valuable alive than dead. Alive they can help serve as a buffer, another opponent that someone else will have to challenge and beat before they can get at us. Dead, they serve no purpose at all. The only time we see a death from combat in Sanctuary tends to be when the two people involved really hate each other."

"Just in case you've been asleep on the job, Vincent and I really hate each other. I've been in plenty of danger in the past without ever needing to square off against any vampires."

I got a cold smile from her. "I'm done talking about this, Alec. Every word you've said has been the truth, but I'm perfectly capable of discerning when someone is trying to deceive me by telling me only part of the truth. I've only continued the conversation for this long because it is vitally important that you understand the extreme importance attached to you manifesting an ability. You are quickly running out of time."

I kept the relief washing through me off of my face, and I was pretty sure that I'd done a decent job stopping it from bleeding over into my scent. She'd assumed that I was trying to put her off the trail of the truth, which I had been, but I'd been trying to keep her going down the path she'd already selected, not steer her off like she'd assumed I was.

"I'm already aware of just how many of Kaleb's plans hinge on me being able to serve as a counterweight to Brandon. I'll take your concerns under advisement, but I hardly expect that anything I could do in the next eighteen hours would allow me to manifest an ability that would make any kind of difference down on the border."

"I wasn't talking about your upcoming tour of duty. Trust me. If you don't manifest an ability soon you're going to look back at our conversation and bitterly wish that you'd moved heaven and earth to heed my warning."

I opened my mouth to ask her what she was trying to get at, but she stood and left the room in a single fluid motion that didn't give me a chance to get any words out. I hurried after her and caught up just outside of the building.

"What are you trying to tell me?"

I grabbed hold of her shoulder to turn her around and force her to acknowledge me, but she pivoted and hit me in the stomach with such blinding speed that I didn't have a chance to do anything more than tighten my stomach muscles to try and absorb some of the force of the blow.

My best efforts weren't enough, not taken by surprise like that, not against another hybrid. She hit me hard enough to knock the wind out of me, causing me to double over in pain as her knee came up and hit my face. A split second later I was looking up at her from my back.

"You don't put your hands on me, Alec. This time was a freebie. The next time you try to impose your will on me in any manner I will kill you and your father's plans can burn."

Mallory turned and walked away without waiting for a response from me. A few seconds later she was onboard the plane and one of the guys from the ground crew was asking me if I was okay.

"Yeah, I'll be fine."

I waved away his offer of a cloth for my nose and rolled back to my feet. My metabolism was already kicking in; the bleeding had nearly stopped and by the time we flew out tomorrow my nose probably wouldn't even be swollen any more.

There were usually at least a couple of cars from the pack at the airport at any given time and today was no exception. The dark blue Honda Civic and the black Nissan Pathfinder both had Kaleb's circular sigil affixed to their rear windows, so I used the standard code to unlock the Honda and a few minutes later I was on my way back to the house.

BOUND

A few years back, two of the locals had figured out our standard unlock code and gone joyriding in one of the pack cars that Kaleb had purchased by the dozen. Kaleb had sent Brandon to teach them a lesson.

Neither guy had been able to walk unassisted for nearly two months. The police had investigated, but nothing had come of it. Actually that wasn't right—nothing had come of the investigation, but after that everyone in Sanctuary had realized that Kaleb had GPS transmitters on all of his cars and that they'd be idiots to touch his property.

Brandon had strutted around like a king after that and I'd realized just exactly how little influence my mother really had. She'd managed to anonymously pay for the worst of the medical bills that Brandon had inflicted on the two guys, but she hadn't been able to do any more than that.

I'd wanted Brandon to end up in prison, or for some kind of civil case to be brought against Kaleb, but both had remained completely above the law, just like always.

I started my drive back to the estate in a bad mood and thinking about Brandon just made things worse. By the time I got home, I was angry enough that I probably would have done something stupid like challenging Brandon if I'd run into him in one of the halls.

Fortunately, he was down on the border and I didn't run into anyone else on my way to my room. I cleaned myself up and headed into the

113

small training room that Kaleb had attached to my bedroom as a reward when I changed to a wolf for the first time.

I'd used it religiously for several years until I'd realized that it didn't matter how much I worked out I still wouldn't be able to match the unnatural strength of someone like Brandon or the supernatural healing that Kaleb routinely used to wear his opponents into the ground before finishing the fight in an abrupt explosion of violence.

The fact that Vincent was now stronger than me was proof that weight training did indeed pay dividends even for shape shifters, so that meant that I needed to squeeze regular training sessions into my schedule on top of the studying that I'd need to get my GED.

I was midway through my fourth set of curls when someone knocked on my bedroom door. Some of the anger that had started to die down while I'd been working out flared up and I stalked towards my door fully intending on giving somebody a piece of my mind. My beast was just as unhappy and waves of power preceded me, beating on the door in time with my steps. I flung open the door and then upon seeing that it was Donovan who was waiting for me, reined my anger in.

"Have I come at a bad time, Master Alec?"

"No worse than normal, Donovan, I'm just not handling things as well today. Please come in."

Donovan gave me a respectful nod and then waited as I turned on the three privacy generators stationed about my room.

"What can I do for you, Donovan?"

"Not for me, sir, but rather for your mother. She sent me to ask if you would be willing to spend the evening with your sister. She's heard that Master Kaleb is quite incensed over the damage to his troop rotations occasioned by her shopping trip with Mistress Rachel and she expects that he will pay her a visit tonight to discuss his unhappiness over her recent actions."

"And she'd rather Rachel not feel like it's her fault for asking Mother to take her shopping."

"Exactly, sir. May I tell her that you'll acquiesce to her request?"

"Yes. I'd much rather spend the evening stewing, but it would probably be good for me to not be by myself tonight. Mother could have just called me and saved you the trip across the house."

Donovan gave me the small smile he used when I questioned the traditions that my family had followed for more centuries than I could even imagine.

"Some things are simply better conveyed one person to another rather than over one of those technological devices that your generation is so fond of."

I shook my head at him. "And by that you mean she couldn't get away herself, but she wanted you to report on my state of mind in greater detail than she thought she'd be able to get by talking to me over the phone."

"Of course, sir. And since the secondary purpose of my visit is now out in the open, may I ask how things went? Your mother heard that you'd been injured and was quite concerned."

"All in all, they could have gone quite a bit worse than they did. James and I were injured, as were two of Jack's wolves, but Jasmin and Jessica came out of it with flesh wounds and James and I will pretty much be back at full strength by the time we land in Arizona tomorrow."

Donovan nodded, but it was obvious to me that he was considering his next question very carefully. "May I tell your mother that your power level has grown?"

I wanted to put my fist through a wall, but I forced my anger back down and nodded. "Yes. I hadn't planned on keeping that a secret from Mother, but I didn't expect for the secret to get out on its own so quickly. First Mallory and then you. At this rate the entire pack will know before I leave tomorrow. Is it that obvious?"

Donovan pursed his lips and then shook his head slowly. "I would say no, at least not for most of the dominants, but we submissives tend to become very good at remembering relative power levels, and you were quite angry just now. Under normal circumstances nobody other than Mallory could tell that anything had changed, but you will need to be very careful to remain in control of your emotions if you want to maintain your secret."

"I seem to be having a harder time than usual controlling my anger today. Honestly I'm not sure how Mallory got so far under my skin, but she sure pissed me off today."

"If I may, Master Alec, I've noticed a definite trend that would seem to indicate that the more powerful one's beast is, the harder time one tends to have keeping one's feelings in check. While you've become quite accomplished and controlled over the years, it is possible that your recent increase in power is going to take some getting used to on a number of fronts."

He was probably right. It made a lot of sense, which meant that I'd have to be even more vigilant than normal for the next little while, but that wasn't what had caught my attention. There'd been a slight change in his expression when I'd mentioned Mallory. It had been so small that I would have almost thought I was imagining it, but it wasn't the first time that it had happened when I'd mentioned her name around him.

"Donovan, just now when I talked about Mallory you...well, it was almost like you flinched."

"Indeed, Master Alec. I have tried for years to break myself of that habit, but it appears that I have not yet fully succeeded."

"Can I ask what happened or is that presuming too much?"

Donovan was silent for several seconds before finally nodding with a jerky motion that was nothing at all like the smooth, graceful, proper movements that normally characterized him.

"I must admit that the story is difficult for me to tell even now. Your mother has no doubt told you that your father was an entirely different man back before you were born, but you may not have realized that many of the pack were likewise different back then. Mallory and I have both been in service to your family since back before your father was born."

I nodded. I didn't tend to think about just how old Donovan was, but much like Jack he'd been around and lived through things that I'd only heard vague references about in history books.

"I fought my feelings for many decades, but the truth was that during our shared service, first to your grandfather and then to your father, I developed feelings for Mallory."

I felt my eyes go wide, but Donovan didn't seem to hold my surprise against me.

"I wish you could have known her back then, Master Alec. She was a strong, brave woman who was consumed by the plans that Kaleb had for the pack. It seemed that nothing was impossible back in those days. Kaleb was outmaneuvering the Coun'hij at every turn and he'd laid the groundwork for alliances with Jaclyn in the south and Ulrich in the north."

"What happened?"

BOUND

Donovan shrugged. "Nobody knows, not even those of us who were inside of Kaleb's inner circle back when it happened. We had a visitor late one night, a man who demanded to be shown to Kaleb's office and who conversed with Kaleb for nearly ten hours before disappearing into the night. After that things slowly started to change. The differences were almost imperceptible at first. Still, I should have seen them, but I was foolishly focused more on Mallory than on Kaleb."

"She betrayed you, didn't she?"

"Yes. In hindsight, looking backwards with a knowledge of who she's become over the last couple of decades, it must seem obvious that she would betray me, but I didn't have that advantage back then. I'd struggled with the possible impropriety of my feelings for years, but finally one day I expressed my admiration for her in stronger, plainer terms than I ever had before. She told me that she was flattered, that she'd sensed a special bond growing between us over the years, but that she hadn't ever thought it proper to act on it before now. She told me that she needed some time to think things over and confirm to herself that a relationship between the two of us wouldn't violate our oaths to Kaleb and the pack."

Donovan's smile was bittersweet. "We spent more time together over the next couple of months. I wanted to press her for an answer, but

I knew that she wasn't the kind of woman to respond well to being pressured, so I kept my silence and just enjoyed the fact that we were together so much more than before. Things came to a head when the two of us ran into Agony."

My breath caught. Agony had been the shape shifter equivalent to the bogyman for as long as I could remember. He was just a hybrid, but his power was one that allowed him to short-circuit the normal healing abilities of a shape shifter. Normally we healed back from nearly anything that didn't kill us and we rarely scarred. Agony could make any wound heal with human slowness and even then they never really healed right, leaving a mass of scar tissue that pulled whenever we moved around and especially when we shifted forms.

"It was a routine patrol. If we'd known that he was sniffing around we would have brought more help, but it was before Kaleb had joined up with the Coun'hij so we weren't expecting Agony to take any interest in us. Besides, we wanted some time alone."

"He knew. Somehow he knew that Kaleb was going to throw in with the Coun'hij."

"Yes, I think he did. I still don't know how, but I think that you're right. He knew that Kaleb was considering an alliance with the Coun'hij and he was scouting around the edge of our territory looking for a weakness, looking for a way into the manor so that he could attack Kaleb."

"What happened?"

"We attacked Agony like the good soldiers we were. Believe it or not, back then I was a respectable fighter. I was no match for a hybrid by myself, but Mallory and I together had Agony on the ropes. I thought that we were going to beat him, and then Mallory was a fraction of a second too slow in backing up one of my lunges and Agony buried his claws in the left side of my chest. It was far enough back that it missed my heart, but it scarred up exactly as you would have expected, which is why I rarely transform any more. After that Agony fled and Mallory carried me back here to the estate."

"Why would she have let you get hurt like that?"

"I think that she had been instructed by Kaleb to do whatever she could to increase the bond between us. She must have thought that her delay would go unnoticed, that I would think that she'd saved my life rather than risking it. She came to me while I was still in bed trying to recover from my injuries and she told me that she wanted to be with me, but that there was something hanging over her head that wouldn't allow it. Of course I begged her to tell me what was stopping her and finally she told me that Kaleb was planning on betraying the pack. She said that she was worried that he would use our relationship to manipulate both of us and that the only way for us to act on our feelings for each other would be for us to run away."

Donovan stared off into the distance for nearly a minute before sighing. "I didn't have access to nearly as much of your father's finances back then as I have now, but I could have easily made off with millions. It would have been enough for the two of us to live out our lives on a small island somewhere safe from Kaleb and the Coun'hij both."

"You told her no."

"I did indeed. I told her that my oath to your father was more important to me than even my feelings for her. I said that if he were indeed to betray us that things would be different, but until then I would have to stand by Kaleb no matter what else might come."

"It was a test."

"Indeed, a most shrewd one at that. I'd never realized until then just how accomplished a liar Mallory was. Her scent, her pulse, her expression, her voice, they were all perfect. I had no doubt that she was telling the truth and I chose to stand by Kaleb regardless. The only clue I had during the whole lead up to their test was the fact that she'd almost let me die, but only minutes after she left my room Kaleb came in and told me that I'd passed, that I'd shown the kind of loyalty that he'd always known I'd possessed."

"At which point he put you in charge of all of the pack finances."

"Correct, Master Alec. It was a cruel irony that not too long after that Kaleb joined the

Coun'hij and I started to realize that everything Mallory had said had been true other than that she wanted to run away with me."

"I'm so sorry, Donovan."

"Don't be, Master Alec. I've had a long time to work through the bulk of my feelings where Mallory is concerned. I related the story now only because I think it's important for you to know what you are up against. Master Kaleb and Mallory are capable of almost any atrocity if they think that it might bring them closer to their goals."

Donovan shook himself slightly and then bowed his head respectfully. "I'll let your mother know that she can send Rachel over at any time."

I watched in silence as Donovan turned and left my room. I went back to my weights and made it through two more sets before Rachel arrived, but my heart wasn't in the workout anymore, so I didn't feel particularly put out by needing to stop to get the door for her.

Rachel wrinkled her nose at me as she stepped into my room. "You've been working out."

"I hardly worked out at all, but I can go jump through the shower if you want me to."

Rachel shook her head. "That's a bad idea if I've ever heard one. If you did that then I'd get bored and go back to Mom's rooms, thereby defeating the purpose of her suggesting I come and check up on you. You're not very good at this spy stuff."

I rolled my eyes at her. "Somehow I'm not surprised that you saw through Mom's attempt at getting you out of the way. It makes life a lot easier though because it means I *could* go shower without worrying that you'll wander off."

"If it's all the same to you, I'd rather you stay out here and talk to me. If I'm by myself then I'll just think about Dad yelling at Mom." Rachel looked down at the carpet and then shrugged. "Mom and I went on a shopping trip, which is what has Dad pissed off."

"Usually she schedules those a week or two in advance to make sure that it causes the minimum amount of fuss possible. What made her change things up at the last minute this time?"

Rachel sighed and tried not to meet my eyes, but I reached out and gently brought her chin up so that she had no other choice.

"Mom got a call from Jack in St. Louis. He told her that you'd been hurt and that he needed some help coming up with a way to keep you there for a day or two. She figured that a request from him combined with us screwing up the schedule for one of the planes would do it. She was right, but now Dad is going to yell at her again."

There was almost more information in those few sentences than I knew what to do with. Apparently Jack was working with my mother, maybe not all of the time, but enough still that they would do each other favors, at least when it came to protecting me.

"I didn't know that Mom let you hear those kinds of things. Usually she sends you out of the room whenever we talk about something important."

Rachel nodded. "Yeah, that's pretty much just for show. If it's just the two of us and a call comes in she rarely makes me leave. As long as we keep up the appearance that I don't know anything then she figures that I'm pretty safe. Nobody will try to sweat me for information if they don't know that I'm privy to most of what she knows. You'd be surprised at some of the stuff that's rattling around inside of my head, Alec."

She said it with a smile, but there was an undertone of worry to her voice.

"What's wrong, Rachel? I mean besides the fact that Kaleb and Mother are in her rooms fighting. There's something else, isn't there?"

"Yeah. Mom has started keeping a secret from me, or maybe I've just started to realize that she's not telling me everything like I thought she was. There's something going on down at the border, something that has her worried, but she keeps dodging my attempts to try to figure out what it is. I don't suppose you know what's going on?"

I shook my head. I could feel a headache coming on. I'd always thought that Mom kept me in the loop on everything and kept Rachel in the dark as much as possible. Rachel had just shaken my worldview in a slight but very real way.

"I don't know, but I'd bet that Jack does. He more or less hinted that something terrible was going on down on the border, but when I tried to press him about stuff, he shut me down in spectacular fashion."

Rachel frowned. "I don't like this. I don't like the fact that they are keeping some huge secret from us. It makes me question for the first time whether or not I can trust Mom. It seems like the stakes just keep getting higher and higher."

"Are you still hoping that Kaleb isn't the bad guy here?"

"I'm not an idiot, Alec. I know that Dad isn't very nice, and I know that he's done some pretty mean things. The fact that I'm holding out a little bit of hope that he's in some way redeemable doesn't mean that I'm going to allow him to hurt me or the people I care about. I'm telling you though that there is something about what Dad is doing that just doesn't add up, and I'm going to keep digging whenever I get the chance to try and figure out what is really going on."

I pulled Rachel into a hug and closed my eyes as I rested my chin on the top of her head. "You're too good for this life, Rachel. Someone as kind and smart as you belongs in the normal world where you can make some lucky guy extremely happy and then have a life where the worst thing you worry about is whether or not the two of you will be able to make your mortgage payments."

"Thanks for the vote of confidence, Alec. You're pretty okay yourself. Out of everyone in my life, you're the one person I still feel like I can trust completely. Please don't betray my trust. I'm not sure that I could survive that."

"Don't worry, Rachel. I'll do everything I can to protect you."

Chapter 7

Alec Graves
Rio Rico Airport
Rio Rico, Arizona

Our plane touched down in Rio Rico a little before noon. We found 100-degree heat and a fearsome reception waiting for us. I'd expected our arrival to be fairly low-key. Rio Rico was a small town with less than twenty thousand people that hadn't even had an airport until Kaleb had decided to make it one of the centers for his war on the southerners.

Instead of the bored local holding a sign with our names on it, we found Brandon, Vincent, and half a dozen other shape shifters from our pack waiting for us. It was like something out of an action movie. The way that the hybrids were all facing outwards, prepared to respond to any kind of threat, gave me the distinct impression that we were in hostile territory.

Alison, one of the wolves who had been sent down to the southern front more than four months ago, stepped forward and pointed towards a line of black SUVs waiting less than fifty feet from the plane.

"The cats have attacked the airport several times over the last two months. The four of you aren't versed in our standard operating procedure, so Brandon has asked that you go take a seat in the cars while the rest of us keep an eye on the plane until it is refueled and begins taxiing."

My beast didn't particularly like being told what to do by a submissive, but I mentally sat on him to keep him from sending out a flare of power that might tip off Brandon or Vincent to the fact that I was more powerful now than the last time they'd seen me.

"You heard the lady, let's get over to the vehicles."

James shot me an unhappy look. Apparently his beast was likewise dissatisfied with the way the chain of command was working, but I was dominant to him, so unless he wanted to start a fight with me out here in broad daylight there wasn't much he could do but follow Jasmin and Jessica to the SUVs.

Once we were inside one of the air-conditioned bubbles of calm, James practically exploded. The surge of power he unleashed into the air around him made my ears pop.

"That was a calculated insult. Brandon should have been the one giving us orders rather than sending Alison to do it."

I locked gazes with James and refused to back down until he looked away. "I think you're probably right that Brandon was insulting us, but just because that was an insult doesn't mean that it was all that it was."

Jasmin looked up with curiosity written all over her face. "What do you mean?"

"Look at them." I pointed at the circle of men and women standing in a loose circle around the plane. "We see Brandon and Vincent back in Sanctuary on a pretty regular basis, but the rest of these guys are out here for months at a time. Even when Kaleb gives them some down time he doesn't usually let them come back to Sanctuary—instead he sends them in twos and threes off to someplace where they can blow off some steam without causing any waves back home. Do any of the people from our pack look the way you remember?"

Jess shook her head. "No, Alison was practically scared of her own shadow before. Now she looks like she could rip me in half without breaking a sweat."

I nodded, not just because Jess was right, but because that was exactly the same difference I'd noticed almost as soon as we landed. The old

Alison never would have given me an order, no matter how politely worded and no matter whom she was representing. This new Alison had chopped her hair into a ragged bob and dyed a light-red streak through it. Everything from her clothes—black cargo pants and a tank top—up to her posture seemed to indicate that she'd been through hell during the last four months and that she was more than able to handle herself in any of the situations she was likely to run into.

We watched as the ground crew finished refueling and checking the plane and then two of the waiting figures left their spots in the circle and boarded the plane. Fifteen minutes later the plane was taxiing down the runway and everyone else was piling into the waiting vehicles. Alison took the driver seat to our SUV and drove with a kind of easy confidence that told me she'd done this many times before and that she didn't expect problems now that we were moving.

We'd left the front passenger seat open, but now I moved forward and sat down beside her. "What's going on down here?"

"We're in the middle of a war; that pretty much says it all."

"The reports we've been getting back in Sanctuary led us to believe that we were winning."

Alison nodded, a short, choppy motion that conveyed her supreme discomfort with where I was steering the conversation.

"We are winning if you just look at the kill numbers. We've killed four or five cats for each of our people that they've retired."

"But that's not the full story because you guys don't look like the winning team."

"Right, well, the truth is that the jaguars who have carved off territory and set themselves up as petty dictators tend to have bastard children by the scores. Even if only a relatively small percentage of those kids turn out to be moonborn, that still adds up to a lot of cats running around down there. Before now, they always spent most of their time fighting against each other, but now that we've gone and stirred things up they are setting aside their differences so that they can fight us."

"So we're way more outnumbered than anyone back home realizes."

Alison snorted. "That's got to be the understatement of the year. Even if every wolf in North America was down here fighting we'd still be outnumbered. As it is we've got only a relatively small percentage of the able-bodied adults down here on the border so our odds are even worse."

"How are you guys holding out against those kinds of numbers?"

"In a word? Brandon. Don't get me wrong, there are a lot of people down here pulling together. We've got everything from some of the Coun'hij's bully-boys to some of the dispossessed who've decided to come in from the cold and help fight the good fight, but it's Brandon who always turns the tide of every fight that he's in. I've seen him take out three cats in three seconds and do it without taking even a scratch in return."

There was a glow in Alison's eyes that made me distinctly uneasy, but either I managed to keep my feelings off of my face or she was just too caught up in what she was telling me to notice anything short of the conversational equivalent to a tactical nuke.

"Two months ago one of the really old cats made the trip up from Nicaragua. The intelligence operation your dad put together saw him coming days before he arrived and it scared the crap out of everyone here. You know how cats just continue to get stronger and faster as they age rather than plateauing out like we do."

I nodded, but Alison seemed to take it as a given that I knew what she was talking about. She resumed talking after only a second.

"Mostly as they get older they tend to carve out little kingdoms in the middle of nowhere and surround themselves with younger cats to serve as bodyguards. Eventually it seems like a few of the lieutenants always get together and kill their boss before splitting up the kingdom and then setting to trying to kill each other. Somehow this guy managed to not only survive a heck of a lot longer than most of his kind, he also won the loyalty of his people such that they willingly followed him up here to tear us apart."

Alison looked away from the road long enough to meet my eyes. "It's almost like a holy war with most of these guys, Alec. You'll have to see it to believe it, but they blame us for all of the centuries of poverty and corruption down there. They want to break into the United States because they think that once they are here they will have the same kind of lifestyle as we've enjoyed for so many years."

"So what happened when he arrived?"

"Hmm? Oh yeah, Anton. He came in as bold as anything I've ever seen and demanded to fight our leader. Brandon stepped forward without any kind of hesitation and then proceeded to fight Anton to a standstill. I've never seen two guys who were so strong and fast. For a minute there I thought that maybe Brandon had finally met his match, but he killed Anton five minutes into the fight, after which Anton's people scattered and we spent the next four days hunting them down and picking them off one by one."

We turned onto a side street and I noticed two guys up on the roof of one of the taller buildings. A couple of seconds later Alison followed the rest of the caravan into the parking lot of a Rest Easy Motel and then put the SUV into park and turned to look directly at me.

"Some of the other older cats were slowly moving north before Brandon killed Anton, but him taking down Anton all by himself scared them enough that they've all moved back to their home bases. Now it's mostly just the younger, more adventurous cats pushing against our territory in an attempt to break through. Brandon is the only reason we're not all dead already and most of the people down here respect him for that despite whatever other faults he might have. I know you and he have had your differences in the past, but if you know what's in your best interest you'll bury the hatchet—assuming Brandon will let you."

We all piled out of the vehicles and then stood there a bit at a loss for what to do next until Alison had made her way around to our side of the SUV.

"There are room reservations in your names at the front desk and there's a copy of our standard operating procedures waiting for you in your rooms. You've got the next eight or so hours to start getting comfortable with what's in that manual. Brandon will conduct a briefing at eight tonight in the main conference room. Trust me, you don't want to be late."

Alison walked off without saying goodbye, and everyone else was already disappearing into the hotel, so I motioned for James and the girls to follow me inside. We got our rooms without any problem and the promised manual was indeed waiting for me. I unpacked my small suitcase and then James knocked on my door before I could sit down and start reading. Jessica and Jasmin were just visible in the hall behind him.

I waved all three of them into my tiny room and then once the door was shut I turned on the two privacy generators I'd brought with me, placing them on opposite sides of the room.

"What are we going to do now, Alec? Brandon is building himself an army of fanatics."

I nodded. "Yeah, I picked up on that too. It's worrying, but for right now our best bet is just to keep our heads down and do as we're told. Hopefully Brandon will leave us together for the most part since we already have all of the dominance issues sorted out between each other. To be honest, I'm starting to wonder what we've been thrown into. Everyone back home knows that Brandon is bad news, but I hadn't heard anything indicating that he was strong and fast enough to take down one of the Ancients like this Anton is supposed to have been. For the first time in my life I think I'm starting to hope that Kaleb knows what he's doing. Someone needs to put the brakes on Brandon or things could get ugly really, really fast."

Chapter 8

Alec Graves
Rest Easy Hotel
Rio Rico, Arizona

I made it through most of the operations manual before it was time to go to Brandon's briefing. I knocked on the doors to James' and the girls' rooms and then we all went downstairs together. I'd thought that there were a lot of moonborn waiting for us at the airport, but that was nothing compared to the sheer number of people packed into the conference room. I counted thirty people and when you factored in the fact that there were probably some of Brandon's people still detached as lookouts and guards, it meant that the actual size of Brandon's force was probably somewhere in the range of forty or fifty warriors, and I only recognized about half of the faces present.

It wasn't something designed to help me rest easy at night. Not only did Brandon have a miniature army more than twice the size of most packs, he'd successfully recruited from outside of the Sanctuary pack, which meant there was a chance that Kaleb didn't even know the full extent of Brandon's power base.

Vincent entered through a side door and then held it open so that Brandon could walk through it. Brandon scanned the waiting shape shifters and then seemingly satisfied that everyone was there, he launched into his briefing.

"We got another anonymous tip last week and the Brain Box, our intelligence group, has finally managed to confirm its validity."

Brandon pulled a remote out of his pocket as someone hit the lights and a second later the overhead projector that had been quietly humming flared to life with a map of northern Mexico.

"A nest of cats have set up an hour west of Santa Ana apparently relying on the sheer distance between here and there to keep them safe. It's taken some work to confirm numbers that far away from our normal area of operations, but the Brain Box puts the group at twenty, only two of whom are old enough to potentially be classified as Ancients."

The projector flashed and the map was replaced by a picture of a compound. "This is an aerial view of their base..."

BOUND

I relaxed into the briefing, memorizing the layout of the compound and making mental notes of how Brandon was deploying his people. It appeared that he had pulled in his thirty best fighters and was planning on using them to storm through the interior of the compound. He was likely more than a match for one ancient, which meant that Vincent and the rest of his people should outnumber the rest of the cats by a healthy enough margin that at least some of the cats would scatter and try to get out of the compound.

Fortunately for us, there were really only two decent routes away from the compound, so Brandon was deploying two more groups outside of the compound to serve as a safety net to scoop up all of the runners.

It was a simple plan that seemed to rely more on Brandon's extreme lethality and our superior numbers than on anything else, but I couldn't see any glaring holes in it. I looked away from the screen and back at Brandon as he started to wrap up.

"...We've got information packets for you all to review on the trip out, but despite the fact that it's outside of our normal theater of operations and a bigger group than we usually tackle, it should be a pretty straightforward job. For the most part you're all staying in your normal units. The team leaders have already been pre-briefed and they'll reach out to anyone who's been moved between teams. Let's kill some cats and all come back in one piece. This could be the propaganda win that we need to get the trickle of recruits to start flowing south again."

Apparently any questions would be answered by the team leaders because Brandon walked out of the room without looking back. James gave me an inquiring look, but I just shrugged. There wasn't anything that we could do other than just sit here and wait for our new team leader to come find us.

A couple of seconds later someone tapped me on the shoulder. "You're Graves?"

"Yeah. This is James and that's Jasmin and Jessica. Are you our team leader?"

"Yes, my name is Juan Ruiz. Let's go find somewhere quiet so that I can bring the four of you up to speed."

Juan caught Alison's eye as he carefully made his way through all of the bodies between us and the main exit. Alison didn't look thrilled about any part of what was going on, but she nodded and started towards us.

We walked for nearly five minutes before Juan turned off into a tiny coffee shop that looked like it was on its last legs. The Hispanic woman behind the counter was well past middle age, but the way she smiled when Juan walked through the door made her seem much younger than she actually was.

Languages have never been my strongest area, so I didn't catch much from the lightning-fast exchange that Juan and the woman carried on in Spanish, but she motioned us towards the back of the store as she continued to talk to Juan.

Alison seemed to know where she was going. She led the rest of us up a narrow flight of stairs which terminated on a small landing, only when we went through the door we found another staircase which climbed up the back of the building. The whole affair seemed to have been cobbled together as an afterthought, but when we finally reached the end of the creaking stairs we found that the top of the roof had been converted into a kind of sunroom paradise.

Alison fidgeted with a couple of dials on an ancient-looking machine and then it roared to life with a gust of cool damp air. "Swamp cooler."

The words weren't said to anyone in particular, and after Alison said them she went over to one of the chairs on the far end of the glassed-off enclosure and used it to get high enough up to crack open one of the windows before plopping down on the faded plastic seat with a sigh of resignation.

It was obvious that Alison didn't want to make small talk so I motioned James and the girls into chairs and then pulled up one of my own. We passed the next couple of minutes in silence until Juan walked into view and let himself into the sunroom.

"Can someone please get that window over there? Swamp coolers only work properly if you give the air somewhere to escape to."

Jessica saw to the window in question while Juan opened a third window and then pulled out a couple of white noise generators and stationed them as far away from the swamp cooler as possible.

"Okay, everyone huddle up. With all of the racket in here nobody should be able to listen in on anything we're saying, but we'll need to get closer or we won't be able to hear each other."

We all moved in, James and the others with an air of curiosity, Alison looking like she was ready to start swearing. Juan let the silence stretch out for several seconds and then waved at Alison. "If you have something to say then go ahead and get it off of your chest."

"Why in the hell did you let us get stuck with them? I didn't expect that we'd get a pair of top-tier hybrids to replace Jones and Rivera, but having these four on our team is worse than having nobody at all. By letting Brandon stick us with them you've painted a big old target on our backs."

I expected Juan to slap Alison down with a roar of power, but he just shrugged mildly and turned to address me.

"You'll have to excuse Alison. She's normally not quite so abrasive, but she hates your father pretty badly."

BOUND

Alison shot Juan a fierce look. "Don't go there. They don't have any right to know."

"Now that's where you're wrong. Your feelings are going to make everyone's lives more difficult and the main purpose for this meeting is to clear the air. Either you can do it or I will. And don't break Reina's chair or I'll stick you here helping her on your days off to pay for a new one."

Alison's hands had been white-knuckled on the arms of her chair, but she let go of the creaking plastic like it was burning her. "I hate you."

Juan shrugged and smiled and I wondered for a second whether or not this was partially punishment for her refusal to properly submit to him.

"I'll tell it then, but I'll probably get some of it wrong since I'm not from your pack and I heard it all secondhand."

"I'll do it." Alison's voice was low and seethed with rage. "I was in love with Sam Giles for years. My mom said he wasn't any good, but that just made me want him more. I was so far gone that I even convinced myself that I didn't mind that he couldn't seem to pick between me and Chloe."

I started slightly. I remembered Chloe, she'd been a couple of years younger than us, but she'd left with her parents about the same time as Alison had been deployed down to the border.

"Right, you probably still believe the official story that her parents wanted to fight the cats so badly that they both volunteered to go down to southern California. Well, that's just another of Kaleb's lies. The truth is that Sam was just using Chloe and me. We formed our own little power bloc that helped keep him safe while he worked for what he really wanted."

Alison looked up with challenge in her eyes. "He wanted to work directly for your dad. He kept telling us that he was studying all of those business books because he wanted to go to college and live a normal life, but it was a bald-faced lie. He wanted to help manage the pack's money because he saw the way that it made Donovan untouchable. He figured it was the best way to secure his future and when Kaleb offered him the chance he jumped at it and cut Chloe and me loose."

"Chloe's parents didn't volunteer in a fit of patriotism, did they?"

"No, they were forced down there because Sam didn't want a reminder of his duplicity hanging around. He and Kaleb would have been satisfied with just sending Chloe away, but her parents wouldn't just stand idly by while she was sent off to die. They started raising a fuss directly to Kaleb so he disappeared them to California and sent Chloe and me here to Arizona."

Juan interrupted. "Alison and Chloe were both assigned to my team, which is how I found out what had happened to them. I tried very hard to keep Chloe alive, but she was just too young, too inexperienced and small. She didn't even last two weeks."

Alison looked like her rage was the only thing keeping her from tears. "My mom is still in Sanctuary pretending like everything is okay because Kaleb personally told her that he'd have me killed if she said anything to anyone."

"And if you cause problems here then Brandon will tell Kaleb and he'll have your mother killed. You both serve as a guarantee of the other's cooperation."

My voice came out low and angry. What had been done to Chloe and Alison was wrong. Kaleb had put a price on the lives of five people; he'd implicitly said that the extra money that Sam would generate for him was worth more than the lives of Chloe, Alison and their parents. I wanted to jump into a car and drive back to Sanctuary so that I could throw myself at Kaleb, but there was a tiny part of me that hadn't given into the rage of my beast, and that sliver of self-control knew that the implications of what Alison had just told me were much greater than she knew.

Sam having been brought in expressly to help manage the pack's tithe and Kaleb's fortune meant that Donovan was at risk in more ways than one, but more concerning was the fact that neither Donovan or my mother had told me anything about what had happened with Alison and Chloe.

I looked down and realized that James had his hand on my chest and that I was only a step away from the door. I'd thought I was still at least peripherally in control, but apparently my beast had been calling more of the shots than I'd realized.

"Sit down, Alec. You too, James. Nobody is going to leave right now, we're not done talking."

Juan's voice was even, but it was still a command and my control wasn't up to keeping my beast from bristling at the order. Power exploded out of me, and it wasn't just the limited surge that I'd been trying to train myself to use, it was everything I was capable of. Waves of energy beat against the walls in a metaphysical rush that caused James to back away from me and all three of the girls to shrink in on themselves in a clear bid to avoid becoming the focus of my ire.

"You shouldn't have done that."

Juan didn't rise to the rage in my voice. "You didn't give me any choice, Alec, any more than Alison gave me one. If I hadn't given you another target to focus on then you and James would have come to blows and you'd be halfway back to the hotel so you could steal a vehicle by now."

The things he was saying were just words, and they weren't capable of deflecting my beast—not now, not without something more substantial to back them up. I roared at him and sent out another crest of power to batter him. This time I did spark a response from him and he unleashed a pulse of energy that was respectable but less than I'd managed even before my recent gains.

"There you have it, Alec. I've much less power than you. Your beast is telling you to attack, to prove your dominance, but what will that really prove? If you kill me then you'll be giving Brandon exactly the excuse he's looking for, and if you beat me without killing me then you'll be the leader of this team but a leader without the knowledge that would allow you to keep all of us alive. Is that what *you* want? You, not the beast that isn't capable of planning more than a few hours ahead."

I wanted to sink my claws into him so badly that it was all I could do to stop the shift that was threatening to tear through me. My whole body was trembling from the need to transform and rend, but the incident with Jack had shown me that I was more capable of mastering my beast than I'd ever realized previously.

I focused on my breathing, letting some of the tension out each time I exhaled, and within a few seconds the shakes were gone and I was enough in control to look at Juan without wanting to kill him.

"Good job, Alec."

The words could have been mocking, but something about Juan's tone told me that he was sincerely impressed, which helped dissipate most of the rest of my beast's anger.

"There aren't very many hybrids who could have done what you just did."

I waved off the compliment. "It doesn't help me stand up to Brandon or Kaleb, so it amounts to little more than a cheap parlor trick."

"With all due respect, it has the potential of keeping you alive when less controlled hybrids would get themselves killed by picking the wrong time and place."

I shrugged and looked around as I heard footsteps coming up the stairs. Reina appeared less than a minute later with a heavily-laden tray of food and beverages. Juan thanked the old lady and handed her a hundred-dollar bill. Once she had retreated back down the stairs he waved at the tray.

"Eat up. She made sandwiches and the drink is an agua fresca with watermelon. We'll be leaving in less than an hour now and you're going to wish you had something in your stomach by the time we get down there if you don't eat now."

I sampled the drink and found it to be delicious. In addition to the watermelon, it had a ton of crushed ice and what tasted like lime juice. I drained the glass and then refilled it from the large pitcher in the center of the tray.

"So what did all of that accomplish other than almost getting you and me in a fight right before we were supposed to leave on an op?"

Juan motioned towards Alison with his head. "For starters, it proved to Alison that you aren't any more of a fan of your dad than she is. That isn't going to magically make everything better, but I suspect it's going to go a long ways towards making it so that we can survive as a team rather than getting cut to ribbons the first time that one of Brandon's plans comes apart at the seams."

Juan took a bite of his sandwich and I waited while he chewed and swallowed. "It also gave you a chance to prove that you aren't just some young hothead who can't override your beast enough to stop from getting yourself killed for no good reason, which means that I can trust you more than I would have otherwise. Not only that, it helped you see that you weren't being told the full story by people you've been trusting."

"You knew that already?"

"Yeah. Even without Alison's story having been confirmed to me via other sources I still would have suspected as much. I've been in healthy packs before. I'm atypical because I don't usually hang around for very long, but I've seen how a pack is supposed to function and everything coming out of Sanctuary smells like a cat that's been dead for six days."

"So you don't trust Kaleb either?"

Juan gave me a hard smile. "I don't trust very many people, and I definitely don't trust anyone associated with the Coun'hij."

"Then why are you down here fighting their war for them?"

"I'm not. I'm down here helping them fight my war. My mother was a human, a lot like yours is supposed to be if rumors can be believed, but she immigrated here from Mexico before meeting my father. I've spent time on both sides of the border, I've seen the pros and cons to both countries and one thing stands out loud and clear with regards to Mexico. All of its problems stem from corruption, which ultimately can be placed at the feet of the shape shifters who've set themselves up as untouchable whether via the drug trade or some other mechanism."

"So you want the cats dead."

"Either dead or following policies more like the wolves follow in North America. I've been fighting this particular war since before Kaleb and Puppeteer were born. I'll take advantage of their current willingness to prosecute it, but that doesn't mean that I'm not looking for a better offer."

"You're taking a massive risk telling us that."

Juan leaned back in his chair and shrugged. "Yes, I am. Not as big of a risk as you might think though, and it needed to be done because you need to know that I'm out here as a potential resource and what my terms are."

"Why me?"

"Because any resistance to Kaleb and the Coun'hij will naturally congeal around you. You're the golden boy Mallory has been excited about for more than seventeen years. Brandon too, but by all accounts he's turned out to be a disappointment from the standpoint of realizing the potential that she saw in him so many years ago."

"I just finished finding out that Brandon is the single most deadly individual in the world, how can he be a disappointment? Puppeteer

BOUND

could probably take him down under the right set of circumstances with enough werewolves, but nobody else even comes close. Besides, how would you even know that?"

"Back when you and Brandon were first born Mallory was so excited she couldn't keep her mouth shut, at least not inside the pack. That changed pretty quickly, but as discontent inside of the Sanctuary pack has grown, her early slipups have become common knowledge inside of certain circles."

Juan took a long drink of agua fresca and then looked back up at me. "As for the other part of your question, Brandon is a disappointment for the same reason that Kaleb is vastly more important to our people than Puppeteer could ever be in the short term. Puppeteer is an example of an ability that serves as a force multiplier for short periods of time with a very limited application. It's become obvious, despite Kaleb's efforts to keep it a secret, that he's dramatically increasing the birthrate there in Sanctuary. That whole bit about him being able to heal faster than anyone else who's ever lived is nothing more than a sideshow. His real power boils down to the fact that his pack is growing four or five times as fast as it should be. That's why the Coun'hij puts up with him. Part of it is that they are running scared of just how big the Sanctuary pack has gotten, but mostly they are greedy. By helping

151

him keep as many shape shifters around him as possible they are creating a population explosion that could expand our numbers by an incredible amount over the next couple of hundred years."

It was like a punch to the stomach. I'd already been forcibly educated as to the fact that I wasn't being fed as much information as I'd thought, but this was something else entirely. There were entire planks that my world was built on that I'd never even suspected existed. I looked over at James and the girls and they looked just as shocked as I felt.

"So they are hoping that I'll manifest some kind of ability that will benefit our people more broadly, something like what Kaleb has rather than something like Brandon or Puppeteer have."

"Exactly. That's why you've been given a ton more rope than most of your fellows and it's also why Kaleb and Mallory have been so careful to keep you isolated from the other packs until now. They didn't want anyone giving you a more complete perspective on your worth out of worry that it would make you more difficult to deal with. They can't afford to go wrong with you."

My laugh was a bitter, mocking thing. "I don't see why. You've just finished telling me that Kaleb turns any pack into a baby factory. If he alienates me it's still only a matter of time until the pack produces a dozen more with as great or greater potential."

Juan shook his head. "Frankly the math behind all of that doesn't interest me in the slightest, but statistically speaking hybrids with your level of potential are extremely rare—think a fraction of a percent of all moonborn births. There was some talk that Kaleb had somehow shifted the odds when you and Brandon were born at the same time, but it's been nearly two decades and there hasn't been a repeat, so it's looking very much like that's not the case. That means that Kaleb and Mallory will probably only get to see another two or three savant births. Mallory is older, she might see one or two less, Kaleb is younger so he might see one or two more, but he won't even be able to identify his potential successors without her. There's always a chance that one of the non-savant level hybrids will manifest a particularly useful power like Kaleb's which has an impact all out of relation to the power required to fuel it, but it's unlikely."

"So Kaleb needs me to solidify his hold over our people and secure his legacy."

"Yeah, that's pretty much the size of it."

I rubbed my temples. I knew it was a bad thing to do from a negotiating standpoint, but I just couldn't help it. Juan had hit me with too much information in too short a time period that had much too profound of an impact on my worldview for me to be able to process it right now.

"You know that telling me this could send me on some kind of egotistical power trip."

"It's possible, but I don't think it's likely, Alec. You've had an awful lot of dirt kicked in your face during the last few years. When that happens you either end up getting to a point where you only look out for number one, or you become empathetic to the people around you. James, Jasmin and Jessica wouldn't be ready to walk through fire for you if you were the kind of person I needed to worry about. Not only that, you're obviously smart enough to eventually figure out that this doesn't actually change anything right now. It might allow you to bluff a little here or there to get something you might not have realized you could get before, but your ability is still nothing but potential. Until it manifests you don't have any choice but to dance to Kaleb's tune."

"But if it does manifest, especially if it manifests into something useful, then I can start calling some of my own shots."

"And with that we've returned to my original reason for letting Brandon put you on my team. When you become top dog—if you become top dog—I want to put a plug in for taking care of the jaguar problem south of the border."

"What if I decide that the best way to take care of the problem isn't to kill them all but to work out some kind of deal with them?"

"If it means that the corruption goes away and that my people get a chance to start building a future for themselves instead of lining the pockets of despots, then you'd have my full support. The truth is that there's no way that we'd be able to exterminate the cats. All they need to do to avoid dying is just keep a low profile. Kaleb's Brain Box employs something like two hundred analysts, and they still end up spending more than half of their time following up on the leads that we get from our anonymous tipster. Without him we would have lost the war months ago. The fact that wolves are more social means that we tend to be easier to identify, which means that the initiative would be completely on their side."

That was another piece of the puzzle that I'd never realized was missing until now. With the vampires it was relatively easy to track them down due to their distinctive scent. Werewolves didn't really have a smell that we could use to identify them, at least not the younger ones, but they were little more than dumb animals and the fact that they created rolling blackouts wherever they travelled meant that we always had some idea of where to go look for them. It seemed incredible, but I'd never realized just how hard of a time we would have finding the jaguars.

"If it is so hard to find the cats in the first place, how did we manage to nearly exterminate the cats back during the time of the monarchy?"

"It was a different world back then. There weren't any cars, so people didn't move around like they do now. It meant that your neighbors knew you, it meant that even if a town didn't believe in shape shifters, which most did back then, they still knew when there was something different about a family. From a defensive standpoint, the few travelers to come north were always suspected until we'd observed them during a full moon and confirmed that they didn't have to fight the need to change forms. From the offensive side of things, we just went from village to village and the villagers pretty much identified the jaguars for us."

I could feel my mind chewing on the problem he'd just presented me, but before I could even begin to find a solution Alison broke into the conversation.

"This is all fascinating and I'm glad that you think we'll be able to play nice with each other, but it doesn't change the fact that Alec and his friends have a massive target painted on their backs. How exactly are you planning on dealing with that little problem?"

Juan shrugged. "If the game were easy and safe then everyone would play, Alison. The truth is that I don't have a solution, at least not yet. The first step will be for Alec to evidence a change of heart where Brandon and Vincent are concerned. If you can start pulling as part of the team, then they'll be less likely to try anything. If they did do something like that they would risk losing the independents like me."

"Do you think that Vincent is smart enough to realize that?"

Alison was tapping her lips with a forefinger as she thought about my question even though it had mostly been directed at Juan.

"I think so. If he's not, then Brandon is and Brandon will certainly make the effort required to explain it to Vincent. Slightly more than a third of the wolves and hybrids here are either dispossessed or from small, unaligned packs. If they start feeling like they can't trust Brandon to keep Vincent from playing favorites that might get someone killed, then they'll leave and our ability to go in against the larger groups that the tipster tends to identify for us would be seriously compromised."

I shook my head. "It's not that I'm unwilling. My biggest beef with Brandon and Vincent has always been the way that they bully everyone beyond the requirements even of establishing their dominance. If they play nice with people here because they need them, then that takes away most of the reason, on my side at least, for friction between us. That all works, but I don't think that they are going to buy it if I suddenly become all chummy with them for no reason."

Juan's smile wasn't the least bit reassuring. "Oh, I wouldn't worry about that. Like Alison said, you've practically got an expiration date printed on your forehead now that you're down here. I suspect that you'll have an extremely good reason to change your behavior towards Brandon and Vincent in very short order."

Chapter 9

Alec Graves
Suarez Compound
Northern Mexico

Once we got the tricky parts of our first briefing out of the way, prepping for the mission went by pretty quickly. Juan filled us in on what we needed to know about the operation and then we were bundled into a helicopter.

Most of the attack force was traveling via the ubiquitous black SUVs that seemed to be the mainstay of transportation for the wolves deployed on the border, but our team had been tasked with plugging the backdoor out of the compound and Brandon apparently felt like our chances of sneaking around from the front without being seen weren't very good.

It meant that we left quite a while after everyone else, which was nice, but it also meant that we were more or less cut off from support. If the rest of the teams ran late for any reason and the cats realized we were hanging out back behind their stronghold then we were going to be in for a very long running fight as we tried to get away without all dying.

The roar of the rotors precluded any kind of casual conversation on the flight out, and the things that I wanted to discuss wouldn't have been appropriate for the pilot to listen in on, so I passed the time while we were in the air alone with my thoughts. It was tempting to stew over Juan's revelations, to try to make plans for the future. I needed to have a very blunt conversation with my mother and possibly Donovan as well, but I knew it would be a mistake to think about that right now.

Instead of focusing on the things that I couldn't address, I instead spent the time calming my beast and preparing myself mentally for combat. Mallory had been wrong about what had triggered me gaining more power, but she'd been right about the difference between what I'd faced back in Sanctuary and the world that I was entering now.

Death had been a possibility anytime I'd faced down a challenger, but if it had happened then it would have been an accident, an oversight that happened despite all of Kaleb's efforts to make sure that I lived long enough to realize my potential. The jaguars we were about to go up against would do everything they could to kill me, and unlike the fight with the vampires, I couldn't even count on the fact that everyone on my own side would be trying to keep me alive.

After what seemed like forever, the pilot came back onto the radio to announce that we were within two minutes of our drop point. Juan responded without hesitation.

"Very good. Slow and come down to within twenty to thirty feet of the ground and we'll dismount."

I could hear the alarm in the pilot's voice as he responded to Juan's order. "Hold on, nobody said anything about that. I'm not accepting any kind of liability when you guys break your legs trying to pretend like you're Navy Seals or something."

"You put a large amount of money on deposit with our boss when you accepted this job. If you don't do exactly as I just told you to, you're going to forfeit the entire sum. We're not going to injure ourselves. Trust me, we've trained for exactly this kind of thing."

The pilot looked at Juan and I could tell that he wasn't going to agree, but Juan chose that moment to send a wave of power at the other man that left him shaking and white. I'd considered adding my own pulse of energy into the mix, but was glad that I didn't after I saw the effect that Juan's demonstration had on the poor man.

"Do exactly as I said, and if you can make it look like you're not hovering over the spot to drop people off, that would be even better. We'll need to drop in two waves."

Juan got a shaky nod in response and then the pilot gestured at a low hill. "Right there. The first set can drop out of the left side of the helicopter and then the other half of you can jump from the right side a second or so later."

Juan clapped him on the shoulder, which triggered a bit of a start in the other man, but the helicopter remained rock steady. The pilot really was as good as we'd been told.

James and Alison opened up the back doors on their respective sides and then Juan was climbing out onto the runners. James shed his helmet and then gave me a look that dared me to go out there next. I hadn't been particularly excited about this part of the operation, but part of being a dominant was leading from the front, so I gave him an unconcerned smile and followed Juan outside.

The buffeting of the air driven downwards by the blades was intense even this close into the body of the aircraft. I hunkered down as far as I could to avoid the danger zone above me where the rotors were whirling like razor-edged banshees. As James joined us on the runner Juan reached down to the running light mounted on our side of the helicopter and ripped loose the wire powering it. As the light died I looked through the open doors and saw Alison kill the light on her side as well.

The pilot gave us a nasty look, but the helicopter didn't waver in its approach. Five seconds later our side of the helicopter dipped towards the ground and the pilot hit the glass with his fist to signal us. It was a nice touch, but we'd already let go, flinging ourselves off into thin air.

As my feet lost contact with the runner, I reached out to my beast and shattered the chains I'd carefully bound it with. My transformation ripped through me with even greater force than normal. When I hit the ground a second or so later I didn't hit with the fragile body that I'd been wearing inside of the helicopter and my hybrid body absorbed the force of the impact without even needing to roll to bleed off momentum.

The hardest part of the whole operation turned out to be forcing my beast back down and shifting back to a human so that I could catch Jasmin as she threw herself out of the helicopter in my direction.

Her wolf body wasn't any more suited to a thirty-foot-plus drop than her human body, so she retained her human form and just prayed that I'd make the shift back in time to break her fall without impaling her with a set of semi-retractable claws.

Jasmin's aim was perfect, I hardly had to move at all to get under her. Jasmin was skinny, even for a girl, but after gravity had a chance to accelerate her for slightly more than a second she still hit me with an incredible amount of force. I got my arms underneath her, but the goal was never actually to stop her from hitting the ground. Instead of decelerating her instantly, I simply started slowing her down several feet before the ground would have done it.

We managed to bleed off most of the energy from her fall so that when she did hit the ground a simple roll allowed her to avoid injury. Jasmin let her roll bring her back up to her feet and then started shedding her clothes.

I looked away for a second to confirm that Jessica and Alison had made the drop safely and then looked back to see Jasmin slip out of her jeans so that she was dressed only in the stretchy ha'bit that preserved at least a degree of modesty.

"What do you want us to do with these?"

Jasmin managed to keep it nothing more than a simple question despite the fact that I knew Alison had to be rubbing her the wrong way. Jess was probably happy to let Alison be dominant to her, but Jasmin's nature wouldn't let her and Alison make it much beyond this current mission without settling the question of who was most dangerous.

Juan shrugged. "Stick them under a rock somewhere. If we carry the day then we'll come back for them. If not, well, welcome to the war, the bad guys will have your scent assuming we survive the rout."

A target painted on our backs indeed. All six of us transformed, one after another in a cool wash of power, and then we set off on four legs. The helicopter had dropped us more than a mile away from the compound, but it would only take us a few minutes to cover the distance between here and there. The hardest part would be avoiding being seen once we got to the top of the hill between us and the compound.

We hadn't discussed a specific formation for the trip between the drop site and the compound, but we fell into a loose double chevron without any scuffles. Alison took point as befitted the wolf with the most time in the trenches, while Jasmin and Jess took the wings. Juan was at the center of the formation with James and I flanking him closely.

Wolves were always able to cover ground faster than hybrids, which dictated our current choice of forms, but no hybrid was completely comfortable fighting as a wolf because we spent most of our time as hybrids.

Combat as a hybrid was all about bleeding your opponent out until you found an opening that would allow you to clinch and end the fight. Combat as a wolf was a completely different animal. Wolves didn't get a chance to bleed an opponent out, and disengaging from a fight usually got you killed. Jasmin was such a good fighter precisely because she didn't second-guess an opening when she saw it. She went for it with every ounce of strength and speed her body possessed and relied on her ability to kill her opponent once her jaws were locked around their throat.

BOUND

Putting the girls on the outside of the group would mean that they should trip whatever ambushes might be out there. It had a brutal, sacrificial feel to it, but they were the ones most likely to be able to avoid an attack in this form and positioning the hybrids in the center of the formation meant that we'd be ideally placed to change forms and then come to their aid within seconds of any attack.

Despite the dark tone of my thoughts, we crossed the dry desolation along our route without any problems greater than needing to dodge the occasional creosote bush or cactus. Only a few minutes after we started out we arrived at the hill that had, up until that point, hidden us from the compound. Juan dropped onto his belly and scooted just far enough to look out over the compound. I followed him, and caught a glimpse of two sentries before Juan signaled me back with a low growl.

The inability to communicate complex thoughts was actually one of the biggest drawbacks to this shape, but Juan had been very clear on our orders for this part of the operation back before we'd even left the coffee shop. We were to hold position until Brandon and the others attacked, and then we would start down the mountain, hopefully making enough noise to stop every cat in the compound from bolting straight towards us.

We'd just missed the new moon, so there was a sliver of moonlight dancing across the arid landscape as we waited. I found a flat rock with a large cactus on one side of it and rolled onto my back so that I could look up at the stars.

A couple of seconds later Jasmin padded over and dropped down next to me. We didn't need to talk for me to know that she was worried about the fight that was coming up. Jasmin put on a good show, but in a lot of ways she challenged other wolves simply because she was worried what would happen if she didn't keep clawing her way up the dominance food chain.

We hadn't had a good chance to just sit down and talk since St. Louis, but I knew that the last fight had been hard on her mentally. Having people burst into flame only feet away from you was a pretty good object lesson in all of the ways that things could go wrong.

I almost shifted back to my human shape so that I could wrap a comforting arm around Jasmin, but I'd already shifted three times tonight and I'd have to shift at least two more times before all was said and done. It was foolish to risk a set of cramps that might strike during the middle of the fight, but I was tempted. The cramps usually struck once we were back in our primary form, but occasionally they occurred when we were wolves or hybrids with predictably catastrophic results if it happened during the middle of a fight.

Instead of shifting I simply rolled back onto my belly and then moved back over to her so that I could rest my chin on her shoulders. A little way away but still perfectly visible as ghostly figures of golden-white light to my wolf eyes, I could see that James and Jessica had assumed a similar position as James tried to reassure Jess, who was the worst fighter in our group. James and Jess weren't any more of an item than Jasmin and I were, and although James hadn't ever really talked about their relationship, I got the feeling that they also felt like there was something missing there—that they should be with someone else, but they just didn't know who.

Juan was still up at the crest of the hill, positioned so that he could watch the compound, while Alison was between him and us, pacing back and forth in an effort either to bleed off nervous energy or keep from cooling down.

I watched the way the silver of the moonlight played with the light shining out from just underneath her skin. It was actually a much better visual feast than anything the stars could have hoped to provide. She moved with a sure confidence that was incredibly appealing and I found myself wondering if she could be the one who would be able to fill in the hole in my chest. I'd never really considered her in that way before, but there was a core of strength to her now that hadn't ever been visible before. It was like the harsh sand of near-constant combat had worn away the non-essentials to her personality that she'd always hidden behind back in Sanctuary.

Jasmin had a similar iron center, but for all that it was more readily visible than Alison's had been, hers was relatively untested. Alison's wolf form was undeniably beautiful and her primary form was likewise enchanting. She'd become a wiry masterpiece and even the single lock of red hair looked good on her. I inhaled to take in a bigger than normal lungful of her scent, which caused her to turn and look at me.

Her glare was unmistakable and made me smile inside. She was all angles and fury on the outside, but I got the feeling that she would be worth the effort it would take to get her to open up, only...she wasn't the one for me. I could appreciate her beauty and spunk, but she still didn't move me the way that the blonde from my dreams did.

My musings were interrupted a second later as Juan slipped down from the top of the hill and nudged all of us onto our feet. Apparently he'd seen something to make him think that the rest of the attack force was in position.

I followed Juan up over the top of the hill and then I saw them, more than two dozen glowing figures working their way towards the compound, using every scrap of glowing vegetation possible to mask their presence as they approached.

Juan and I started down the hill, moving quietly, but not making any special effort to remain hidden. The other four stayed hidden and unmoving just out of sight exactly in accordance with Juan's plan. It took the cats' sentries exactly thirty seconds to spot us and raise an alarm. The yelling and sudden explosion of movement down in the compound worked exactly as planned and Brandon's main combat teams killed their first two cats in the confusion before anyone else down there realized that they shouldn't have been focusing all of their attention on Juan and me.

I heard James and the others start down the hill at the same time that Juan and I launched into full sprints. The hope was that our numbers would cause the cats to pause for a critical few seconds as they tried to establish where the real attack was coming from.

We were running fast enough that it only took us a couple of heartbeats to drop down to where we couldn't see over the wall anymore, but it looked like the plan was working. I saw powerfully glowing figures streaming out of various buildings inside the compound and forming up in a loose group that was mostly facing our direction. We were still a hundred yards from the outer wall when a chorus of howls and growls filled the night.

I could hear the crash of bodies and someone from our side yelling commands as our teams inside the compound engaged the cats. Juan slowed to a stop, allowing James and the others to catch up to us as we waited to see if any cats would try to come over the wall. The plan called for one of the teams inside to secure the rear exit first thing, but although the wall was more than twelve feet high, it was mostly there to keep out local predators because it couldn't stop a full-grown southern shape shifter.

Under other circumstances I would have said that it would be impossible for a mere three hybrids with a matching number of wolves to bottle up all of the cats who would be looking to run away once they realized that they were outnumbered and outclassed, but Juan had assured me that only the most desperate would try to go over the wall. Doing that would take them extra precious seconds, during which time they'd be vulnerable to attack from our hybrids.

I'd bought into his explanation so completely that for a split second I refused to believe my eyes when I saw nearly a dozen cats come running towards us. I blinked a couple of times and then realized that they'd exited through the door, which apparently hadn't been sealed off like the plan had said it would be.

Juan shifted into the hulking shape of his hybrid in a sun-bright flare of power and I followed suit without thinking about the change. As hybrids we once again had vocal cords that were roughly analogous to those of a human and I heard James swear as he completed his transformation.

"What's the plan now, oh fearless leader?"

"Don't worry too much about trying to contain them, that's an impossibility given the fact that they now outnumber us. Just try to keep yourselves in one piece and we'll deal with the fallout of so many having escaped afterwards if any of us survive."

Juan's words were calm and unhurried, but I knew we were in serious trouble. The mass of cats racing towards us was shifting around too much for me to tell whether any of them were glowing with the extra light you'd expect from one of the Ancients, but even if the Ancients were both still inside of the compound we were outnumbered and while hybrids tended to outmatch the younger jaguars, even the younger jaguars tended to be more deadly than wolves.

James, Juan and I formed a spearhead with the girls trailing along behind, only just before we clashed with the cats Juan did something completely unexpected. Between one step and the next Juan reached down and picked up a long branch that was the better part of ten feet long and as big around as my leg when I was in human form. Before any of the cats could adjust to the fact that they were facing someone armed with more than just the normal claws, fangs and talons of a hybrid, Juan impaled one of them with the branch and then swept the branch, and the cat he'd stabbed, through the rest of the group springing at us.

It was a masterstroke and it gave us a chance, however slim, of surviving the next few minutes.

A cat hurled himself at me, but Juan had obviously rattled him because his timing was off and he wasn't as fast as he should have been. I plucked him out of the air with my right hand, and ignored the way that his claws ripped into my arm. He writhed around with a strength and violence that I wasn't expecting and for a second I almost lost my grip on him. Wolves were capable of flailing about in an attempt to break free, but his claws gave him leverage that exceeded anything I'd ever been up against before.

The claws on my right hand started to lose their grip on him, but I'd held him relatively immobile for just long enough and my left hand joined my right, sinking claws into his flesh and ending his life with a couple of carefully-aimed slashes.

I'd taken too long to kill my opponent. Juan was streaming blood down his right side, but he'd killed another cat and was holding a third one at arm's length already. The disarray triggered by Juan's opening attack had evaporated and it seemed like a solid wall of cats was coming towards us now.

A particularly large cat looked like he was going to attack Juan, but at the last second he executed a lightning-fast change in direction and threw himself at me instead. I was focused on a different cat who was obviously lining up to attack James, so I was out of position. I knew that there wasn't any way I was going to manage to get my hands between me and my attacker, so I dodged left and winced slightly as his claws tore through the top of my right shoulder.

If I'd been a hair slower he would have had a shot at my neck and I probably would have been dead, but there wasn't time to dwell on that. My evasion had brought me around to where I could see James, who had a jaguar fastened to his front tearing at his stomach and chest while he used one hand to hold its fangs away from his neck and the other to try to get to something vital before it bled him out.

It wasn't a good position for James to be in, but it was a lot less concerning than the two cats who had circled around behind him so that they could attack from the one direction hybrids were least equipped to defend.

I yelled, but I already knew that he wouldn't be able to respond in time, not with the first cat savaging him like it was and a fourth cat approaching attack range from the front as well. The cat who had gone sailing past me a split second before was probably angling for a killing grip on my back as well, but I threw myself towards James anyway.

The cats were too focused on their target and the distance between us was blessedly short, so I managed to catch both jaguars by surprise. The bigger cat had already left the ground and was arrowing towards James, but I snatched him out of the air with both hands settling for a bad hold on him rather than no hold at all.

The smaller cat spun around as I grabbed her partner, but I just sank the talons on my right foot into her side just behind her shoulder and hoped that I'd get lucky and hit her heart. Stabbing the female threw off my stride, which was probably the only thing that saved me. A split second after my talons skewered the smallest cat I got hit by a hammer blow of force from behind that sent me sprawling.

I tried to lead with the cat in my claws, driving him into the ground and using him to cushion my landing. I let my fall convert into a roll, hoping to crush the cat that was furiously clawing at my back. I misjudged my momentum and rolled all the way back onto my feet only to feel another impact as someone else crashed into me.

I caught bits and pieces of the fight going on around me as I went flying head over heels yet again. James was bleeding from dozens of wounds large and small and he'd dropped to one knee, but he had his one remaining opponent immobilized and looked to be only seconds away from ending that portion of the fight.

As I landed on my side something grabbed hold of my left hand, tearing it free of the cat it had been buried in and rolling me over onto my stomach. It was a dangerous position to be in because it left my back exposed and vulnerable, but someone else had hold of my right leg and they were stretching me out in an effort to keep me from being able to free myself.

I looked to the side and saw that the small female who had been focused on James had been knocked free of my talons and was circling, looking for an opportunity to grab hold of another of my appendages so that she could help immobilize me while the big cat on my back finished me off.

I realized that this was the end, that I only had a few seconds left, but rather than just giving up I unleashed the full measure of my beast's power and pulled with every ounce of force my massive hybrid body could generate.

The jaguar in my right hand convulsed once before I let him drop away, and then I focused all of my efforts on pulling my arms and legs in close enough that I'd at least be able to meet death on my feet. The cats pulled with everything they had, but I felt my left hand and right leg slowly inching back underneath me. I looked to the side to see how long I had before the female latched onto my right hand, and saw a bright blur crash into her. Jasmin had hold of the back of her neck and she planted and started whipping the cat back and forth with everything she had.

Juan suddenly appeared and tore away the cat who had been tearing at my right leg. I surged to my feet, using my right hand to help lift the cat dangling from my arm up to where my fangs could latch onto its neck. A second later there was another dead jaguar at my feet and only then did I realize that there wasn't anything on my back. I turned around just in time to see Alison finish off the huge cat who had come within inches of killing me.

I opened my mouth to thank her for saving my life, but my knees buckled and blackness claimed me before I could get a single word out.

Chapter 10

Alec Graves
Rest Easy Hotel
Rio Rico, Arizona

Apparently I'd been injured even worse than I'd realized when I'd passed out at the compound. Judging by how relieved Jasmin had looked yesterday when I'd finally opened my eyes back at the hotel, it had very much been touch and go as to whether or not I was going to make it.

Even with my newly-accelerated healing abilities I'd still been down for nearly forty-eight hours before I finally rolled out of bed without assistance. I was feeling pretty good now—twenty-four hours later—but our medic, a tiny woman named Francesca, seemed almost as rattled by how close I'd come to death as Jasmin had been. I'd been ordered not to participate in any kind of combat operations for at least another two days.

I was pretty sure that she'd underestimated my recuperative abilities by a significant margin, but that wasn't necessarily a bad thing. I needed every edge I could get down here on the border and if she was underestimating me then everyone else would be too. Besides, she had a point in that replacing the amount of blood that I'd apparently lost didn't happen overnight, even for one of the moonborn. The last thing I wanted right now was to end up in another fight for my life only to find out that I was a half-step slower and weaker than normal.

I'd gone to the hotel's outdoor pool yesterday out of desperation. I'd spent too much time lying around in my bed and I'd needed an activity that would get me outside but also avoid running me into the ground in case I wasn't fully recovered.

I'd expected to get some sun and take a long nap, and gotten something completely unexpected instead. I was headed to the pool even earlier today than yesterday, partially because I was feeling better than I had yesterday, but also because I was eager to see if the steady trickle of people who had come to visit me would repeat itself.

There was one hall in the hotel that for whatever reason had been built slightly narrower than the rest of the halls. Some idiot had placed a long series of decorative tables along one side, which made it so that while two normal people could walk past each other in it, if either of them happened to be very big it became a lot easier for one of them to just get out of the way and let the other pass.

Predictably it had turned into a dominance extravaganza. For the most part the moonborn down here on the border were less concerned with dominance posturing, at least outside of their own units, but there was no getting around the fact that there was still going to be some dominance issues any time you put a large number of wolves and hybrids together in one place.

Vincent and his team were the worst. Where the other teams tended to stick to themselves for the most part, Vincent's people seemed to go out of their way to strike sparks off of members of the other teams. The fact that they were the ones who most often fought alongside Brandon in the heaviest bits of fighting meant that Vincent's team overall was considered the most elite set of fighters we had. That should have been enough for them, but instead they seemed positively obsessed with rubbing everyone else's noses in the fact that they were currently the top of the food chain.

As luck would have it, I ran into Vincent in the challenge hall, as it had become known. Actually, it would have been more accurate to say that Vincent practically ran into me. Despite the fact that I was nearly to the end of the hall and he would have only had to wait for a couple of seconds for me to be out of his way, he stepped into the narrow passageway and made it clear that he wasn't planning on giving way to me.

The sheer arrogance and rudeness he was displaying was enough to set my teeth on edge and awaken a surge of anger from my beast, but I just gritted my teeth and stepped off into the tiny space between two of the tables so that he could pass by.

For a second I almost thought he looked disappointed that I didn't get in his face, but whatever emotion I was having a hard time identifying was quickly replaced by a broad smile.

"It looks like you've finally learned your place."

"I've had it rather forcibly demonstrated to me that accidents happen on battlefields. I have a feeling that I'll get plenty of fighting in against the cats without needing to go around looking for fights with other hybrids."

I was walking a very thin line and I knew it. The act of having gotten out of his way was inherently submissive, but if my words were either too aggressive or too submissive, either one, he'd never believe that my recent changes were sincere.

"Yeah, too bad about that. I'm sure glad that something worse didn't happen to you or one of your friends."

The insincerity practically dripped off of his words, but I just gave him a tight smile and waited for him to continue walking by. Given my druthers I would have just walked away from him, but that wasn't proper behavior coming from a subordinate. Several seconds passed before Vincent's grin got even broader and he turned and continued on down the hall.

"I might have some errands for you to do later, Alec."

My jaw clenched from the effort of not telling Vincent what he could do with his busy-work chores, but I managed to get out of sight without responding to that final taunt that he'd tossed over his shoulder.

Judging by the scents waiting for me on the breeze when I opened the door outside, Alison, Jasmin and Jessica were all already at the pool. I'd stopped by James' room before heading to the pool, so it wasn't a surprise that he wasn't there too. He was recovering nicely from his wounds, but although he hadn't been injured as badly as I had been, he also didn't have a metabolism that was quite as supercharged as mine. He'd probably need all of the next two days to finish healing.

I came around the corner and any thoughts of James fled from my mind as I got my first view of the three girls in their swimming suits. Alison probably already had a swimsuit before we'd arrived, but Jasmin and Jess must have borrowed one of the SUVs to go shopping at some point yesterday.

All three were wearing two-piece outfits that left long expanses of stomach and shoulder bare and I idly noticed just how good of a job they'd each done in selecting a color that suited them perfectly. Jasmin's black swimsuit went perfectly with her darkly-tanned skin, while Jess' frilly white top and bottom matched perfectly with skin so white you could be forgiven for thinking that she was some kind of alabaster doll that had never been intended on being taken outside where she might be damaged.

Alison on the other hand was wearing a bright red outfit that was perfect for her lightly tanned skin and the strand of red hair that she'd re-dyed sometime between our last operation and now. It really was too bad that I couldn't shake my obsession with the mystery blonde from my dreams. I was about to spend the day with three incredibly beautiful women, but even when faced with such breathtaking perfection I still couldn't help but think of the girl from my dreams.

"I didn't expect to find the three of you here today."

Jasmin put her hand up in a languid wave without looking my way, while Jessica turned towards me and smiled in a way that made the huge sunglasses she was wearing even cuter than they'd been a second before. It was Alison however who spoke.

"Orders. Juan saw your visitors yesterday and thought that maybe it might be smart not to have clandestine conversations out in the open without taking certain precautions."

I opened my mouth to ask her what she meant, but she seemed to read my mind. She reached over to the portable music player sitting on the table next to her and turned it up to the point where it would serve as a kind of makeshift white noise generator.

I nodded as I realized that also explained the seating that the girls had chosen for themselves. They'd arranged themselves into a half circle with two empty chairs in the center, presumably for me and any visitors I might have.

I picked the chair closest to Alison and gently lowered myself down into it as I considered whether or not to pull my shirt off. The truth was that the wounds had all turned into thin white scars already, but it would be foolish to reveal that fact to anyone who happened by, so the shirt was going to have to stay on.

I set my book, some cookie-cutter spy thriller, down beside me and then turned to Alison. "I haven't had a chance yet to tell you thanks for pulling that jaguar off of me. I asked Juan where you were yesterday so that I could properly show my appreciation, but he told me to mind my own business. I'm glad that you're here today. Thanks."

Alison shrugged. "You would have done the same thing for any of us. In fact, I'm pretty sure that you did exactly that for James. Besides, my having put that one down wouldn't have helped much if Jasmin hadn't gotten that female who was lining up to jump you too."

"I told Jasmin thanks already."

"Okay, so it sounds like we're all square then."

It was obvious that she was trying to get me to shut up and leave her alone, but I was fascinated by the change she'd gone through. She'd survived and Chloe hadn't. Did that mean that survival here required some kind of extreme change like she'd undergone, or was that just her way of dealing with everything that had happened?

"Can I ask you a question?"

"Sure, you're dominant to me and everything, so it's not like I can beat you into leaving me alone or anything."

"I'm not going to use the fact that I'm bigger and stronger than you to pry, Alison. If you don't want to talk to me you can just say so and I'll leave you alone."

She let her black sunglasses droop down to the point where she could look at me over the top of them. "You're serious?"

"I'm not Kaleb. I've got my own share of issues, but I do at least try not to be a jerk to people who've saved my life."

"Fine, you get one question, but I may or may not answer it depending on what it is."

"Why do you dye your hair? It has to be a pain to re-dye it every time you shift forms."

Her fists knotted up and for a second I thought that she wouldn't answer, but after a few heartbeats she relaxed and then just shrugged.

"You do seem to have a way of seeing right to the heart of things."

I shook my head. "I don't think so. Ever since I left Sanctuary all I've done is find out just how blind I've been, just how much was going on underneath the surface of things that I never even considered might be going on."

"Yeah, but that is because you trusted people who were doing their level best to keep you in the dark. I think that you're more perceptive than you're giving yourself credit for right now."

It was my turn to shrug. "Well, thanks for the vote of confidence."

I leaned back and opened my book up, but I saw her sit up out of the corner of my eye.

"You're really just going to leave it at that? You're not going to press me for an answer to your question?"

"No. You know what I'm curious about, but it's your choice whether or not you want to fill me in. Even if it were smart to try and beat an answer out of someone who is going to be watching my back over the next few months, it still isn't something I'd do."

Alison sighed and then dropped back onto her chair. "You and I are more alike than I like to think about. We both trusted the wrong people. The dye disappears after every shift so you're right, re-dyeing it all of the time is a total pain, but I do it to remind myself that I trusted the wrong person. I do it because it's a reminder that I'm going to be paying for my mistakes for the rest of my life, however short that may turn out to be. The burden of dyeing a strand of my hair multiple times a week is a small symbolic gesture of the bigger burden that Sam and your dad left me with."

"It doesn't have to be forever."

Alison's laugh was mocking, but it somehow didn't trigger any kind of response from my beast.

"You're right. If I could figure out a way to kill Sam and Kaleb and then run away somewhere so that I didn't have to risk my life in a purposeless war that can never be won, then I could stop dyeing it."

"You think you're stuck, that you don't have any options."

"Yeah, I think that because it's true. You can be all Pollyannaish about things if you want. That doesn't have to stop us from working together, but don't let your optimism get in the way of doing your job. I'm resigned to the fact that I'm not going to make it out of here alive, but that doesn't mean that I'm going to be okay with you putting me in extra danger because you refuse to see the world as it really is."

I opened my mouth to respond but she jammed a pair of earbuds in and flipped open a magazine. I'd obviously pressed too hard, but I hadn't been able to help myself. Alison hadn't ever seemed to need my help before. She, Sam and Chloe had formed a tiny little power bloc that hadn't been very tough, but which also had taken great care to keep its head down so that nobody would have a reason to grief them. The old Alison hadn't needed me, but the new Alison did whether she realized it or not.

I forced myself to look away from Alison in the hopes that not having her in my field of vision would help me get my frustration under control. Jasmin caught my eye and turned over onto her side.

"You can't help everyone."

The words were more mouthed than actually said so as not to carry over to Alison, but they didn't make me feel any better. It seemed like everyone needed help and I wanted to help them, but I didn't even have the power to keep my closest friends safe, let alone random people who didn't want my help.

Actually, if I were to be completely honest, I couldn't even protect myself, and that rankled maybe the most of all. My beast was convinced that we should be the top dog and I desperately wanted to believe him, but every time I turned around it seemed like someone new was curb-stomping us.

I gave Jasmin my best impression of a reassuring smile and then flipped my book back open. I wasn't in the mood to read anymore, but at least it gave me an excuse to break eye contact.

Once I had the book open, habit took over and I found myself scanning down through the words. I'd been reading for less than five minutes before I heard footsteps. I looked up a second later to find that we'd been joined by one of the independents currently working with the primarily Sanctuary-staffed army.

Abram belonged to one of the packs based in Montana and before now I'd exchanged all of five words with him. He was a hybrid and one whom I suspected most other hybrids tended to underestimate on a regular basis. The muscle shirt he was wearing highlighted the arms and shoulders of a serious bodybuilder, which would have been enough to make most people back down if not for the fact that he was only five-eight.

There was often a link between the size of an individual and the size of their alternate forms, so conventional wisdom would have said that Abram would be on the small side as a hybrid, but conventional wisdom would have been wrong. I'd seen his hybrid form and it was nearly as big as Brandon's, although not as strong.

"You mind if I sit down here next to you, Alec?"

"Please do, Abram. How is your team all doing?"

He carefully sat down on the white plastic chair with the air of someone who was used to accidentally breaking things.

"We're all okay. I had one person get opened up from shoulder to flank when Vincent failed to bottle up the cats like he was supposed to. They started to flank us and it looked like things were going to be touch and go there for a second until they broke out the back door towards you guys. My wolf will be okay though, she's a tough one."

"You guys are on light duty then too?"

"Pseudo-light duty. Brandon doesn't usually send out a team that's down two or more people, but he occasionally sends one out that's only down one person, especially if it's a wolf that's missing rather than a hybrid."

I gave him a nod. "I'm glad to hear that everyone is okay, or at least will make a full recovery."

Abram looked over at Jessica and Jasmin and raised an eyebrow. It could have meant a lot of different things, everything from simple appreciation of two pretty girls to concern that they were close enough to overhear us, but I was pretty sure I knew the actual meaning based on how some of my other conversations had gone yesterday.

"Jasmin, Jess, could you please work your magic?"

Both girls reached over to the portable music players next to them and turned them up. Alison seemed to be dead to the world, but she'd turned her player up before grabbing her iPod and sticking her earbuds in.

"This is a delicate matter, but I just wanted to stop by and let you know that I don't approve of how that last operation went down. I don't have any proof that it was intentional, but despite being a bunch of colossal jerks, Vincent's guys are actually quite good in sticky situations. I've never seen them miss the timing on an op that badly."

I nodded carefully. "My history with Vincent isn't a secret, at least not among the Sanctuary pack. I would be lying if I said that I didn't think about the possibility that he was trying to send me a message."

"That's the thing; Brandon is supposed to be above that. A good third of the people down here don't owe any kind of allegiance to him or Kaleb either one. We came here because we believe in the cause. We want to see the cats pushed back, and Brandon's ability combined with the backing of the Sanctuary pack means that this is our best chance to make a difference without running afoul of the Coun'hij."

I nodded. It made sense. Jaclyn, the leader of the Tucson pack, actually had an ability that let her put individual cats down even faster than Brandon, but her ability didn't work as well against the more powerful cats. She still could have served as the focal point for another coordinated offensive against the southerners but for the fact that she was openly disparaging of the Coun'hij. She wasn't saying anything that a lot of other people weren't thinking, but they weren't saying it out loud and she was, which meant that in her own way she had an even bigger target painted on her back than I had on mine.

Throwing your lot in with Jaclyn would be a really quick way to put yourself into a position where you might end up fighting Puppeteer instead of the cats that you'd signed on to fight.

Abram continued on, oblivious to the thoughts running through my head. "The thing is that this only works as long as we independents know that we're going to be treated at least as well as you guys from Sanctuary, and that you guys from Sanctuary are being treated okay."

"I can understand that. Nobody wants to be sent on suicide missions or used as cannon fodder."

"Right, and the stakes are even higher. There are hundreds of shape shifters north of here who could come help and make a huge difference in this fight, but they don't because they're scared. A bunch of us were hoping that putting up a big win like this last operation would help pull some of those able bodies down here to help, but it actually looks like it had the opposite effect."

This was new. Neither of the others from yesterday had mentioned this particular tidbit.

"What do you mean?"

"People aren't stupid, Alec. All of North America pretty much knows that you and Brandon have bad blood between you. When you get critically injured in the first operation you're on, despite being put in a secondary spot where you shouldn't have been in all that much danger, it's naturally going to make people worried that if they come down here they might get caught in the crossfire."

"I see your point, but I'm not sure what you're proposing."

"Eat a little crow. It seems like you've already started doing that, but keep it up. This war is too important to risk having everything blow up in our faces because Vincent is too stupid to keep the dominance games back here where they belong rather than out there in the field."

I let my face harden. "That's asking a lot. Even assuming I can bring myself not to get into things with Vincent, what's to say that he won't just then use that as an excuse to cause me even more grief?"

Abram shrugged. "You're not stupid either. You know as well as I do that the deck is stacked against you. You can either go down in a blaze of glory and screw this entire war up, or you can swallow your pride a little and hopefully live long enough to be able to go back home. If you choose the second option, then I'd be willing to let Brandon know just how thin the ice he's standing on is getting. If you get hurt under any kind of suspicious circumstances, then he could see a third of his force walk out on him with no further warning."

"What if there was another option? One that gave you a chance to fight the cats, one that gave you a hope of winning rather than just an endless round of bloodletting, one that still kept you out of trouble with the Coun'hij?"

"Unless you've developed magic powers that I haven't heard about then there isn't any other option, kid."

"You're right, there isn't any other option, right now, but what if there was?"

Abram took a deep breath. "If there was another option then you could come talk to me and I'd hear you out. If you were too crazy then it wouldn't buy you anything, but I'd at least listen."

"Thanks, Abram. That means a lot. I'll do my best not to make any more waves with Brandon or Vincent, and I'd appreciate anything you could do to help make sure that there aren't any additional…accidents while we're out on the field."

Abram gave me a tight nod and then stood and left. Jasmin watched him go and then looked over at me. "You're playing a dangerous game, Alec."

"I know, but I don't feel like I have much of a choice. Maybe you're right, maybe I can't save everyone, but if we don't do something then everything is going to keep getting worse and worse."

"Have you ever considered the possibility that maybe there isn't anything that can be done to fix the world? There are just too many people trying to ruin it."

"If I don't try, then I'm no better than the ones causing all of the problems."

I got a shrug in response, but any further response I might have offered up was preempted by Juan's arrival.

"I'm glad to see that the girls showed up to give you cover like I asked them to."

"Yes, thank you. It made my most recent conversation a little more straightforward than the first two."

"I thought it might."

I waited to see if Juan was going to pry, but he seemed happy to leave me with my secrets. It was possible that he just expected that he'd be able to pump Alison for information later, but I didn't think so. He seemed genuinely to only care about his war against the cats. He'd sent the girls to act as a screen just because I was a part of his team and he wanted to keep his team out of trouble, but he was happy to otherwise leave me to my scheming.

After a few seconds of silence Juan looked over at me again and sighed. "I've been doing some more poking around. It was definitely Vincent who was responsible for the back door."

"Yeah, I just had someone else confirm that for me as well today. That definitely means that he was out to get me."

Juan nodded. "Yeah, but I'll go you one better. Brandon doesn't always tell even the team leaders who is going to cover which role. I'm not sure why, it's one of his worst failings as a leader, but I think it's because he doesn't completely trust us. I finally ferreted out who originally had the back door assignment and it wasn't Vincent. The team leader who originally was supposed to cover the exit said that Vincent showed up partway through Brandon's briefing and demanded that the roles be swapped."

I resisted the urge to rub my temples. "So it was all Vincent's idea then, which means that Brandon may not have it in for me as bad as I thought."

"Yeah, but that's a big maybe. It could have been that Brandon just didn't see the opportunity to put us in the crosshairs until after Vincent pointed it out to him, or it could even mean that Brandon's playing a much longer, much more devious game than we're giving him credit for. It's always possible that he saw a way to put us in danger, but that he orchestrated everything so that it would look like Vincent had been behind it."

"I really hate this kind of double-and triple-think."

"Yeah, me too, but unfortunately that's the way the world works in the big leagues."

Chapter 11

Alec Graves
Rest Easy Hotel
Rio Rico, Arizona

James was back on his feet, but he was obviously not at one hundred percent. He was a little paler than normal and he moved with the slow care of someone who had discovered that it hurt if they moved too fast and pulled at still-healing wounds.

His wounds actually looked pretty good now, but obviously his injuries had taken a mental toll on him. He didn't look very happy to have to sit and wait with everyone else for Brandon to show up so that the briefing could start.

Actually, he wasn't the only one who looked unhappy. There was a different feeling to the room than there'd been at the last briefing and I was pretty sure that it had a lot to do with the fact that everyone here knew that Brandon had let Vincent take a shot at us. It was the kind of thing that sent a little thrill of satisfaction through me, but I sternly reminded myself not to let my success so far go to my head. It was always possible if I got to be enough of a problem that Brandon might just decide to have me eliminated despite the risks.

I took a deep breath and then pushed all of that to one side and let myself think about the last couple of days. I'd had a surprising amount of fun at the pool. It had been nice to just kick back and do nothing for hours at a time. Jasmin, Jess and I had laughed and joked until my face had hurt from smiling so much. Alison had even thawed out a little there by the end, which had been an added reward.

Lazy summer days by the pool. Given the amount of money behind the Graves name some people might have expected that I'd done little more than sit around like that so far in my life, but the truth was that Kaleb had kept me pretty busy almost as far back as I could remember. I'd always had at least a little time to do with as I'd wanted, but although there was a small pool back home, pack life had never really lent itself to lounging around at a pool so I'd always found other ways to spend my limited free time.

I wouldn't have expected being down here on the border to change any of that, but it had. Knowing that we could be sent into battle with only a few hours' notice had lent our downtime an odd kind of vividness that I'd never experienced previously.

It was probably true that I'd get restless if hours spent at the pool was the sole sum of my existence, but resting in the sun with three beautiful women close at hand, even if I couldn't quite see myself with any of them, had been the perfect way to spend the last few days.

James had come out to join us for a couple of hours yesterday and Juan had even swung by and spent an hour or so with us. It hadn't been planned, at least not that I'd been able to tell, and I hadn't expected such a short time together to make any kind of significant difference to our cohesion as a group, but it had. Instead of being spread out with Juan in one spot, Alison in another and the rest of us in a third, all six of us had chosen to stand together while we waited for the briefing to start.

My musings were interrupted by Brandon's arrival. He strode into the room like he owned it; he didn't seem to notice the new tension that was present in the room.

"Thank you all for coming today. I'd planned on simply briefing you all on the latest target that the Brain Box has identified for us, but I'm afraid that something else has come up."

Brandon pulled his remote out of a pocket and turned off the lights at the same time that he brought the projector online.

BOUND

"Just this morning we got word of four deaths in a little town east of here called Hereford. The police and town officials are busy suppressing any mention of the murders because all four people were 'savaged by some kind of large, clawed beast.' The Brain Box has been trying for the last several hours to obtain photos of the wounds in question, but so far they've been spectacularly unsuccessful. Some of the hacks that they've been using lately to compromise target IT systems have been identified by the greater security community and new hotfixes are slowly making their way out to state and local government computer systems. We could be flying blind for several weeks until our intelligence assets manage to find new ways into the systems that we need access to."

Brandon let that tidbit of news sink in for a moment and then clicked a button which caused the map of Arizona to appear on the screen.

"As you can see, Hereford is very much inside the territory claimed by the Tucson pack and ideally we'd just leave the investigation to them, but as is their normal practice lately they aren't returning any of my calls."

It was a weak attempt at a joke, even from Brandon and not just because it highlighted the fundamental rift between the Coun'hij and most of the rest of the wolves in North America.

"It's traditional to leave the policing of their borders to each individual pack, but given that

199

this particular incident has the potential to cause our existence to become disseminated to the general public, I've been asked to provide a team to help deal with things in Hereford."

There was a low rumble, not discontent exactly, but at the very least surprise. The Coun'hij had dedicated troubleshooters who dealt with any kind of threat that could cause our secret to be pushed out into the open. It was unheard of for the Coun'hij to require extra help just to deal with a few deaths like this. Not only that, it was the kind of assignment that had the potential to blow up in a person's face.

If you did a good job and destroyed any and all evidence that would cause people to keep asking questions, then at best you might get a pat on the back. If you screwed things up and missed some critical piece of information then you could pretty much count on your life going to crap.

Brandon seemed to realize that his presentation wasn't very convincing. "I should clarify. The Coun'hij will be sending in one of their specially-trained troubleshooters to clean up the evidence, they just need one of our teams to go provide some support so that their guy doesn't get ambushed by whatever killed those humans."

That was a slightly better prospect. We were all a lot more comfortable with a bodyguard role than with any kind of information suppression, but some of the Coun'hij's troubleshooters had a pretty bad reputation. Worst of all was the fact that Brandon hadn't indicated that the group who went on this op would be getting any kind of reprieve from whatever Brandon had in the works before the murders in Hereford hit his radar. Running back-to-back ops without at least a couple of days' downtime between them was a recipe for a mutiny, which was probably why Brandon was essentially asking for volunteers rather than just ordering a team to go take care of things.

The silence grew to the point where it was obvious nobody was going to say anything and Brandon's frown grew in lockstep to the ticking of the clock.

"Vincent, I hate to order anyone to do this task given that it shouldn't even be our job and that we'll still be going forward with the operation first thing tomorrow night, but your guys are some of the best we've got."

I'd seen Vincent at a loss for words on more occasions than I could count, but usually that was because he was mad and his relatively limited vocabulary was failing him. I'd never seen him unable to speak and looking uncomfortable at the same time.

"I…ah, that is, I think you're forgetting about that matter you wanted me to deal with. I don't see how I could do both, not unless you were okay with postponing that other thing…"

Brandon looked like he wanted to spit nails and a pulse of power roared through the room before he got himself back under control.

"No, you're right. Someone else will need to go to Hereford. Finishing the preparations for your other assignment takes precedence."

I could tell that I wasn't the only one surprised by what Brandon had said. In theory, Brandon was subordinate to the Coun'hij and therefore this secret mission he'd assigned to Vincent shouldn't be superseding the job in Hereford.

Without really knowing why I was doing so, I leaned forward and whispered to Juan. "I really think we should volunteer for this one."

Another team leader would have just told me to shut up. Juan did give me an odd look like he was trying to figure out what my angle was, but after a couple of seconds he cleared his throat.

"We'll go to Hereford."

Brandon shook his head. "You're down two people right now. In fact, your team is part of the reason that I haven't been pushing for the main op to be put together before now. You're not back up to full strength until just before the op goes live."

Juan shrugged. "We can leave James here so that he doesn't get set back at all. Alec seems to be raring to help out, so who am I to tell him he has to stay here?"

His bland tone seemed to indicate just how stupid he thought I was being. It drew a chuckle from a few of the shape shifters who'd been close enough to hear me ask him to volunteer, but apparently Brandon at least hadn't been able to hear my whisper to Juan. A flicker of something that almost looked like confusion crossed Brandon's face and then he nodded.

"That works for me. Thank you for being willing to help out. You guys should go ahead and get on the road now. We can bring you up to speed on the big op once you are back here tomorrow morning. I'll let my contact on the Coun'hij know that you're the ones he needs to get in touch with."

Chapter 12

Alec Graves
Highway 82
Southern Arizona

Juan managed to keep his questions to himself until after we got on the road. Once Brandon dismissed us, Juan waved at James to stay for the briefing and then led the other four of us out into the hall.

"Get an overnight bag and the standard first-aid supplies. I'll meet you all out in the parking lot in ten minutes."

Alison shot me a dirty look as we all scattered back to our rooms, but that wasn't entirely a surprise. By convincing Juan to volunteer us I'd just put us all in danger again more than twenty-four hours before we'd otherwise have been put into harm's way.

I made it out to the parking lot a full three minutes before the deadline that we'd been given and found Juan already there waiting for us.

"You'd probably like an explanation."

Juan grunted. "Not here."

Over the next few minutes the three girls trickled out of the hotel and we all climbed into the SUV that Juan had picked out. At a nod from Juan, Alison got behind the wheel and we were off.

I opened my mouth again to explain my reasoning, but Juan held up a hand as he pulled out a small electronic device and pushed some buttons. We waited for a couple of minutes while the device beeped and flashed and then Juan nodded to himself and put it away.

"Okay, the car's clean. A few of us independents have organized a watch schedule that allows us to keep two of the vehicles in the motor pool under surveillance. We can't guarantee that someone couldn't slip a transmitter onto them, so we have to still use a portable bug sniffer, but at least keeping an eye on them like we do means that nobody can wire them with something more complicated that doesn't require a transmitter."

I shook my head in astonishment. "I never would have guessed that you'd all be so paranoid down here."

"Don't let anybody fool you. Putting big wins up is nice from the standpoint of recruiting, but it doesn't matter for crap if there isn't some kind of support structure down here that lets people feel safe. Half of the independents down here wouldn't have ever agreed to come help if a couple of us hadn't come down here first and set up some basic precautions."

My mind was whirling. It seemed like every time I turned around something else caught me by surprise lately. I'd known that Juan and the others were worried about Brandon turning on them, but I hadn't realized that they were quite so organized.

"This isn't the only security measure you guys have in place, is it?"

"Of course not, but don't bother asking what else we've got in the works. You're a pretty straight shooter, but you're still from the Sanctuary pack. Instead, how about if you tell me what made you think it was a good idea to volunteer us for this particular assignment."

I nodded. "Okay, that's fair. The truth is that I'm not sure I can point to a single reason, it's more like a bunch of small things that made this feel like the right decision. Firstly, it extends an even bigger olive branch out to Brandon and Vincent by showing them that I'm willing to take orders and even volunteer when the need arises."

"You're assuming that Brandon will eventually hear that you were the one that pushed for us to volunteer."

"Yeah. As paranoid as you guys seem to be about the idea that he's spying on you, it seems like a safe bet."

"That could backfire on you if it makes the independents think that you are too firmly in Brandon's pockets. What else?"

"I figured that there is a chance that being out on this assignment will bring us into contact with some of the Tucson pack."

Juan's right eyebrow rose a fraction of an inch. "It's possible, but why is that desirable? Jaclyn is pretty well known for not liking the Sanctuary pack in general and your father in particular."

"You and a few others have recently given me a crash course in the fact that everyone I run into is going to have some kind of agenda. The only way for me to hope to get a complete picture of what's really going on is to get more points of view than I have right now. Jaclyn seems like a decent source to help counterbalance some of the propaganda I get fed when I'm back home."

"Assuming she doesn't just kill you out of hand."

"That would be pretty shortsighted of her."

"Jaclyn isn't considered to be the most well-grounded individual out there. She'd pretty much have to be a little crazy to put the Coun'hij on notice like she has."

My mouth went a little dry, but I managed a shrug. "I guess if she kills me then she kills me, but she's going to be a lot more likely to believe me now when I'm operating from a position of weakness than she would be later on if I approach her after I manifest an ability."

"You probably have a decent point there. Any other reasons?"

"Yeah, I guess one last big one. Somebody—or something—killed four people who shouldn't be dead right now. I don't know if it was cats or not, but I want to help put whomever was responsible for those murders down. I know that you're big on stopping the cats, but it feels to me like lately we've been spending way too much time bickering over who's the biggest, toughest predator on the block and not enough time protecting people who can't protect themselves."

Juan shook his head. "We're not as different as you think, Alec. I want the cats gone for the same reason that you want to end whatever killed those people. I want those who are still alive to have a better life, just like you."

"So you're not going to hold this all against me?"

Juan looked over at Alison and then shrugged. "*I'm* not going to, but I'm probably not the one you need to worry about."

Alison muttered something that sounded like 'highhanded jerk' and then turned onto the main highway.

BOUND

We'd been driving for twenty minutes before Juan got a text from an unlisted number that contained nothing more than an address and a time. A quick text to Brandon confirmed that the text had come from whomever the Coun'hij was sending to contain the incident, but we still didn't have any idea who we'd actually be working with.

It quickly became obvious that we were going to struggle to hit the deadline that we'd just had imposed on us, so Alison swore under her breath and sped up a little more. The radar detector inside the SUV didn't chirp even once and I thought we were making pretty good time right up until Juan's phone buzzed again three minutes before we were supposed to be at the meeting spot.

Based on the expression on Juan's face he expected the text to be a reprimand for not having been there early, but after reading the actual text he shook his head in astonishment.

"It looks like we've got an odd one."

Juan passed his phone around and my insides jumped in nervousness.

I've been delayed, but I'm getting reports of some kind of fighting happening on the west end of town. I'll meet you next to the water tower as soon as you can arrive.

I handed the phone to Jasmin so that she could read the text and started looking for the water tower. A second later Juan found it on his side of the car.

"Change of plans, Alison. We're headed towards that water tower. Turn right here and I'll see if I can find a route there on the GPS."

My first thought as we arrived and Alison brought the SUV to a screaming stop was that it was odd for the water tower to have been put off to the side of the town away from where everyone lived. It made even less sense for the town this small to have such a large abandoned industrial park, only at second glance the area didn't look abandoned. There wasn't any graffiti or broken windows. In fact, everything about the area looked like an active, operational industrial zone except for the fact that the night was unbroken by a single working light for at least three or four blocks in any direction.

Juan offered up the explanation at the same time that I realized what was going on.

"Werewolves, and more than one or two if they've taken down so much of the electrical grid."

My blood ran cold as I realized just how much danger we were in. Given that werewolves were bigger than any hybrid and able to neutralize most abilities, it was rare for a pack of wolves or even a group of hybrids to come out on top in a fight against werewolves unless they outnumbered the werewolves by a considerable margin. Like say maybe three to one. There was a chance that we could deal with two werewolves if we had a little bit of luck on our side, but there was no way that we could defeat three or four of them and Juan was probably right that it would take more than two werewolves to black out so much of the city.

Jasmin looked as worried as I felt, and Jess was positively jumping back and forth from one foot to the other, but it was Alison who asked the question.

"So what do we do? Jump back in the SUV and get out of here?"

Juan shook his head. "The guy from the Coun'hij said that there was fighting. As wolves we'll probably be faster than the werewolves, so we can always run away if push comes to shove, but we should at least get some intel."

I opened my mouth to point out that the Coun'hij had forbidden picking fights with werewolves, but shut my mouth without saying anything. Juan was right. At the very least we were going to have to clean up after these werewolves, but it was more than that.

We were probably outnumbered and in a position where all we could do was run away, but if that didn't turn out to be the case, then a part of me wouldn't shed any tears if we were forced to engage and kill a werewolf or two.

Werewolves were nothing more than mindless killing machines and while Puppeteer had been able to use them to good effect in places like St. Louis, that didn't justify the order that had come down from on high forbidding the moonborn from killing werewolves in anything other than self-defense.

"Leave the keys in the car and leave the doors unlocked. If we get chased back this direction we're going to need to be able to leave in a hurry."

Juan shifted onto four legs in a crackling rush of power and one by one the rest of us followed. My beast seemed extra eager today and I cut loose with a stronger flare of power than I meant to release. Nobody else seemed to notice though and a second later we were all following Juan off into the unnatural darkness that you could only find where man had killed all of the vegetation and replaced it with artificial constructs of metal, glass and concrete.

As we got closer the lights started flickering at irregular intervals. I would have said that it had to be yet another werewolf getting closer to the scene of the fight, but rather than the flickering being the result of more lights dying, it was caused by blocks of lights out on the edge of the blackout turning back on for a second or two before once again browning out.

We rounded a corner and I saw my first real, live werewolf. It was huge, which went without saying, but the thing that struck me the most was the way that the light it emitted, the light that was part and parcel of being a living organism, looked subtly wrong.

The wind shifted directions slightly and the werewolf spun around as it scented us. I expected Juan to turn and lead us back towards the SUV at a dead run, but he charged forward, transforming into a hybrid as he crossed the distance between us and the werewolf.

Apparently Juan's actions took everyone else by surprise too because there was nearly a second pause before we all charged after him. I opened the mental cage where I housed my beast, asking for just enough power to shift forms again so that I could meet the werewolf as a hybrid, and my beast responded with another tsunami of power that ripped me from one form to another in a fraction of an instant.

My beast was ready, eager even, to exchange blows with the werewolf, but despite my words earlier, part of me was busy thinking about the repercussions of what we were about to do. Puppeteer was brutal when it came to enforcing the prohibition against killing the earthborn. He didn't manage to punish every single offense, and I was pretty sure that most of the people who ended up punished were already on the chopping block for other reasons, but even so killing a werewolf risked having half a dozen werewolves under Puppeteer's control showing up one night to execute you.

Juan eased any concerns with a single sentence a split second before he closed with the werewolf. "We have no way of knowing whether or not our contact from the Coun'hij has been dragged into this fight already."

It was a slightly threadbare excuse, but it was the kind of thing that kept people alive when the Coun'hij got around to reviewing the results of some fight. The fact that we could say we'd been sent to neutralize any threats to our contact from the Coun'hij should be enough to shield us from the Coun'hij.

That all flitted across my mind as I crossed the three remaining steps to the werewolf and then there wasn't time for any thoughts that didn't relate directly to my immediate survival.

The werewolf slashed at Juan as the lights flickered again, but Juan lunged to the right in a blindingly explosive move that kept him just out of reach of the werewolf's deadly claws. It was an impressive display of speed that I'd never seen bettered by anyone else before.

I was only half a step behind Juan so I hit the werewolf on its right side, digging my claws into its arms in an effort to slow its turn as it tried to follow Juan around as he flanked it on the other side. I felt strong, stronger than ever before, but I still wasn't a match for the sheer brute strength that the werewolf commanded so casually.

Despite my best efforts the werewolf pulled its right arm free of my claws. The action left bloody ribbons where my claws had ripped through the werewolf's flesh, but there was no sign that the pain slowed my opponent in the slightest as it reversed directions connecting with an elbow to my face that threw me back into the side of the building behind me.

BOUND

I had a brief instant to be grateful that I'd been struck with the werewolf's elbow rather than the razor-sharp back edge of its claws, and then I hit with enough force that I saw stars as my head connected with one of the metal structural members hidden in the wall.

If the werewolf had just been facing Juan and me, we would have lost the fight right then and there, but a chorus of yips and growls told me that the girls were in the fight now too. My vision cleared just in time to see Juan take four long slashes to the chest as he tried to dance back out of range after an aborted attack that had probably been intended to distract the beast so that the girls could spring.

Juan's attack served its original purpose, if not quite in the way he'd intended for it to. Jasmin used the fact that the werewolf was momentarily focused on Juan to jump and clamp her jaws down on the back of its right arm roughly where the triceps muscle would have been on a human.

Jess and Alison latched onto the back of the creature's legs, ripping with their jaws for nearly a second before they and Jasmin all three had to drop away and try to dart back out of range of its counterattack.

Jasmin and Jessica were just fast enough to dodge out of the way of the werewolf's claws, but Alison was a few inches too close and got slashed all the way from her shoulder down to her back leg. She was bleeding profusely and I could see bones showing through in a couple of spots, but Alison gamely spun around and prepared to spring at the werewolf again.

I'd managed to pull myself back to my feet while the werewolf had been busy savaging Alison, and I hit it from the side. I couldn't generate enough force to knock it over, but I did jostle its arm enough that its next attack missed Alison by several inches.

More importantly, the werewolf's momentum from that last swipe at Alison meant that it couldn't spin back around fast enough to stop me from sinking both claws into its back and getting my right foot set into the meaty part of its leg.

The werewolf spun around as I jammed the talons on my right foot into its other leg, but it was a heartbeat too slow. It had allowed me to get set and I was holding on for everything I was worth. Juan came in from the left side, grabbing the werewolf's left arm with both of his claws at the same time that Jasmin sank her teeth once again into its right arm.

Between the two of them and me the werewolf was carrying an extra eight or nine hundred pounds and even its unnatural strength wasn't up to doing that without slowing down noticeably. I felt the werewolf change directions again, spinning to the left in an attempt to bring Juan into reach of its right hand and its fangs, but this time I used the brief instant when it had no momentum to lever my right foot up higher on its body.

I felt Jess hit the beast a second later, tearing into its leg in an effort to hamstring it. Juan dropped away only inches ahead of the claws that would have opened him up from stomach to chin if he'd tried to continue to control the werewolf's left arm.

With the werewolf's left hand free Jasmin was in increased danger, but she let go and danced back just before the werewolf could savage her. Alison joined Jess in an effort to damage the creature's legs enough to bring it to its knees, but it swiped at the two of them and the only thing that saved them from serious injury was that they were partially shielded from the attack by the werewolf's own bulk.

I used the distraction they provided to move my other foot higher as well as going for a new hold with my left hand. It was risky and I knew it as I made my move, but I could tell that the girls especially were tiring. Faced with the choice between potentially being bucked off of the werewolf or moving too slow and watching one of my friends die, there really wasn't any option but to move more quickly and hope that I could manage to hold onto the werewolf for just long enough to kill it.

My claws must have hit a particularly sensitive spot because the werewolf suddenly howled and threw itself back into a wall in an effort to dislodge me. It probably would have succeeded except for the fact that Juan charged forward and hit the creature hard enough to spin it around so that its right shoulder took most of the force of the impact with the building.

The werewolf's roar brought answering howls from two more of its kind and my breath caught as I realized that I'd completely forgotten about the other werewolves that we'd known had to be in the area. The werewolf we'd been fighting had just given away our position and we probably only had seconds before we'd be up against three or even possibly four of the things. We needed to disengage now, but that was going to be almost impossible with Alison hurt and me stuck on this werewolf's back.

Times were as desperate as they were likely to get. The werewolf's vulnerable head and neck seemed to be miles away from my current position, but I knew that wasn't the case. The distance was only a matter of feet, but it was feet that I was having to cover slow inches at a time.

The werewolf rebounded off of what was left of the wall and slashed at Juan in a blur that was too impossibly fast to follow. I would have said that there wasn't any way for her to manage it, but Jasmin somehow latched onto its wrist and once again her weight threw off the werewolf's timing and speed just enough to save Juan from being disemboweled.

BOUND

I took the biggest gamble of my life and banked everything on the assumption that the werewolf was going to reverse its course once again and spin right in an attempt to put Jasmin down before she could disengage and retreat back out of range. I launched myself up and to the right in an effort to preempt the werewolf's moment and as my claws and talons all came free of the werewolf's back I saw it blur into motion as its lunge to the right combined with my leap to create an incredible amount of relative motion.

My entire world narrowed down to the werewolf's neck and the slow arc of my left hand as I fought to bring it around so that the two would meet. It seemed for a second as though I was going to miss, but then the wolf's motion brought its head down a few precious inches as it tried to sink its claws into Jasmin who'd dropped to the ground and was trying to duck the attack.

The claws on my left hand sank into the werewolf's neck just below its jaw and I felt my arm strain in protest as my momentum was abruptly redirected with my left hand as the pivot point. Out of the corner of my eye I saw Jasmin dodge the werewolf's first swipe by a fraction of an inch, and then I was sailing over the creature's right arm as inertia brought me around in front of it.

I saw something like surprise in the werewolf's eyes as both of my feet sank into its chest and then my right hand was buried in its neck as well and I used the leverage provided by my feet to rip both sets of claws through the side of its neck as I threw myself backwards.

I'd been able to feel the werewolf's claws arrowing towards my vulnerable back, and I'd half expected to die, but my clunky back flip launched me a few inches above the trajectory of the werewolf's claws. I landed heavily on my knees and looked up just in time to see the werewolf drop to the ground in a spray of blood.

"Jess, go get a first-aid kit now!"

I followed Juan's gaze and felt my throat tighten up as I saw that Alison was lying on the ground surrounded by blood. She'd transformed back to two legs, which meant that she was either critically injured or dead, but as I dropped down next to her I saw her chest slowly rising and falling.

I must have shifted at some point because when I went to apply direct pressure I did so with human hands rather than hybrid claws, but I didn't remember forcing my beast back into its mental cage in order to change forms.

"Don't die on us, Alison, Jess will be back in a minute."

My voice broke as I said whatever came to mind in an effort to keep her with us while I held her wounds closed and tried not to think about her odds.

Jasmin dropped to her knees next to me and placed her hands next to mine in an attempt to help stanch the bleeding, but I somehow *knew* it wasn't going to be enough.

Juan's voice cut through the mental haze that was rapidly taking me over.

"Alec, back on your feet. I need you in your hybrid form. Someone is fighting those things and our best hope of keeping Alison alive is to go help kill those other werewolves before they come over here and end us all."

I shook my head. The threat of the other werewolves had somehow become a distant cloudy thing when compared to the imminent death of the pretty girl who'd just spent the last few days lounging around the pool with me.

Juan's backfist knocked me to the ground. He hadn't put any real strength behind it. He was still a hybrid and I'd been in my primary form so if he had put any real oomph into the blow it probably would have snapped my neck.

As attacks went it was remarkably restrained, but my beast didn't view it as such. A surge of power lashed out of me as a transformation ripped through my body. I'd never felt my beast so enraged, but the power that had been unleashed was only a shadow of what I'd displayed in St Louis.

I hadn't been expecting the sudden flare of rage from my beast, so I hadn't been prepared for it any more than I'd been prepared for Juan's backfist. Under those circumstances I should have practically lit the area up with a power storm, but it was almost as though the power that my beast usually drew on was being funneled somewhere else.

That all passed through my mind almost as an afterthought because my real focus was on trying to bring myself back under control enough not to try and kill Juan. I succeeded, but it was a close thing. As my breathing came back under control I turned back towards Alison, but Juan lunged toward me in a move that was only half feint.

"If you go back to her then I'll kill you myself. We need to get in on that fight or we're all as good as dead."

"You don't know that."

"Maybe not, but that won't stop me from killing you."

I felt my lips draw back from my fangs but the sound of four feet sprinting back our way told me that Jess was at most seconds away from helping Jasmin.

"Fine, we'll do it your way, but if she dies then I *will* make sure you join her within minutes."

Juan's smile showed his fangs and seemed to say that his beast would likewise welcome a chance to see who was truly dominant once and for all, but after holding my gaze for a second he turned and started off towards the sound of fighting.

As I followed him I wondered if the other battle had just started up, or if it had been going the entire time and I had just been too focused on our battle to notice anything else. Our contact's reports of fighting from this area certainly suggested the latter, which was disturbing. A leader needed to be able to keep enough presence of mind to deal with the larger picture as well as the fight he was involved in or his people would eventually be outmaneuvered and killed when someone blindsided him with something he should have seen coming from a mile away.

Juan led me round a corner and suddenly we were in the middle of another battle. This one was shape shifters against werewolves also, but where there'd only been five of us and one werewolf, here there were two werewolves with what looked like another one dead a few feet away.

The battle was too fluid and there were too many figures, wolves and hybrids alike, darting in and out for me to count how many people had faced off against the werewolves, but there were a number of bleeding forms scattered around the periphery of the battle and it seemed that whatever had been gained by one werewolf being killed had been offset by attrition in their own ranks.

"We help with the one on the left."

Juan sprang forward even as the words left his mouth, but I hung back for just long enough to see how his presence would impact the fight. Juan tried to catch the werewolf from behind but it spun around and slashed at him, forcing him back just long enough for it to catch one of the original hybrids it had been fighting with claws to the shoulder.

The other hybrid reeled back away, but in the same instant that the werewolf's claws had touched her, the lights had flickered again. I filed that curious bit of information away as I stepped in and slashed the werewolf's arm as it turned back to deal with Juan. The werewolf shrugged off my attack, but there were enough of us now that we'd forced the werewolf completely onto the defensive.

The hybrid who had caused the lights to flicker darted in and slashed the werewolf across the chest at the same time that the other hybrid from the same pack grabbed the werewolf's arm. I was pretty sure that the second hybrid had simply been trying to protect the first hybrid, but it created the perfect opening for me as well and I took it without thinking about what would happen if I was too slow.

I jumped over Juan, who'd just been knocked down by the werewolf, and although I didn't land as well as I had on the werewolf that we'd just finished killing, I still managed to get both hands and feet buried in the werewolf's back well enough to ride out the next couple of seconds as the werewolf tried to knock me free.

Juan grabbed hold of one arm at the same time that the two hybrids from the other pack grabbed the werewolf's other arm. The werewolf threw itself backwards into a light pole in an attempt to crush me, but the combined efforts of all three hybrids was just barely sufficient to slow it down so that the impact knocked the wind from me rather than shattering bones as it otherwise probably would have.

Gasping for breath as I was, it was nearly more than I could handle to maintain my hold on the werewolf's back. The werewolf staggered slightly and I looked down and saw that a pair of wolves had attached themselves to the creature's legs while a third wolf was dangling from the arm that Juan was fighting to keep immobilized.

"Hurry up and kill the damn thing already!"

The words came from the larger hybrid, the one who had made the light flicker, and the voice was unmistakably female despite the distortion introduced by the fact that she was in her hybrid form.

In one sense her frustration and urgency was completely understandable, but I was the one who had just nearly been crushed to death and my beast didn't take kindly to her tone. Another roar of power escaped me and this time it was very nearly as strong as I'd ever felt it before. There was still the tiniest feeling that something was siphoning away a portion of my vitality and energy, but as the power washed out of me and crashed into the female hybrid it seemed to take my exhaustion and weakness with it.

The werewolf flung Juan and the wolf away, which then caused the two hybrids from the other pack to release it so that they could avoid being stabbed, but I easily rode out the sudden shift in direction and then repositioned myself higher in two explosive movements.

A second later I was high enough up to reach the werewolf's throat and it dropped to the ground as its life leaked out of the arteries that I'd just severed. Everyone else who had been involved in the fight was as much as a dozen feet back by that point in an effort to avoid being caught up in the werewolf's death throes, so they made it over to the last werewolf well before I was able to untangle myself and go help.

This time there was nothing of strategy or finesse to the kill. The hybrids and wolves, Juan included, who had been fighting the werewolf I'd just killed threw themselves at the werewolf, joining the moonborn who had already been fighting it in a writhing ball of claws and fangs.

Two hybrids made it onto the last werewolf's back and started climbing it while everyone grabbed an appendage and pulled. The last werewolf was dead within moments of the second one dying and then we were left staring uneasily at each other.

The female hybrid was the one who broke the standoff. She looked around, seeming to verify that the lights were all back on, and then ordered her people to see to their injured. Only after everything seemed well in hand did she turn back to Juan and me.

"I'd ask you what you're doing here in my territory, but I already know. Brandon sent you after I refused to return his calls, didn't he?"

Juan nodded and then apparently decided that it was time to deescalate things and shifted back to his primary form.

The female hybrid looked at the ha'bit that all of our people wore and wrinkled her nose in disgust before looking pointedly at me. Shifting forms was more difficult than I expected it to be. This time my beast was working at cross purposes to me, trying to maintain our current form rather than shift down to something less durable and fast. If the Tucson pack decided that they wanted us dead then there wouldn't be much we could do to stop them other than running for the SUV and hoping that we were faster than them, but my beast didn't always think in those kinds of terms.

It took what seemed like a frozen eternity to force my beast back into its metaphysical cage, but it finally yielded to my will and I shrank back down to my human form. The female hybrid stared at the two of us for several moments before following suit and discarding her towering hybrid shape.

The Tucson pack didn't follow the Sanctuary convention of wearing ha'bits, so she was completely naked, but she seemed less bothered by that fact than I was.

"I'd just kick you out of our territory, but I'm afraid that I owe you one. We came expecting to fight two vacuums but prepared for three. That fourth werewolf would have torn through us like tissue paper if you hadn't taken care of it for us."

She sighed and then stepped forward and offered her hand to Juan. "My name is Jaclyn. I'm the alpha of this pack."

Juan looked more than a little uneasy at the prospect of touching her hand, but I couldn't blame him. Jaclyn's prowess in single combat would have been respectable even without the ability that she'd manifested decades ago, but with it she was unmatched by any other hybrid I could think of offhand.

Brandon was stronger and faster than she could possibly be, but Jaclyn was able to funnel a powerful electrical charge through her hands and feet, delivering the equivalent of a massive Taser blast into whomever she happened to be fighting.

Pieces started to click into place inside of my mind and I blurted out my observation without thinking.

"It isn't just your hands, you can charge your whole body. When the werewolf cut you across the shoulder the lights flickered, which had to be you delivering a jolt that partially overwhelmed its natural absorptive ability."

Juan's mouth clicked shut and then he shook his head at me in resignation before turning back to Jaclyn and taking her hand.

"I'm Juan out of the Colorado Springs pack and this is Alec."

Jaclyn was smiling as she shook Juan's hand, at least right up until he provided my name without also telling her which pack I was from.

"Graves?"

I nodded. "Yes, but Kaleb and I don't see eye to eye on most things."

Jaclyn rolled her eyes at me and didn't extend her hand. "That's pretty much the kind of transparent lie I'd expect out of Kaleb's spawn, but I expected better based on what I've heard about you, Juan. I'm not entirely surprised to hear that you've ended up down here on the border killing cats with that piece of trash Brandon, but I thought you'd at least have enough integrity not to let Kaleb turn you into some kind of demented babysitter."

Now that Jaclyn had shaken his hand without zapping him, Juan seemed much more relaxed. He smiled at Jaclyn as a pair of white SUVs pulled up and some of the people she'd sent away piled back out of the vehicles with first-aid kits and various other supplies in their arms.

"Kaleb didn't have anything to do with this. He apparently decided that Alec needed to be blooded and once Alec was sent down here Brandon stuck me with him. Alec's been a pleasant surprise though. He volunteered our team for this at least partly because he was hoping to get a chance to talk to you."

"Your life is so bad you were hoping for a quick end?"

I shook my head. "I was hoping to be able to get your take on everything that is going on. Since I arrived down here I've started finding out a lot of things have been kept secret from me. I figured that the best way to get a clear view of what's actually happening is to talk to people who are dramatically opposed to Kaleb and everything he stands for."

"That's it?"

"I had hoped to also be able to convince you that I'm not my father, that I'm someone who you could someday work with under the right set of circumstances, but I know that's a long shot."

One of Jaclyn's people handed her camouflage cargo pants and a black tank top; she slipped them on without looking away from me.

"Kid, you've spent so much time in the dark that you won't even be able to see the truth when it's shoved right in front of your face."

"Try me."

"Some things can't be conveyed through words, Alec. Some things you have to see with your own eyes to believe."

"Fine, so take me wherever it is and show me."

"I can't do that, not without putting my people in an unacceptable level of danger."

I threw my hands up and shook my head at her. "I'm really trying here, Jaclyn. I don't know how to convince you, not in the short amount of time we have before our contact on the Coun'hij arrives and we have to go babysit him."

Jaclyn went white. "You didn't tell me that someone from the Coun'hij was on their way."

Juan stepped up to answer that particular question. "We figured it was obvious. We didn't know what was going on here, we just knew that the humans had found bodies with wounds they couldn't explain. The Coun'hij is sending someone to make all of the evidence disappear. We're just along to protect whomever it is that they've sent."

"Everybody get the wounded into the SUVs and then I want the entire area doused with vinegar! We don't have much time, people."

I opened my mouth, but two sets of footsteps interrupted whatever it was I'd been about to say. An unfamiliar man stepped out from between two buildings. Jasmin was following him and she looked so uncomfortable that I started towards her only to have Juan pull me up short.

"Is everything okay, Jas?"

"I think so. Jess and I got Alison stabilized and we were in the middle of loading her into the car when this guy showed up. I think he's from the Coun'hij, but he hasn't said a word yet. So far all he's done is gesture for Jess to stay with Alison and for me to follow him."

The Tucson pack had gone almost completely still. There was still a little movement out on the edge of things, mostly people who hadn't seen the Coun'hij's operative yet. Jaclyn looked like she wanted to spit.

"Just for the record, none of you are welcome in our territory ever again. Anyone who arrives in the company of that thing permanently puts themselves in my bad graces."

Juan didn't look particularly happy about Jaclyn's pronouncement, but he didn't seem prepared to argue with her.

"I don't understand. It's not like we had a choice, we were just given a time and a place and told to meet him here."

"Saying you don't have a choice is just a coward's way of rationalizing their cowardice, kid. You guys have until tomorrow morning to finish up whatever work he has to do to wipe all of this under the rug and then you'd better be gone. I can't kill Oblivion without bringing the entire Coun'hij down on me, but I'm willing to see how far your daddy is prepared to go to avenge *you* if you're not gone by sunrise."

Things were moving too fast and I didn't have any of the background information that I'd need to make sense of them. I wanted to ask what was so bad about this particular operative, but before I could say anything a four-legged shadow detached itself from a wall and threw itself at the operative.

I didn't realize that it was one of the Tucson wolves until after she was airborne. She'd taken me completely by surprise, but the guy from the Coun'hij didn't even blink. He dropped down to one knee so that the wolf sailed over his head and then the operative casually reached up and let his fingers run along her side as she flew past him.

I expected the operative to shift to hybrid form so that he was prepared for the wolf's follow-up lunge, but the operative simply stood back up and watched as she hit the ground and rolled bonelessly for several complete revolutions before coming to a stop.

Every other wolf from the Tucson pack took a step forward as though planning on attacking, but Jaclyn yelled for them to stop. Her control of her pack was absolute and everyone skidded to a stop leaving a strange kind of scene with the operative on one end, Jasmin at his back looking like she wasn't sure she was on the right side of the fight, and more than a dozen moonborn on the other side looking like they wished they could tear the operative to bits.

I'd never seen anything to match what the operative had just done. The ability to kill with a touch when not even shifted to a combat form surely made this shape shifter even more deadly than Brandon or Jaclyn either one.

"What just happened?"

The words slipped out of me of their own accord, but when Jaclyn turned her glare on me I refused to back down. After a couple of heartbeats Jaclyn looked at the operative once more, but he simply smiled and made a gesture that seemed to say that he was waiting for her to explain everything to me.

"That's Oblivion. He's the Coun'hij's top troubleshooter because he doesn't just sweep evidence under the rug and leave people as laughingstocks when they can't back up their fantastical stories, he destroys the memories of anyone who's seen anything the Coun'hij doesn't want to go public. Jane isn't dead, but she might as well be. Everything that made her an individual is gone. She's been wiped clean and the child he's left in her place won't even remember her own name."

"He's been here before."

It was more a statement than a question but Jaclyn nodded in agreement. "Yes, he's been here before. That's why Jane attacked him. Oblivion did the same thing to her sister last year. Most packs don't even suspect that the Coun'hij has someone so insidious at their beck and call, but our pack got called into help after an op down here went sideways and Oblivion lost most of his protection detail. Jane's sister did or said something to piss Oblivion off and he wiped her clean. It was one of the things that pushed me over the edge where the Coun'hij is concerned."

Oblivion returned Jaclyn's glare without any expression on his face and then turned to Jasmin and motioned for her to pick Jane up and carry her to her pack mates. I stepped forward to help her but Oblivion grabbed my wrist. My beast had understood the significance of what had happened to Jane, and tried to break free, but I held onto control of my shape by the slimmest of margins.

It was one of the hardest things I'd ever done, but shifting to a hybrid wouldn't save me if he'd already decided to scoop out everything that made me the person I was. I had a split second to wonder whether or not it would hurt to have all of my memories stripped away, but then he released me and shook his head. Once he was satisfied that I wasn't going to help Jasmin, he waved for me to follow him into the darkness.

Chapter 13

Alec Graves
East Dixon Lane
Hereford, Arizona

Oblivion led me through the darkness until we were back at our SUV. Jess gave me a worried look as we got close enough for her to see us, but I gave her my best reassuring smile and then turned to Oblivion to see what he wanted us to do next.

Still using nothing but gestures, he had me help Jessica unload Alison out of the vehicle and then he climbed into the driver's seat and I sat down in the passenger seat next to him.

We passed the drive into the center of town in silence and I was left wondering why I was even along for the ride. The werewolves were dead, so Oblivion didn't need protection from them, and Oblivion didn't seem to have any reason to fear the Tucson pack, not given the sheer power of his ability.

Oblivion had punched an address into the GPS before leaving the industrial park, and following the device's directions led us to a quiet little neighborhood that wouldn't have looked out of place anywhere in the Southeastern United States. Oblivion parked us on the street and then after double-checking the address one last time, he motioned for me to follow him as he left the SUV.

Oblivion knocked on the door to a white-brick house and then waited until a tired, middle-aged Caucasian man answered it.

"What do you guys want...?"

The homeowner trailed off as he got a chance to take in the tattered, bloody state of my ha'bit. He stepped back and made as if to slam the door in our faces, but his human reflexes were no match for Oblivion's moonborn speed.

Oblivion grabbed ahold of the man's arm with one hand as he pushed his way inside of the house and then put his other hand over the man's mouth to make sure that he couldn't cry out. Feeling more like a villain than I ever had at any time before in my life, I followed Oblivion into the house and watched as the man in Oblivion's arms started shaking.

At first I thought it was the natural result of being terrified for his safety and that of his family, but then I noticed that his eyes had rolled back up inside of his head. After a few moments Oblivion took his hand off of the man's mouth and moved it up to the man's forehead.

The convulsions gradually died down until the man was motionless, at which point Oblivion gently lowered the man to the ground and then turned and looked at me. I got a frown as though Oblivion was noticing my appearance for the first time. Oblivion ordered me back to the SUV to put street clothes back on over my ha'bit, which I did and then I returned to find that neither Oblivion nor the man had moved while I was gone.

"Who is he?"

Oblivion looked around and then pointed at a frame on the wall. I got close enough to read it and found that it was a medical diploma.

"The coroner?"

Oblivion nodded and then gestured for me to pick the coroner up and follow him. The house was surprisingly big and I initially marveled at the sure way that Oblivion led me upstairs and directly to the man's bedroom. It shouldn't have been a surprise, not in someone who could pull memories out of a person's head, but it seemed wrong for Oblivion to be so comfortable inside of someone else's home, a home he'd never set foot in before tonight.

The coroner's wife was apparently a sound sleeper because she didn't even stir until I set her husband down into the bed next to her.

Oblivion was already on her side of the bed by the time I put her husband down, but he didn't touch her until after her eyes fluttered open and she looked up at him.

The process of draining her was eerily similar to what had happened to her husband and after only a short time Oblivion released her and motioned for me to follow him once again.

I almost couldn't believe my eyes when Oblivion opened the door to a child's room. When he took a step towards the bed of a girl who couldn't have been any older than ten I grabbed his arm, forgetting for a moment just how dangerous he was.

Oblivion just looked at me, but the expression on his face was enough to bring me back to myself, to remind me of the fact that right now I existed on his sufferance.

"There isn't any reason to drain her dry."

Oblivion shook his head and held his hand up with his fingers spaced far apart. He slowly brought his fingers together until they were nearly touching and then nodded.

"You're not destroying everything? Just the memories that have to do with the werewolf kills?"

I got another nod, which caused me to release him. I had no real reason to believe him—anyone who worked for the Coun'hij directly wasn't exactly trustworthy—but the simple fact of the matter was that there wasn't anything I could do to stop him.

Destroying the little girl's memories went much more quickly than the process had gone with her parents and she didn't convulse nearly as badly as they had. I wondered how much of that was because he wasn't destroying as many memories or if it was some function of the fact that she didn't have as many memories to search through and her memories were somehow less solidly fixed inside of her mind.

Oblivion motioned me out of the room and then quietly pulled the door shut behind him. A couple of minutes later we were back inside the SUV and pulling away from the curb. Oblivion didn't bother with the GPS unit at any point after that during the night. Apparently he got the directions to his next victim's house directly out of the minds of his previous victims.

Over the next couple of hours we visited the chief of police, a detective and a news reporter. Surprisingly it was the news reporter who was the most paranoid. It was hard to know whether that was because of her profession or because she was a woman, but she was the only one to check out the window before opening the door and even when she opened the door she left the chain on. It didn't save her though. She was in the middle of asking Oblivion who we were and what we wanted when he straight-armed the door with enough force to rip the chain free of the door jamb and knock her unconscious from the force of the door hitting her forehead.

I noticed that Oblivion was much more careful during our time in the reporter's house. He used his sleeve to avoid leaving fingerprints on her bedroom door and when my phone started to ring he forbade me from answering it with a stern headshake.

Apparently he could erase any mental evidence that we'd been there, but there wasn't anything he could do to explain away the broken chain or the spectacular bruise she was going to have on her forehead.

Once we were back in the SUV he motioned for me to go ahead and check my phone. As he got the car moving towards the next victim I got my phone out of my pocket and saw that I'd missed a call from Juan. He picked up after only the second ring.

"You're still alive then?"

"Yeah. I even seem to have all of my memories too."

"How would you really know if that was the case or not, Alec?"

I reviewed the night and couldn't find any blank spots, but when I looked over at Oblivion he just smiled.

"I guess I'll never really know."

"Yeah, well, life is just full of those kinds of mysteries. How much longer are you guys going to be? Jaclyn and the rest of her pack are getting restless."

I turned back to Oblivion. "How many more people do we need to pay a visit to?"

Oblivion held up three fingers but then he shrugged.

"So three you know about but you may find out about others from these three?"

I got a nod. We'd managed to communicate fairly well despite Oblivion's inability or refusal to talk.

"It sounds like we've got at least another hour and a half, Juan. How is Alison doing, will she be okay?"

"She'll live. Jess and Jasmin got her pretty much stabilized, but it turns out that the Tucson pack carries whole blood with them when they go on these little excursions. Once Jaclyn was satisfied that all of her people were stabilized she grudgingly allowed one of her medics to transfuse a unit of blood to Alison, which has her all of the way out of the woods."

"That's good news."

There was a pause and then Juan cleared his throat. "Have you talked to Oblivion about the fact that we were fighting werewolves when he arrived?"

"No, it hasn't come up yet."

"Bring it up. You need to make sure that he understands that we got into that fight because we were worried that he had already made it to the meet before us and been drawn into a fight with them."

"Okay, I'll talk to him about it."

"Thanks. There are a couple of people here who are very nervous about what's going to happen. Killing werewolves is still very much proscribed by the Coun'hij."

After I hung up I caught Oblivion looking at me.

"You heard Juan?"

I got another nod, he didn't look particularly unhappy, but there was still an element of risk to what I was about to ask.

"Do you agree that we had a valid reason to engage the werewolves?"

Oblivion pursed his lips and then slowly nodded. Apparently he was telling me that he knew saving him hadn't been our primary concern, but that he was willing to let our sin go without reporting it up to Puppeteer.

"What about Jaclyn and her people? Are you going to cause them problems?"

There was more of a pause now. Oblivion let me stew in silence for a couple of minutes before he shook his head.

It was a clear break with the rules that the Coun'hij had established, but for some reason I believed him. I'd taken a risk by asking about the Tucson pack separately because it had acknowledged the fact that they hadn't been fighting under the same pretext we had, but it seemed to have paid off.

There was something about the way that he'd answered that had my mental antennae tingling. I knew I should leave it alone, but I just couldn't seem to bring myself to do so.

"You didn't want to hurt Jane, did you?"

Oblivion refused to meet my eyes. He stared out at the road for nearly five minutes without providing any kind of response. Finally as we pulled to a stop in front of our next target he shook his head minutely. The movement was so slight that I almost could have believed that I'd imagined it, but it had happened.

Oblivion was possibly the coldest single individual I'd ever met, but he didn't seem to take any joy in what he was forced to do as a result of his service to the Coun'hij. As we walked up the steps to steal the memories of yet another person, I wondered what could make someone agree to serve the Coun'hij in such a terrible role.

Chapter 14

Alec Graves
Sierra Vista Municipal Airport
Sierra Vista, Arizona

By the time that Oblivion and I had scrubbed the memories of the inhabitants of Hereford to his satisfaction it was nearly sunrise. Jaclyn and her people had helped Juan and the others relocate up to Sierra Vista, so Oblivion rerouted his helicopter pilot up there while I drove us to the Sierra Vista Airport.

Juan and the others had destroyed all of the evidence of the fight in the industrial park, and Oblivion's last stop before we left had been to break into the morgue and torch the bodies that had originally caused people to start asking questions.

I was worn out and hoping that Jess or Jasmin had managed to grab an hour or two of sleep so that I'd be able to sleep on the way back, but the sight of the group waiting for us at the airport washed away my exhaustion with a shot of adrenaline.

It wasn't just Juan, Jess and Jasmin waiting for us like I'd expected. Jaclyn was there too and she'd brought along four of the biggest, meanest-looking guys I'd seen in a long time. Oblivion was menacing, but it was an understated menace. These guys on the other hand looked like they ate small children for breakfast.

Juan didn't look particularly happy, but he and the girls were a couple dozen feet away from Jaclyn and her people, so I assumed that we weren't in immediate danger. Still, I parked the SUV a ways away from everyone.

Oblivion gave me an approving nod and then checked his phone and left the SUV. I half expected some kind of heated confrontation between Jaclyn and Oblivion, but he simply ignored everyone and headed towards a helicopter that was sitting on the tarmac fifty yards away.

I waited to see whether Oblivion would look back, but he disappeared into the helicopter without ever acknowledging my presence, or anyone else's for that matter. A couple of minutes later the helicopter was airborne and rapidly heading north.

Juan waved me over as soon as the helicopter had disappeared in the distance. I put the SUV back in motion and followed him over to a pair of white SUVs. As soon as I put my vehicle into park one of Jaclyn's guys opened the back of one of their SUVs and a big sigh of relief made its way through my tired body.

Alison was looking like she'd been beaten to within an inch of her life, but she was sitting up unassisted and looked like she was going to be okay once she got some rest and time to heal.

I bailed out of my car and gently picked her up.

"I can walk, you big oaf."

I shook my head. "You can't even stand right now."

"How would you know?"

"Because you never in a million years would have agreed to sit there while Juan and the others were standing all of the way over there if you had any other choice."

She harrumphed like an old woman, but she stopped complaining as I carried her over to our SUV. In human form I'd always expected her to be light, but now that I actually had her in my arms I was surprised at just how little there seemed to be to her.

She was still the fiery, deadly young woman that she'd been yesterday, but she was also woefully frail and I was more conscious than ever of just how little it took for one of us to be killed even with all of the benefits inherent in being a shape shifter.

I set Alison inside of our vehicle and went to help buckle her up, but she swatted my hands away and told me to stop being such an old woman. I smiled as I backed away from the car with my hands up in mock surrender, and then felt all levity drain from my face as I turned and found myself face to face with Jaclyn.

"You're an interesting problem, Alec Graves."

"I'd like to be something other than a problem to you."

"I know. That's actually what makes you such a problem. If I really believed that you didn't mean a word of what you said to me last night then you wouldn't be a problem, you'd just be another name waiting to be crossed off of my list when the Coun'hij finally loses control of everything."

"So you do believe me!"

"Calm down, Graves. Yes, I believe you, at least that you've got good intentions, but that doesn't change an awful lot. The situation is too complex and you're just not ready."

I felt like I was banging my head against a wall.

"So help me get ready."

"Even assuming I was willing to help you out, it's not that easy. There would be significant risks to you."

"I'm prepared to run risks."

Jaclyn shook her head. "I'm not. Thanks again though for helping bail us out last night. I lost a couple of good people in that fight, but I probably would have lost everyone if not for your help. You've got a respectable amount of power at your beck and call by the way. Did you notice the way your beast ponied up extra energy when the fight was against a werewolf?"

I had to consciously force myself to close my mouth. "You mean that's normal?"

"Not for everyone, no, but for some of us it is. There's something about going up against werewolves that makes the truly dominant among us fight harder. It's like even our beasts know that the werewolves are wrong on every level, that they need to be wiped off of the face of the earth."

"That's why you fight them even though it's been prohibited."

Jaclyn nodded. "That's part of the reason. Nobody in their right mind would hold a rattlesnake to their chest, but that's exactly what the Coun'hij is trying to do. They want us to protect the werewolves when the more sensible course would be to make sure that we don't let them grow in numbers to the point where they can turn on us."

I nodded. There were definitely some valid points behind her argument. The piece about our beasts providing more power for fights against werewolves was interesting too. It meant that the full degree of my power was still a secret. She thought that when she'd yelled at me during the fight the night before that she'd seen my full power plus an increase due to the fact that we were fighting a werewolf.

Instead what she'd seen was slightly less even than what I'd displayed to Jack, because some of my power had been somewhere else.

"Okay, well, if you change your mind please let me know. I need to get my footing, I need to know the things you're worried about telling me. It doesn't matter how dangerous the process of learning them is."

Jaclyn shook her head, but she held out her hand to offer the handshake she'd refused to give me the night before.

"I don't change my views on those kinds of things, Graves, but just in case, I'll keep you in mind."

The words were exactly what you'd expect out of someone who was worried that she was being spied on, but hidden in her palm was a scrap of paper. I did my absolute best to keep my surprise off of my face, and based on the fact that her face didn't even flicker as I took the paper and casually stuffed it into my pocket, I was pretty sure that I'd succeeded.

Jaclyn had something to tell me after all.

Chapter 15

Alec Graves
Bisbee Municipal Airport
Bisbee, Arizona

Jaclyn's paper had contained today's date, an address on the outskirts of a town called Naco, and an injunction to be there at four p.m. sharp. Convincing James to come with me had been the easy part. Convincing Jasmin and Jessica to stay at the hotel and cover for the fact that the two of us were gone was much harder. Getting out of the hotel without anyone seeing us was somewhere between the two extremes of difficulty.

James was looking a lot better with another day of rest under his belt, but I was sincerely hoping that we'd be able to avoid a fight today. I wasn't sure that either of us was in good enough shape to get in a fight this afternoon and then turn around and run an op for Brandon tonight.

Actually, getting out of the hotel was a lot easier than I suspected getting back in would be. The Rest Easy apparently did most of its laundering onsite, but that was during normal times when the hotel was running with a significant number of empty rooms. Brandon's decision to make the Rest Easy the base for all operations against the cats meant that the hotel was nearly one hundred percent booked and had been for weeks.

The owners were doubtlessly turning handsprings of joy, but it had caused the hotel manager some difficulties. For instance, keeping all of the linens clean had required ferrying a load of laundry over to another hotel in town at least twice a week.

Jasmin had hit on the idea of smuggling us out in the laundry trucks and it had worked like a charm. She and Jess had grabbed a couple of the large carts that the hotel staff used to transport dirty linens and brought one to each of our rooms.

The concept of riding around in a basket full of other people's dirty sheets was mildly gross, even despite the fact that as a shape shifter I was immune to pretty much any disease you could think of. I compensated by stripping the sheets off of my own bed and laying one down on top of the rest of the laundry and then using the other one to cover myself with. The last thing I saw before Jasmin covered me up with some clean towels from my bathroom was Jasmin rolling her eyes at me.

It was more than a little unnerving to sit quietly in the basket and just hope that the plan went off without a hitch. In theory we should be okay. We couldn't completely mask our scent, but nobody would think twice if they caught a whiff of James or me around the baskets or along the trail that they were taken between our rooms and the truck. The logical answer, that they were just smelling the sheets that we'd slept in, was the right answer, just not the complete answer.

The real risk was that one of the other shape shifters would get close enough to the carts to hear our heartbeats. All of the material packed in around us should go a long ways towards muffling the sound of our pulse, but it was the one part of the plan that had given me the most concern from the start.

Luck was with us though and half an hour after I climbed into the cart I felt the unmistakable movement of a vehicle in motion. James came out of his pile of laundry at the same time that I climbed out of mine and then we just waited quietly for the truck to arrive at the other hotel. Once we were there we watched until the driver was distracted chatting up one of the girls who worked on the housekeeping staff and then snuck out of the truck.

The next phase of my plan relied on the fact that Donovan had been siphoning money off from Kaleb's investments for the last two decades. Most of the embezzled funds went to an account under one of my mother's aliases, but Rachel and I both had significant balances with several national banks under pseudonyms of our own.

James and I walked into one of the banks in question and walked out twenty minutes later with twenty thousand dollars which we used to first rent a car from the local vehicle dealership and then charter a helicopter to take us from Nogales International Airport to Bisbee Municipal Airport. James had thought that chartering a flight was excessive, but it was a lot faster than driving all of the way to Naco and it had the benefit of meaning that if we wanted to we could return a different way than we'd come.

We rented another car in Bisbee and made it to Naco twenty minutes before four. I didn't really know what to expect. It was possible that Jaclyn just wanted to meet up somewhere she knew would be safe from any kind of spies, but her manner when she'd handed me the note hadn't matched up with that. She'd been convinced that she was putting me in danger and I'd decided before James and I even left that we'd be very careful about how we approached the meet.

We left the rental car in a grocery store parking lot four miles away from the address Jaclyn had given me, and then we walked out into the wilderness that butted up against the edge of town. It took less than two minutes to lose ourselves in the underbrush and hills enough that we could strip out of our clothes and shift to four legs.

I'd scouted the address as extensively as I could using the satellite maps available on my phone. That had allowed me to plan a route for us from the grocery store to the meet without crossing through town.

There were still risks even after everything I'd done to try and minimize them. Everything from the possibility that we were walking directly into a trap to the slim chance that we'd be seen in our wolf forms and someone would start asking the kinds of questions that I'd just spent the night helping Oblivion erase. From a distance we could be mistaken for the wolves that had once roamed freely through various parts of the United States, but anyone who got a good look at us up close would know that we were much too big to be normal wolves.

The air was remarkably still, which was good because it meant that we didn't have to worry about factoring the prevailing wind into our approach route, but it left me feeling curiously blind. I'd been outside in all kinds of weather in Utah, but this was the first time that I'd experienced a day where the air was this still. For people who were used to getting more than half of their situational awareness via their nose it was a worryingly vulnerable environment to be in.

We felt exposed enough that we traveled through the scrubby, brown desert underbrush a lot slower than we usually did, but we still managed to arrive at the meeting place more than ten minutes before four. The location was part of Naco, but it was set off from the rest of the city. A ring of low hills completely blocked the rest of the town from view and made it difficult to find a good observation point, but I'd found a likely-looking spot via my orbital recon earlier.

Working from nothing more than memory I managed to bring us to within fifty feet of the spot I'd picked out, which was good because it meant that we wouldn't be leaving a scent trail all over the hills. Even better, the spot exceeded my hopes. Not only was it big enough to house James and me semi-comfortably for an hour or two if necessary, it had plenty of low scrub brush that would break up our outlines and help keep us hidden from anyone conducting a visual scan of the hillside.

James and I settled down and waited to see what would happen. Four p.m. came and went and by the time four-thirty arrived James was clearly antsy and I was starting to get a little nervous myself. If something didn't happen soon we were going to run out of time. As it was, we were already cutting our margin of error for getting back before leaving for Brandon's op thinner than I wanted to. Brandon was supposed to brief Juan who would then brief the rest of us minus Alison, but even so there was a limit to how long we could go without making an appearance back at the hotel.

Five more minutes crawled by with excruciating slowness and then a pair of SUVs came around the bend in the road that led between the main town and our little cul-de-sac. James shifted as though preparing to head down, but I stopped him with a low growl. These SUVs were black rather than white. It was looking like this wasn't a simple meet with Jaclyn after all.

One of the SUVs stopped just on our side of the hill that separated the two sections of town, but it parked oddly in the middle of the road almost like it had undergone some kind of mechanical failure and been forced to make an emergency stop. Two guys that looked strangely familiar despite the distance got out and moved around so that the SUV was between them and us.

The second SUV pulled right into the center of the little suburb and five guys exited with a swagger that would have told me who we were watching even if I hadn't recognized Vincent.

My mind flitted back to the briefing when we'd volunteered to go down to Hereford. Vincent had said that he couldn't make the trip down to the border and guarantee that he'd be able to be back in time to execute some other mystery op for Brandon. This had to be the op, but it didn't make any sense. I'd been watching the local news recently as a way to anticipate where we might be deployed and there hadn't been even a whisper of any kind of violence in Naco.

There hadn't been any power outages to signal that they had werewolves in the area, there hadn't been any blood bank thefts to indicate there were vampires moving in, there was no legitimate reason for Brandon to be deploying Vincent's team this deeply into the Tucson pack's area.

Once everyone was out of the SUV, two of Vincent's guys unloaded two crates out of the back of the vehicle. It took them only a couple of moments to assemble what looked like a miniature cell tower and then I got the biggest shock of the day.

Vincent shifted. One second he was his normal, arrogant human self and then the next he was a hybrid. It was full daylight and there was nothing to prevent anyone looking out their windows from seeing him walking around bigger than life. It went against thousands of years of tradition and everything that the Coun'hij supposedly stood for.

Despite everything I still half expected Vincent to go charging off towards some threat that I hadn't seen yet, but instead he simply held out his hands and waited while one of his guys pulled an odd contraption out of the second crate and started strapping it onto Vincent's left hand. When Vincent's guy finally stepped away Vincent had large metal gloves strapped to his hands.

BOUND

It was another violation of the laws that the Coun'hij had set forth after overthrowing the monarchy. Hybrid-usable weapons had reached their pinnacle under the last king and then had disappeared almost overnight once the king vanished, but even then it had been swords that had been used, not odd clawed gloves that didn't seem to actually extend the reach of the wearer.

Something similar might make sense for a human as it would transform their hands into claw-tipped weapons, but hybrids already had claws.

One by one Vincent's men all shifted into their hybrid forms and then were equipped with the gloves from the crate. Finally there were just two guys left who walked over to one of the houses and kicked the door in.

It took only seconds for the screams to start, at which point I shifted back to human form and grabbed ahold of James to stop him from rushing down there. It wasn't what I wanted to do. I wanted to change over to a hybrid and run down and start killing Vincent's guys, but the only thing that would accomplish would be to add James and me to the body count.

The screams as the two guys still in human form pulled people out of the first house caused the rest of the neighborhood to look out their windows. Once people realized that their phones weren't working and saw that they wouldn't be safe inside of their homes, there was an exodus as people rushed outside in an effort to either get away or to go help the first few victims. They were being killed by hybrids wearing the weapons that I now realized were solely to make the kills look like they'd been done with the curved claws of a jaguar rather than with the straight claws of a hybrid.

Brandon had hoped that a victory would bring down more recruits, but when that hadn't worked he'd set about creating an atrocity to see if that would serve as a better motivator for the wolves and hybrids in the unaligned packs.

None of the humans ever had even the slightest chance. Once the people were outside of the protection of their houses, Vincent and the other hybrids tore through them like they were nothing more than paper dolls.

Some of the residents brought out guns, but they were simply outmatched. Vincent's guys could smell the gun oil and powder residue on the weapons as soon as they exited the house and no mere human was the equal to the speed of a hybrid.

Several of the gun owners were cut down before they could even get their guns in play and, for the rest, the hybrids simply ducked behind buildings and continued their rampage while one or two of their number stalked the gun owners. As long as the gunmen didn't move they didn't have any targets, but as soon as they started moving around they were taken out by enemies who could smell them and hear their heartbeat from a dozen feet away.

It was the most one-sided battle I'd ever seen, but my heart went out to those who were trying to fight back. They were in a bad situation, but at least they were trying and that was more than I was doing.

A few people made it into their cars and partway down the road, but instead of trying to ram the SUV blocking the road they tried to go around it which slowed them down. Even worse, they were then faced with two more hybrids who were more than capable of driving a fist through the driver's-side window and breaking their necks as they went flying by.

Some of the fleeing humans had made it to the base of the hills by that point, but the two shape shifters who'd been going door to door and pulling people out into the street simply shifted to wolf form and chased them down.

The tiny sliver of my mind that wasn't paralyzed by a roiling combination of anger and outrage wondered whether jaguar and wolf fangs were similar enough that those last few kills wouldn't break the illusion that this had been done by a group of cats.

It felt like the attack lasted hours, but I made myself sit there and watch the entire thing. By the end the humans who remained had realized that fighting and fleeing were both equally futile and some of them simply dropped to the ground and waited for one of the monsters down there to come by and kill them.

Once there wasn't anyone living visible anywhere in the neighborhood, Vincent ordered some of his guys to begin gathering up the corpses that had been killed by the wolves while others went door to door, looking for survivors, no doubt simply by listening for heartbeats.

I tore my eyes away from the carnage below and checked the watch that I'd carried in my mouth the entire way from the grocery store. It seemed like hours had passed but the whole thing had taken less than half an hour.

James tried to protest when I ordered him to follow me back to the car, but he knew as well as I did that there wasn't anything we could do here to make a difference.

We slipped over the top of the hill and raced back towards the grocery store where we'd left the car. As I ran I wondered how long it would be before the cold, numb feeling inside of me would disappear. A part of me thought that if it ever disappeared I'd have somehow failed a basic test of humanity. The people who had just been murdered back in Naco deserved more than for me to just go back to my life and pretend that nothing had happened.

Chapter 16

Alec Graves
Rest Easy Hotel
Rio Rico, Arizona

We made it back to the car and then to the airport without any problems, but I could tell that James was angry at me. He was practically leaking power the entire helicopter ride back west, but he managed to keep himself under control with what was probably a herculean act of will. I was especially grateful for that considering that if he'd said all of the things he'd wanted to say then the pilot would have overheard and we would have had even bigger problems.

I'd had a couple of over-complicated plans that might have offered a chance for us to get back into the hotel without being seen, but in the end I discarded them all and James and I just dropped off the car and jogged back the last mile or two between the dealership and the Rest Easy.

It was foolish to take chances, especially given what James and I now knew, but I felt like I was going to explode. I wanted to do something completely reckless like publically denounce Brandon at the next big briefing, but I knew that would just result in the death of me and my friends as well as all of the independents down here. Brandon would just stage another battlefield and tell the rest of the world that he'd been attacked by a numerically superior group of cats and some losses had been unfortunate but unavoidable.

I couldn't do that, but it felt like I had to do something at least a little risky so I settled for us jogging back to the hotel rather than sneaking in as I knew we should.

Juan intercepted us at the side entryway. "Where have you guys been? I've been putting Brandon off all day. If you'd been five minutes later you'd be in some serious hot water. Brandon has called an emergency briefing. Come on."

I practically saw red, but I let Juan all but drag me through the hotel to the conference room reserved for our use. We were the last ones to arrive. Brandon was even there already, and we got a frown in response to our tardiness. Jasmin and Jess both looked at James and me with concerned expressions so I managed a smile to try and reassure them. The expression felt wrong on my face, but I knew the girls needed to calm down or we'd be giving Brandon one more reason to suspect that something was wrong.

Brandon surveyed the group one more time as though confirming that everyone he was expecting had arrived, and then cleared his throat. "I'm afraid that a complication has come up. The Brain Box has just informed me that there has been some kind of incident on the southern end of the Tucson pack's territory. Jaclyn is still not taking my calls, so it's looking like we're going to be forced to send another team down to investigate."

One of the other team leaders raised a hand and Brandon nodded for him to ask his question.

"Does this mean that we're going to reschedule the op that was supposed to go down tonight? Vincent's team has been gone all day, so we could be as much as two teams down."

Brandon shook his head. "You're correct that Vincent's guys have been gone all day. I dispatched them to the west on a critical mission this morning myself, but I got off of the phone with Vincent a few minutes ago and he's confirmed that he'll be back in plenty of time to still hit our original timetable for the deployment."

I wanted to scream out that Brandon was a liar, but he'd picked his words carefully. He probably had sent Vincent west this morning, but driving west for an hour before looping around back to the east to kill a bunch of innocents wasn't quite the same as being sent on a mission to the west. Brandon's pulse hadn't ever even hiccupped and every other person in the room would leave thinking that Brandon had just told them that Vincent's mission was to the west.

Brandon continued without missing a beat. "Given that we'll only be down by one team, I'd like to proceed with the original op. I have, however, given some thought to who best to send east and I think that since this recent incident has all the earmarks of a low-risk assignment I'd like to send Juan's team. You guys just finished a rather brutal deployment less than twenty-four hours ago and it just makes sense to give you the easier mission rather than sending you into the fire again already."

Juan was nodding in appreciation, but I found myself interrupting.

"No. I mean thank you, sir, but we'd really rather help with the main operation. Alison is obviously going to have to sit things out no matter what else happens, but the rest of us are in fighting shape and raring to go."

Juan turned towards me with a surge of power. I'd just effectively challenged his authority in front of every single person in the briefing, and neither he nor his beast appreciated my brashness. Maybe it was more of the substitute recklessness that I'd shown earlier, but I responded back with a wave of power that was greater than anything else Juan had ever felt out of me. It wasn't quite my full strength, but it was enough to make everyone around us step backwards a couple of feet. In another time and place we would have been at each other's throats already, but Brandon's prohibition against fighting in public was still in effect, and James had stepped up to my side with his own flare of power as Jasmin and Jessica had moved around so that they were at my back.

It was a clear vote of no confidence in Juan as the leader of our team and it had probably just burned up a ton of the goodwill I'd garnered so far among the independents, but I was not going to be put in a position where I had to come back and tell everyone that cats had massacred those people. I couldn't because I'd know that it was a lie and everyone would be able to tell that I was lying even if I tried.

Brandon sent out a blow of power that exceeded anything Juan or I were capable of generating. "That's enough! There will be no challenge match right now. Alec, I know you're new here, but even if you somehow managed to beat Juan you wouldn't become the team leader, it would just mean that you'd be assigned to a new team."

I shook my head, but my eyes never left Juan's face. "I don't want to challenge Juan. I think he's a great leader and I'd vastly prefer to stay in his team. I just really want to be involved in the main operation tonight."

Like so much of the communication between our kind, every word I'd just said was the truth, just not the truth in its entirety. Even so, everyone nearby could tell that I was sincere in my admiration for Juan and I could see that my comments had even put Juan off balance a little bit.

"We're going to have words later on, Alec, but I'm not necessarily against helping with the main operation if Brandon has a spot that only needs five of us, since Alison is out."

Juan's words seemed to satisfy Brandon, and this time when he asked for volunteers he had several teams offer to take the job that everyone was sure would be a milk run. Brandon quickly reviewed the main op and then dismissed us all to meet with our individual teams.

Juan didn't even wait for the conference room to clear out before getting in my face. "What do you think you're doing, Graves?"

"I'm sorry, Juan. I can explain, but do you have somewhere private we can go first?"

He'd hit me with a lash of power, but my complete lack of response on the metaphysical plane seemed to be puzzling him. After a couple of seconds he nodded and led the way out of the conference room and down the hall. We detoured to pick up a wheelchair for Alison, who started to protest that she could walk just fine on her own right up until she noticed the tenseness between Juan and me.

By the time we arrived at Reina's shop and were conducted up to the solarium, twilight had fallen. Juan kicked on the swamp cooler while the rest of us opened up a couple of windows and arranged a couple of anti-snooping devices.

"Okay, Alec, spill it."

"James and I snuck out of town today. You'd probably already figured that out, but what you didn't know is that when Jaclyn shook my hand this morning she slipped a note into it. It had a time and a place on it along with today's date. That's where we went."

Juan threw his hands in the air. "Do you have any idea how much danger you put yourselves in? Jaclyn can get away with flipping off the entire Coun'hij, but neither of you have anywhere near that level of power. I know I put your feet on this path by telling you that your mother and Donovan were keeping stuff from you, but you've gone too far the other way now. You're going to get yourselves killed."

I nodded. "You may very well be right, but I can't change what I saw this afternoon."

Something in my tone must have given away more than I'd realized. Juan looked back and forth between James and me with an odd expression on his face.

"What are you talking about? What did you see at the meet with Jaclyn?"

"Brandon's having humans killed and staging it to look like it was some kind of raid from south of the border."

James' words came out sounding dead and monotone, but they still put a charge into the air that was all beyond anything I'd ever experienced previously. All three of the girls looked like they wanted to ask questions, but the dominance chain was simply too strong for them to interject a comment into a discussion between two dominants when the matter was as serious as this one was.

"You're crazy!"

I shook my head. "No, Juan, we both saw it. That's where Vincent and his guys have been all day and that's why Brandon is sending a team to Naco. Vincent's guys strapped some kind of clawed weapons onto their hands so that the wounds they inflicted would look like they were done by jaguars and then they killed dozens of people."

Juan slumped down in his chair. I could tell that he wanted to disbelieve what James and I were telling him, but the pieces fit together much too well for that. This was exactly the kind of thing that Brandon needed right now, and hard as it was to believe that anyone would order the death of so many people solely in the hopes that it would bring more troops down from the north, Brandon really was capable of doing it if anyone was.

"What have I done?"

It was a time for brutal honesty. "You've supported Brandon by killing jaguars, but more importantly you've helped put in place all of the controls that make independents willing to come down here and fight for Brandon and Kaleb. We need to stop that. The best thing in the world is for Brandon and Kaleb to spend all of their time fighting the cats because while they waste their strength against each other it allows us to start preparing to stop them."

"You're talking about some kind of coup? Do you have any idea how impossible that is?"

I nodded. "I do. Maybe not as much as you, but I know that our odds of winning are so close to zero that for all practical purposes anything we do probably isn't going to make a difference. I can't continue to support Brandon and Kaleb though. There are people resisting them—look at Agony and Dream Stealer. Those two haven't let the odds stop them from fighting and there is always a possibility that we can convince others. You said it yourself that Jaclyn has pretty much already told the Coun'hij to go screw themselves. Just the fact that she sent me to watch that massacre says that she's passively working against Kaleb. How much more would it really take to bring her over to the point where she's actively working against them?"

"A lot, Alec, it would take a lot. All three of the people you just mentioned are major powers in our world, but Agony and Dream Stealer can afford to actively work against the Coun'hij precisely because they don't have any friends or family that the Coun'hij can use against them. Jaclyn has an entire pack and a daughter to worry about. She'll never do anything that will put her daughter truly at risk."

A knot formed in my stomach. With everything else that had happened recently I hadn't thought about Rachel. Mother was a consideration too, but lately I wasn't sure how much she was really on my side or not.

Juan was right. It was one thing to throw yourself into a fight against the Coun'hij knowing that they'd do terrible things if they caught you, it was quite a different prospect to put people you cared about into harm's way.

"We've got to do something, Juan."

"For now I can start quietly letting the other independents know that Brandon staged the murder scene at Naco to make it look like it was cats instead of Vincent. That should cause the word to slowly percolate up to the various packs and make sure that Brandon doesn't get the influx of recruits that he was hoping for."

"How do we get the independents out of here? Every independent we lose down here is one more person who won't be able to stand against Kaleb if the opportunity arises."

"I don't know, Alec. It's not like every independent down here could just pack up and leave all at once without causing Kaleb to ask a lot of questions. I think the best we can hope for is to stop the flow of recruits in and then those who are here will have to gradually leave as they can come up with good reasons why they have to go back home."

"As the number of independents starts to drop, whoever is still here is going to be in a lot more danger."

"I know. It's the exact opposite problem from what we had when we started operations with Brandon, but it's exacerbated because at least then Brandon had a compelling reason to treat us well so as not to preclude the possibility of additional reinforcements arriving."

Chapter 17

Alec Graves
Three miles south of Lochiel, Arizona
Northern Mexico

I could tell that Jasmin and Jessica were still in shock from the revelation James and I had shared, but I couldn't do anything at this point but hope that they'd be able to shake it off enough not to have it interfere with their ability to fight.

Juan seemed to be handling the news better, but I could tell that he was still a little off of his game. He'd finished briefing us on the latest version of the operation and then we'd made it back just in time to form up with the rest of the teams for transport down to the ambush location.

This was an operation that had been solely put together by the Brain Box rather than originating from Brandon's anonymous source and then being vetted by the Brain Box. I wasn't sure that it should make any kind of difference either way, but for whatever reason I was more nervous about this deployment than either of the last two.

The Brain Box had apparently identified a shipment of drugs that was being run up into the United States by one of the drug cartels that had especially heavy backing from a group of fifteen jaguars who'd spent the last decade or so kicking out all of the competition from their home city of Zacatecas. I was unclear on whether or not the authorities even realized that Zacatecas was where ten percent of the cocaine in the United States originated, but apparently the cartel had been having problems with a couple of the other regional drug gangs and as a result they were especially worried about making sure this particular shipment made it across the border.

The Brain Box had a long list of hacked email accounts that indicated that the Zacatecas crew had turned to their usual MO and escalated by including nearly a dozen jaguars to serve as guards for the shipment as it made its way north. If they continued with their normal procedure those guards would then pay a visit to the competing cartels and kill everyone they could find, but thanks to some more fancy hacking the Brain Box had a complete roster of who was going to be along for the ride as well as the route and schedule for the caravan.

Brandon had decided that we would intercept the convoy just short of the United States border, all of which explained why we'd spent the last hour in the darkness alongside the road setting up a series of tire shredders and vehicles such that we could block off the road in seconds.

The Brain Box apparently had aerial eyes on the convoy, and about the time that we all left Rio Rico they confirmed that the number of guards still matched up exactly with the count from the emails that had tipped us off about the operation in the first place.

A couple of minutes before three a.m. we got the signal that the convoy was only ten minutes out and that there were no other vehicles between us and them, so we sprang into action. The tire shredders were flipped to the 'shred' position and the SUV blockade was rolled into place.

Our team was on the north side of the road along with some other people from various teams while Vincent's team and Brandon were on the south side. The thinking was that the terrain to the south was less rugged and therefore we could reasonably expect that most of the bad guys would try to flee south once they realized how much trouble they were in.

Brandon had also positioned a few wolves around the ambush site in a rough circle a hundred yards or so from the road. Jaguars are usually faster than wolves, so the hope was that the wolves would be able to intercept and at least slow down any of the cats who broke free of the main fight and made a run for it. If everything went according to plan then we'd be facing an outnumbered group of cats with a few humans thrown in and we'd have the element of surprise on our side.

My shoulders tensed up as I saw the first SUV appear around a bend in the road. A second SUV followed less than twenty yards from the first, and then a large semi came into view next. Two more black SUVs rounded out the convoy and the next couple of minutes passed agonizingly slowly as we waited for the vehicles to enter our trap.

Brandon had positioned our team on the extreme western edge of the ambush site, so I was able to see our targets well before they had any possibility of seeing our roadblock. The rest of our teams were pretty well hidden, but still visible if you knew where to look. I watched as the same ripple of anxiety that I was feeling slowly swept down both sides of the road as each new wolf or hybrid was able to finally see the approaching group of cars.

The reaction by the lead car was almost perfect when they saw that the road was blocked ahead of them. They must have had radios, because all five vehicles started to accelerate at the same time. Trying to ram their way through our blockade was risky, but they couldn't reverse course quickly, not without losing the semi-truck and the tens of millions of dollars of drugs it was carrying.

They'd all slowed down to negotiate the final curve in the road, which meant that they were starting from a less than ideal velocity, but they still would have been able to break through if not for the tire shredders which they hit less than a second later. Within a few heartbeats the first two SUVs and the truck were all on bare metal rims and the last two SUVs' tires were smoking as they stopped just short of the shredders.

Four more of our SUVs rolled into place behind the convoy and then Brandon shot off a flare and all around me people were shifting forms in a multi-pointed roar of power. My hybrid legs tore into the hard ground underneath me as I joined everyone else in sprinting down towards the road.

At close range humans with guns simply aren't much of a threat because of how slow the operators are, but we were starting out far enough away that I'd been worried that five or six guards armed with fully automatic weapons might do some damage before we got close enough to neutralize them. Hybrids are generally big enough and our internal systems are redundant enough that we are hard to kill with anything less than large-caliber rifle fire, but a pistol shot to the head could still bring us down and the wolves are much less resilient.

My concerns meant that I was hyper-aware and looking for weapons, which explained how I ended up as the first person to realize it was a trap. People were piling out of the SUVs just as expected, but rather than splitting into two groups, one of which was armed and the other of which dropped down onto all fours as they transformed, every single one of the guards shifted with a lash of power and charged towards the hybrids and wolves attacking them.

"It's a trap!"

My words hadn't even had a chance to begin fading away before Brandon started yelling for everyone to push on and attack.

I'd slowed down slightly when I realized that the cats were prepared for us, but I heeded Brandon's orders and crashed into a large male jaguar a second later. There was nothing of finesse in the exchange of blows. He jumped at me with quickness that I wouldn't have thought I'd be able to match, but I somehow managed to get an arm up between the two of us and I picked him out of the air and plunged my claws into his side.

I'd been lucky and I knew it, but as I dropped his lifeless corpse to the ground the back of the semi-truck opened up and three more men jumped out and suddenly the odds had tilted against us.

With one squad detached to Naco, the security team that had stayed back at the hotel, and a few people like Alison still on light duty, we were down to twenty-three effectives onsite at the ambush. We'd been expecting twelve cats and half a dozen humans, which would have meant that we'd essentially have them outnumbered by about fifty percent, once you factor in the fact that we had some wolves out to catch leakers rather than stationed where they could get right into the fight.

Instead, we were up against twenty-one cats, counting the three that had been hidden inside of the trailer with the drugs. Suddenly we were outnumbered and fighting a holding action until the wolves out on the perimeter could arrive and help tilt things back in our direction.

I ducked another cat and then ripped a smaller female off of James' back, but she writhed out of my grasp before I could kill her. Out of the corner of my eye I saw Jess and Jasmin double-team the jaguar that I'd just dodged, but there was still something tickling the back of my mind. In order to have planned this ambush the cats must have had a pretty good idea of how many people we could field. I didn't see any way they could have known that we'd be down a team, so counter-ambushing us with such a small number of shape shifters didn't make any sense.

Another cat tried to attack Jess and drive her off so that she couldn't assist Jasmin, but Juan got ahold of the cat's ribs and slammed it into the ground hard enough that I heard bones break. Before Juan could follow up and finish off his injured opponent, two more cats threw themselves at him. One cat latched onto his leg and the other hit him higher up, gaining a purchase on his chest as its back legs tore into his stomach. He needed help, but another cat was circling me and I knew if I turned my back on it that I'd be dead within seconds.

Down on the south side of the road our forces were even worse off than we were. Whether by accident or design, the cats had sent most of their numbers down there and I could see that they were being pressed badly by the sheer weight of numbers arrayed against them. Vincent and his guys were almost all fighting more than one opponent and bleeding in several places, but the real show was being put on by Brandon.

I'd never seen Brandon go all-out before, which meant that I'd never realized just how much he'd been holding back in all of the fights I'd seen him in before. He wasn't just fast, he seemed to flicker from one place to the next without actually crossing the intervening distance. Brandon killed two cats in three seconds while I was watching out of the corner of my eye and I suddenly realized he was right. He just needed the rest of us to hold on for another minute or so and he'd swing the odds back in our favor all by himself.

My opponent suddenly switched directions and threw himself at James, but I managed to move with him and I got a couple of claws into his feline body. It wasn't much more than a flesh wound, but it threw off his timing and trajectory enough that James was able to spin around and land a couple of blows of his own.

We were in the middle of a total free-for-all. I jumped in and tried to keep the cat James had been fighting up until that point occupied, which positioned me perfectly to see Brandon's plan finally finish unraveling.

The three shape shifters who'd been in the back of the semi with the drugs had been slow to engage, but as I got a decent look at them for the first time I realized that all three were nearly half again as big as any of the other jaguars we were fighting. As Brandon started in on his third kill the three big cats split up with one heading towards us and the other two heading to the south side of the road.

James had somehow left my new opponent with a limp, which was going a long way to counteract the fact that he was obviously older than any of the cats I'd fought so far. The difference in speed and strength was noticeable, but I juked one direction and then waited until he was committed and threw myself forward with enough force that I managed to get both sets of claws on my cat before he could land and change directions.

We went rolling across the ground from the force of my spring, but I managed to keep superior positioning and as I dropped another lifeless body to the ground I looked up to see a trail of bodies between where the three bigger cats had been a few seconds before and where they were now.

Ancients. It finally made sense. They'd sprung the trap with a smaller number of cats because they'd figured that the sheer deadliness of their three most powerful cats would be more than enough to offset both Brandon's considerable gifts and any quantitative disadvantage they would be suffering under.

It was obvious that the two Ancients on the south side of the road had planned on engaging Brandon simultaneously, but they'd taken too long to identify him. Those precious few seconds had allowed Brandon to cut down the bulk of the cats that had been trying to swarm Vincent's team under and now Vincent and his guys had thrown themselves at one of the Ancients in the hope that they could keep it distracted long enough for Brandon to kill the one he was fighting and then turn around and save them.

There was no question in my mind but that Vincent's guys would need rescuing. They were keeping their opponent on the defensive by sheer weight of numbers, but even while on the defensive he was landing respectable blows that were taking a toll on the hybrids facing him.

The fight between Brandon and the other Ancient was nothing but a blur. I couldn't tell who was winning because I couldn't even follow what was happening in the fight. I had a second to hope that Brandon's supercharged strength and speed was enough to carry the day and then a hammer blow of force hit me between the shoulders.

I'd committed the cardinal sin and allowed myself to become so distracted that I lost track of what was going on in my immediate area. The mere fact that I wasn't dead by the time that I hit the ground told me that I hadn't been knocked over by one of the cats, and I rolled to my feet to see that Jasmin had thrown herself at me to keep the third Ancient from executing me on his way towards Juan.

I thought Juan was a dead man, but he flung himself to the side with speed I hadn't known he possessed, and his evasion was just enough that the Ancient couldn't fully compensate. Instead of a killing slash to the neck Juan took a set of claws to his shoulder, but the massive jaguar probably would have killed him a second later if not for the arrival of two of the wolves who had been out on the perimeter. Both wolves jumped the Ancient at the same time that James finished off his latest opponent and moved in to help them.

Jess and Jasmin were only a leap away and I was only a couple of seconds behind them, but the Ancient killed one of the wolves and savaged another before any of us could arrive to assist. It looked like James got a claw or two into the jaguar as it jumped back out of range of the gang converging on it, but it was hard to tell for sure and if he had, then he'd paid for the blow with a set of deep slashes to his chest.

Somehow we'd finished off all of the other cats who had made it over to engage us, and it looked as though the other team on the south side of the road finally had the upper hand in their fight. A couple of their people were already headed this way to help deal with the Ancient, but it was going to be too little too late.

The second wolf, the one who had been hurt so badly a few seconds ago, was back on her feet, but she was so punch-drunk that she staggered away from the rest of us before anyone could stop her. The Ancient only needed a few feet of separation to make his play to finish her off.

A black-furred glowing streak of light pounced on the injured wolf and the rest of us threw ourselves at the Ancient in an attempt to save her. It was like fighting a wraith. I slashed at the cat, but my claws found nothing but empty air and a second later lines of fire tore their way across my chest.

My ribs held and protected my heart from the vicious attack, but the force of the blow knocked me backwards. I saw Jasmin flung away with blood dripping down her side and Jess knocked into James so that he couldn't interfere with what came next.

There was a frozen heartbeat where I could see the Ancient as it gathered itself and sprang at me. I didn't have to be able to see the arc of its trajectory. I was stumbling and off balance, there was no way that something as deadly as this jaguar had already proved itself to be was going to miss such an easy kill. I got my claws up roughly where I thought it would hit me only it didn't hit me because a massive form had been interposed between the two of us.

The Ancient hit with enough force that it actually managed to knock Juan over. I experienced another of those odd instances when I could see exactly what was happening despite the jaguar's unnatural speed. Blood fountained away as the Ancient opened up multiple arteries all up and down the inside of Juan's arms and then I sank my claws into black fur and made a fist around a set of feline ribs.

After hundreds of years of life, after decades of being all but invincible on the battlefield, having someone bury their claws inside of their flesh like that must have been so inconceivable that the Ancient panicked. Instead of doing the right thing and attacking me, the Ancient jumped away in an effort to break my hold.

The effort was nearly successful. I was pulled off of my feet and it felt like my arm had nearly been dislocated, but I managed to keep ahold of the cat and dragging me like that meant that

James was able to time the landing and rake long furrows down the jaguar's other side.

Jess was only a fraction of a second behind him and she managed to lock her jaws around a back leg high enough up that she was mostly safe from the raking attack of the other back leg.

The Ancient tried to make up for the lapse earlier and attacked me with a level of brutality that exceeded anything I'd ever experienced before. I tried to use my grip on its ribs to keep it away from me, but I simply wasn't strong enough. Despite my best efforts, incredibly powerful jaws closed on my upper arm and I felt the huge bone that was the next best thing to indestructible shatter from the pressure even as my inner arm was shredded by two sets of deadly claws.

I willed my fist not to relax, but it seemed somehow disconnected from my will and a fraction of a second later the Ancient was free and turning on Jess. The blood loss had created a sense of exhaustion inside of me and I wanted so badly to just close my eyes and go to sleep, but I forced them open long enough to see that the Ancient got only a single slash to the side of Jessica's face, thankfully missing her eye, before the two wolves from the other team arrived and helped James pin the jaguar down just in time for Brandon to show up and kill it with a single blow.

I looked down and realized that I'd transformed back to human form without intending to. It was a bad sign, but it was hard to be too worried considering that I should have been dead several minutes ago, that I would have certainly been dead if Juan hadn't thrown himself in front of me. I rolled over and found Juan. When the Ancient had leaped at me there at the end so that it could break my arm it must have pushed me back toward him because we were surprisingly close.

"Did we get it, Alec?"

"Yeah, it's dead. All three of them are."

Juan smiled. I'd never seen anyone look as pale as he did at that moment. It was obvious that his shift back to human form hadn't slowed the bleeding enough. I was probably going to die and I was only losing blood from one arm not two like he was.

"Why, Juan? You should have let him have me. I'm dead anyways."

"No, Alec. You're important. We aren't going to get very many more chances to save our people before the storm breaks over us."

I wanted to ask him what he'd meant, but it was no use. Juan was dead and I would be joining him in the next few seconds.

Chapter 18

Alec Graves
Graves Estate
Sanctuary, Utah

I'm not sure how I survived. I've tried to put together some of the pieces, but James, Jasmin and Jessica have all been extremely reluctant to talk about what happened and I haven't had any opportunity to talk to any of the independents down in Arizona.

The bits and pieces that I managed to tease out of my three friends didn't make me feel any better. One of our SUVs had been stocked with several units of blood, but there hadn't been enough blood to go around to everyone who needed it. The fact that I was alive almost certainly meant that someone else was dead who otherwise would have been saved. Considering the sheer amount of blood that I'd lost it was possible that saving me had cost more than one life.

James and the others were less reticent when it came to questions about what had happened once everyone got back to Rico Rio. Kaleb and Brandon were trying very hard to spin the operation as a smashing victory, both internally to everyone in Sanctuary and to the rest of the packs, but it had apparently been obvious to all three of my friends that the few independents who'd survived and even most of the Sanctuary people had felt like we'd had our heads handed to us.

I tended to agree. Killing twenty-one cats, three of which had been Ancients was an impressive feat, but it hadn't been worth losing nearly that many of our own people. The Brain Box and Brandon had been suckered and we'd committed to the wrong operation instead of biding our time and killing that many cats over the course of a few engagements where the odds were on our side and we could engage without losing most of our force.

Juan hadn't made it. When I'd first woken up in my bed in Sanctuary I'd thought that maybe his death had been some kind of terrible nightmare, but Jessica's face had told me otherwise. The scars were already fading, but I could clearly see where she'd taken a set of claws while trying to keep the Ancient pinned down enough for everyone else to pile on.

BOUND

Jess had mistaken my expression for concern over her appearance and had hastened to reassure me that she was fine and that the scars would be gone within a few weeks, but she was trying to bandage the wrong metaphorical wound. Even her joke about not being able to wear a swimsuit at the pool now that we were back didn't tease much of a smile out of me.

Even back then, before I knew the full toll we'd paid to bring down the Ancients, I'd still known that it had been heavy and that Juan hadn't survived. I'd been sad, but I hadn't understood the full weight of that particular loss yet. That understanding didn't come until later when James and Jasmin arrived to check up on me.

Juan had been my connection to the independent packs. He'd had credibility with them that I didn't have, and might not ever have now that he was gone. Not only that, I'd doubtlessly alienated some of his friends when I'd made the scene at the briefing and refused to go on the assignment to Naco.

It had been James who had asked what we were going to do about the people Brandon had ordered killed in Naco. The four of us had decided to go on a short walk as a way of getting out of the house. Only seconds after we'd gone far enough that the house was no longer visible he'd brought up the single biggest unanswered question and I had been forced to tell him and the girls that I didn't know how to proceed.

Vincent had apparently survived as had more than half of his team, so one way or another it was virtually guaranteed that we'd be hearing about more incidents from the border where humans were killed by the southerners.

Despite his efforts to convince everyone that the operation had been a success, Kaleb had issued a slew of orders as soon as he received word of Brandon's losses. Several of the pack who'd been scheduled for downtime were ordered back down to Arizona along with a few members of the pack who had never been considered particularly suitable for pitched combat.

Most surprisingly of all, Kaleb had ordered Brandon to ship Jasmin, Jess, James and me back up to Sanctuary. It hadn't particularly made sense for Kaleb to pull four fighters out of Arizona considering all of the knots he was tying himself into so that he could get more fighters down there to reinforce Brandon, but the order had apparently been non-negotiable and one of the planes had arrived only an hour or so after we'd arrived back in Rio Rico.

I'd still been unconscious when James had carried me onto the plane and it had taken to the air. I'd remained unconscious for nearly forty-eight hours and as nearly as I could tell Kaleb hadn't asked after me a single time while I'd been out.

Mother had been a different matter altogether. She'd sent Donovan over several times to check up on me both before I woke up and since. I'd spent the last twenty-four hours ducking her. I wasn't ready to see her yet because I wasn't ready to discuss the things that she'd been keeping from me. There was a subsidiary benefit that my staying away from Mother would help convince Kaleb that I could finally be brought over to his side of things, but as much as I tried to tell myself that my evasions were part of a larger scheme, I knew the truth.

Once I talked to her there was a chance that I'd have to acknowledge the fact that I couldn't trust either of my parents.

The summons that came from Kaleb thirty minutes after my friends and I returned from our walk was hardly a surprise. He might not care enough to check in on me when there was still a possibility that I might not recover, but now that I was up and walking around he no doubt figured that it was time to put me to work.

James and the others looked reluctant to let me out of their sight, but I waved them away and told them that I'd meet them in the garden once Kaleb was done with me. I turned around to follow Kaleb's messenger, a young kid named Thomas, and instead found Rachel blocking my way.

"I know that you're avoiding Mom, but are you avoiding me too?"

"I'm not avoiding you or Mom either one, Rachel."

It was a bald-faced lie, but my friends were far enough away that they wouldn't be able to catch me in the lie and Rachel and Thomas had only human senses.

"Just for the record, Mom didn't send me to check up on you. I came on my own initiative just because I've missed you while you've been away."

I sighed. "I missed you too, Rachel, but I need to go see Kaleb now. Can I swing by your room in a couple of hours?"

"Right, you're totally not ducking Mom."

"We don't always have to talk in her presence, Rach, but if that's what you want I'll swing by her rooms and we can talk there."

The words came out without my really having thought them through, but I realized that it was time to stop prolonging the inevitable. Once I was done with Kaleb, I would go talk to Mother and find out once and for all where things really stood between us.

Rachel looked at Thomas, who was practically hopping back and forth from one foot to the other with worry over the possibility that he might get into trouble for not bringing me back quickly enough. Rachel scrunched up her mouth the way she tended to when she was trying to make a decision and then stood up on her toes and whispered in my ear.

"Something isn't right, Alec. Mom has been acting a little weird since before you left, but it's just getting progressively worse. I still don't know what's happening down on the border that has her so secretive, but Kaleb visited last night and she's been a complete wreck ever since. If you're going to push her to find out what she's been keeping a secret from us then today's the day to do it."

A wave of emotion washed through me. I didn't need to ask Mother what was going on down on the border because I already knew all about it. I knew, but I hadn't told Rachel yet—in fact I hadn't even thought about telling her before she brought the issue up.

Maybe in my own way I wasn't any better than Mother after all.

"I'll see you in an hour or two, Rach. We'll talk then and I can fill you in on everything that's happened to me since we last talked."

Rachel gave my hand a squeeze and smiled back over her shoulder at me as she walked away. Thomas gave a big, dramatic sigh that was probably much louder than he meant for it to be and then led the way off to Kaleb's office.

Kaleb was typing something on his computer when I arrived. He waved me towards one of the leather chairs.

"I'll be just a minute."

I sat down and looked at his office with new eyes. It hadn't changed while I'd been gone, but I had. The massive sword, built to a scale that made it suitable for use by a hybrid, dominated the space behind him in a way that it never had before. It was a piece that didn't fit with the public image Kaleb projected of a dutiful member of the Coun'hij, but it explained so much.

Swords like that had once been common in every house. They made a single hybrid more deadly than any but the most dangerous of the Ancients and they allowed the warrior who used them to be nearly the equal of a werewolf all by themselves.

Most of them had been destroyed, a few probably existed hidden away by some of the loyalists to the monarchy, but this was the only one I knew of that was openly displayed. Kaleb had never taken it into battle, but the mere fact that he displayed it was a subtle sign of rebellion—an indication that he didn't stand for quite the same things as the rest of the Coun'hij.

I was certain that Kaleb had been the one to hit on the idea of creating the clawed gloves that Vincent and his men had used to slaughter dozens of innocents. Kaleb really was the architect of every wrong I'd encountered over the last few weeks. Rage started to rise up inside of me as my beast awoke and started amplifying my feelings, but I forced my emotions back down and let a cold kind of numbness take over.

I needed Kaleb to think that he could trust me, that I'd finally turned the corner after all of these years, and was someone that he could mold into doing whatever dirty work he needed done.

"You've learned some self-control while you've been away. That's good."

Kaleb followed my gaze and then frowned slightly as he saw that I was looking at the ancient sword that had stood silently behind him for more than two decades.

"That's one of my few failures. Before you were born I spent a lot of time trying to unlock the secret of creating more swords like this one. Do you know that modern metallurgists are still having problems figuring out how the Damascus blades were made in India? All of our modern science and we still can't create swords with as fine of an edge or as hard of a metal."

"I didn't know that."

"Neither did I, at least not until I started paying for tests to be run on this monster. I eventually had to stop because every time I let someone new run any kind of analysis on it they came back wanting to release their findings to one peer-reviewed journal or another."

Kaleb tapped on his desk with one finger as he strolled down memory lane. "There are trace elements in the metal that the scientists couldn't even identify at the time. The periodic table has grown quite a bit since then, but I still wonder from time to time if I had it analyzed now whether or not there would still be an element or two in it that the eggheads still haven't managed to identify yet."

"I didn't think that most of the newer elements that they've identified over the last few decades were very stable."

"You're right, they aren't, but as nearly as I can tell those ancient swordsmiths had found a way of stabilizing normally unstable elements inside of the steel. That sword is five percent lighter than an equivalent blade made of steel, but it has a hardness that approaches what you'd find in a diamond."

"How is that possible?"

"I don't know. The tensile strength was tested at thirty percent better than steel too. The tester wanted to push it to the point of failure but I wouldn't let him. Back then the sword was a symbol of everything that we'd lost. Swords like this were what allowed our ancestors to drive the cats back down to the darkest jungles in South America. In a very real way the monarchy was founded at least partly on the strength of these weapons. I thought that if I could create more of them it would pave the way for a new golden age for our people."

It was always possible that Kaleb was simply playing me, but I didn't think that was the case. The regret in his voice was too palpable for it to be contrived and he'd had no way of knowing that I would focus on the sword when I came into his office.

"What happened?"

"I grew up and realized that it was going to take more than symbols and dreaming to keep our people from being exterminated. We have vampires breeding like lice on both coasts and the cats applying more pressure against the border with every year that passes. I stopped dealing in the realm of make-believe and started living in what was. I think that you've started making the same transition over the last few weeks and I wanted to call you in here and let you know how proud that makes me."

I'd tried to mentally prepare myself for this meeting, but I knew I was about to be tested in ways that I'd never been tested before. I wasn't a good enough liar to control my breathing and pulse in an outright lie, but there was a decent chance I could mislead him if I chose my words carefully.

"I've definitely had my eyes opened to things that I'd never considered before now."

Kaleb nodded and smiled. "I could tell from the reports I got back from Brandon. I don't buy that you've buried the hatchet with him any more than he does, but the simple fact that you're willing to pretend that you did so as to avoid causing more problems is a good start. It means that you're finally starting to realize that there are problems that you can't just charge blindly at and hope for providence to save you somehow."

I nodded. My nod had more to do with the fact that I should have realized that even nearly being killed by Vincent's efforts wouldn't be enough to justify an actual change of heart, at least not in Kaleb's mind.

"You do know that Vincent nearly got me killed right?"

"Of course I do. That was always a chance, but frankly you didn't leave me any choice but to send you down there and hope that combat would wear you down a little."

I took a deep breath. "Since we're being so honest with each other I'm just going to point out that Brandon led us into an unmitigated disaster."

Kaleb nodded, seemingly pleased by the fact that we were carrying on a dialogue for once. "Oh, it was bad, there's no question about that. My intelligence assets have done quite a bit of digging and it's starting to look like Brandon's presence caused a bigger stir even than I expected. I always figured that putting a group down there and kicking off active offensive operations would bring cats out of the woodwork to try and kill our people, but I didn't count on Brandon killing so many of those so-called Ancients of theirs."

The frown was back and Kaleb's fists went white as he tried to control his anger over what had happened.

"Those animals are the real power south of the border and they've always been happy to let the younger cats throw themselves at us because it serves to take some of the pressure off of them. The truth is that until Brandon came along we never had a good way to deal with an Ancient who decided, for whatever reason, to come adventuring out north. Back in the day two or three hybrids with swords were generally a match for a single Ancient, but now that we have to take them with our claws our options are severely limited."

Kaleb held up a finger. "Jaclyn might be able to knock one of them down with that electrical jolt of hers. She's used her ability to good effect against some cats who were approaching the end of their second century, but by all accounts even then she only knocked them down for a few seconds, so it's possible that a cat who is pushing three hundred years might be able to just shrug off any charge she's capable of generating."

A second finger came up. "Puppeteer is capable of bringing down an ancient by using three or four werewolves, but Puppeteer tends to be a clunky kind of tool. He's a bit like a nuclear weapon. If you've got a stationary target and plenty of time to prepare he can burn it to the ground, but he doesn't do as well against small, mobile targets because it tends to take him so long to round up a group of werewolves and sic them on whatever you want killed."

I already knew where he was going. "Which means that mostly we just have to use the third option, which is swarming them under with superior numbers."

"Yeah, and you saw how that went. Those damn cats are so fast that it's hard to get enough bodies in close enough proximity to them to bring them down. Even once you've got enough people there fighting them it still comes down to a matter of luck as much as anything else and they always leave a big pile of bodies behind them."

I realized that I was rubbing the arm that had been ripped open three days before. I forced myself to stop, but it was one of the harder things I'd done in recent memory. The nerves were knitting back together at a record pace and I already had most of the feeling and mobility back in my fingers, but healing at that speed took a toll and more often than not it felt like my arm was on fire.

"We definitely had a lot of luck on our side."

Kaleb waited until I looked back up and then smiled at me. "You had a lot of luck, but it was still an impressive accomplishment. That's part of what helped convince me that you're starting to realize your potential. Mallory stopped by while you were sleeping to check you out, so I know that you didn't manifest an ability or anything, but you still showed the kind of speed that not many normal hybrids ever manage. You kept your friends and everyone else on that northern side of the road alive."

"It wasn't me who saved everyone, not really. Juan stopped the Ancient from killing me when it first tore into us. Without him I would have been dead."

"I know. I have to say that I'm sorry that Juan died, but he made the right decision. He was instrumental in convincing members of other packs to go down there and help us in our fight, but at the end of the day that fight wasn't as much of a disaster as you think it was. There are only a very limited number of cats as powerful as the three you guys killed. Just living for a long time doesn't guarantee that a cat will manifest that level of power any more than becoming a hybrid guarantees that someone will eventually manifest an ability. We just took three of their kings off of the board and although we lost a lot of people we didn't lose any of our key pieces."

This time I couldn't stop at least some of my rage from leaking through and the white noise generator crackled and popped as some of the energy that escaped me bled over into the physical plane in some way that it never had before.

"It's possible that you're right, but right now I don't particularly appreciate you calling us all pawns."

Kaleb waved my concern away. "No offense was intended, and you know it. More importantly, you're not one of the pawns. The truth of the matter is that I've been very careful with regards to who I've sent down to the border. Wolves, yes, by the dozens, and hybrids even, but not young hybrids who Mallory says have the potential to manifest an ability. The only two exceptions to that rule have been you and Brandon. I'm trying very hard to keep from losing anyone truly important to the fighting down there."

Kaleb sighed and then waved his arm around in a gesture that seemed to take in the house and even the estate beyond it.

"Our population growth is actually coming close to matching the cats now and that hasn't happened in centuries. As long as we're careful about who we lose and keep our key individuals, those with the potential to make a profound difference in the long term, out of the fighting then a war of attrition isn't completely a bad thing. Brandon's discovery that the cats massacred all of those people in that border town hasn't had the impact I would have expected as far as galvanizing more people to volunteer to go down and fight the good fight, but sooner or later we're going to see the recruits we need down there. In the meantime, in a lot of ways, this is the opportunity we've been waiting for."

Kaleb seemed to be waiting for another metaphysical outburst from me, but I had a death grip on my beast and I was doing my level best to stop it from acting up. Having the energy from my beast melt into the real world enough to cause electronics to go on the fritz, even slightly, was new. In another time and place it might have been an interesting phenomenon, but right now it was just one more thing that I had to control if I was going to keep Kaleb from realizing that I knew he and Brandon were behind those murders.

A little bit of energy still slipped out, but it was understated compared to how bad it could have been and Kaleb seemed to think that it was outrage over the deaths of the humans—which it was, just not in the way he thought.

"Brandon's support among the pack is the weakest it has ever been. His staunchest supporters were down in Arizona with all of you and some of them are dead now. Those members of the pack here in Sanctuary who supported him are shaky right now too. They've either lost friends and family in the fight against those three Ancients or at the very least their confidence in his judgment and ability to lead has taken a severe hit."

"What do you want me to do?"

"Now is the time for you to begin trying to cement *your* support here in the pack. James, Jessica and Jasmin are a decent start, but you're going to need many more at your back if you're to serve as a counterweight to Brandon. If your ability had manifested itself already it would make your task much easier, but you're not going to get a better chance than right now."

It was perfect. Kaleb was asking me to do exactly the thing I'd been planning on already. He wanted me to build a power bloc that could be used to counter Brandon's influence, and I would build a following to the best of my ability, but the goal would be to stop both of them rather than just Brandon.

"I can see the wisdom in what you're asking. I'll do my best to circulate among the pack and befriend everyone. I'd like to make a request though. I'd like Alison to be brought up from the border. I think she's already got a degree of loyalty towards me after our time together on Juan's team."

A look of annoyance flashed across Kaleb's face. "You're missing the point. A bunch of teenage wolves aren't going to secure your spot. You need to gather hybrids, preferably experienced ones. Once you have a solid core of dominant fighters, the submissives will naturally gravitate towards you. This isn't about making friends with people, Alec. Shape shifters don't want leaders who are their friends, they want leaders who can protect them when something bigger and meaner than them comes along."

I opened my mouth to respond but he talked right over me. "I've made sure that the story about your fight with the Ancient has been circulated widely through our pack, both here in Sanctuary and elsewhere, which will help make your task easier. Even so, until your ability manifests you need to build a coalition of hybrids who are weaker than you, who you can defeat in a challenge match if they become problematic, and hybrids who are more deadly than you, but whom you have some other hold on—usually either because you can throw money at them or because they want a slice of the security represented by those that you've made submissive to you. That's the secret recipe to being a pack alpha and you need to get that through your head. Starting with nobodies like Alison just makes your job harder because you give off the appearance of weakness. By starting with submissives you essentially tell everyone that you don't believe you can manage the dominants who are required to make a pack function properly. Do you finally understand?"

"I understand that you're refusing to recall Alison despite the fact that she's been down there as long as anyone and all without ever getting a chance to come back home for some leave."

"My hands are tied with regards to Alison. Once you're running your own pack and I'm not sheltering you from the realities involved, you'll quickly realize that sometimes you have to trade favors to keep your most valuable people happy. That means that the less valuable members of the pack get stepped on sometimes. Alison isn't dominant and she doesn't have any skills that are particularly valuable. She's done nothing to provide herself with a single ounce of leverage."

"Very well. I'll go start putting together my power base."

I stood to go. It wasn't the right tone to take with Kaleb, but I couldn't seem to help myself. Besides, after the things I'd said already it would be much better for me to leave, even in a huff, than stay and say something worse.

"Sit down, Alec. I'm not done yet."

I sat down and did my best to hide the tremor that was starting to develop in my legs and hands.

"I've been trying to lay the pieces out so that you could draw the proper conclusions, but it's obvious that despite your recent strides you still don't understand the core of how the game is played. Brandon is operating from a much weaker position than he was a few weeks ago, but he's still the single most deadly wolf in our pack. I downplay that fact at every turn, but the truth is that he could cut his way through every single hybrid I could field against him and take over the pack at any point."

Kaleb sighed and leaned forward in his chair. "Right now Brandon knows that he's lost influence and it's making him push harder than normal. In many ways, until you do manage to create some kind of counterweight, I'm even worse off than I was before. Back when he had more power he was actually less pushy, but he's still too powerful for me to ignore if he decides that he really wants something."

My mind flashed back to my last fight with Vincent and the favor that Brandon had wanted out of Kaleb.

"What's he asking for? What does he want?"

"Rachel."

My whole world seemed to vibrate like an enormous gong the tiniest fraction of a second after it had been hit. The outer edges of everything were still absolutely motionless, but I could feel tremors starting up here in this room that would quickly make their way out to everything I knew and I could somehow feel that it would be ages before the vibrations would die back out.

"I don't understand."

My voice sounded calm, dead even, and it took me a second to realize that it sounded calm because inside I was absolutely still. The massive blow that Kaleb had just struck to my life had started everything moving, but somehow in my center the vibrations had canceled each other out. Even my beast was quiet, but it was the motionlessness of a predator in the instant just before it strikes.

"Not for himself, for Vincent. He's dealing with the same problem on a smaller scale that I'm dealing with. Vincent is pushing Brandon. He's had his eye on your sister for a couple of years now and Brandon doesn't feel like he can put Vincent off anymore. I've already told him that it's a go. The two of them are flying up tonight to collect her."

"You're talking about slavery."

Kaleb's hand hit his desk hard enough that the thick wood buckled. "I'm talking about the way that pack life works. Jessica runs and fetches for you at the slightest crook of your finger. That's no different than this. Rachel doesn't have the strength to stand on her own. She's had a pleasant life up until now because *I've* been protecting her.

Just like I protect your mother, just like I protect even you to a lesser extent. I'm at the end of my strength, Alec."

Kaleb stood. "It's come down to a decision as to whether I protect Rachel or I protect the rest of the pack, and I won't sacrifice dozens of people for her. I can't afford to let the fate of minor pieces stop me from doing what needs to be done. Not even my own daughter can be allowed to destroy everything I've worked for. I keep my position as the head of the Coun'hij solely based on the size of this pack and the fact that Brandon backs my every move. Our pack has just suffered a major loss. If I do anything to alienate Brandon then Puppeteer and the rest would tear through this pack like a tornado."

It was obvious that our interview was over. I stood and turned to leave and this time Kaleb didn't stop me, but he did call out to me before I made it to the door.

"It's already decided, Alec, but I wanted to at least give you a few hours' heads-up. You'll need some time to prepare yourself. You can't afford to get in Vincent's or Brandon's faces about this. Brandon is on a hair trigger and I can't interfere if you do something to really piss him off."

I looked back at him and nodded, but he already had his phone out and was muttering something about needing to use a different room for the next few days until his desk could be repaired.

Chapter 19

Alec Graves
Graves Estate
Sanctuary, Utah

I called James as soon as I was out of earshot of Kaleb's office.

"I'm not going to be able to meet up with the three of you in the garden like I'd originally planned."

"Okay, is there anything that you need us to be doing right now?"

I debated my answer and then told him a partial truth.

"Brandon and Vincent are going to be in town later tonight. Obviously if things get tense for whatever reason we can't face Brandon down, but it might be a good idea for you guys to get some rest in between now and then so that you're fresh for whatever the night might bring."

"Okay, will do."

I put my phone back in my pocket and started towards my mother's rooms. It was past time to find out just exactly how much she knew.

I opened the door to her solarium and walked inside without knocking.

"Hello, Alec. I wondered when you would be by."

"You've been lying to me."

She held a hand up in my direction and looked over at Rachel. "Rachel, can you please give us a few minutes?"

Rachel looked back and forth between the two of us and then shook her head. "I want to stay. I'm tired of being left in the dark. Something is going on and I need to know what it is."

Mother looked at me. "Please, Alec. She doesn't need to be in on this conversation. Please, not like this."

A part of me wanted to refuse her, to tell Rachel right here and now exactly what our mother had been involved in, but there was a chance that she was right. Rachel didn't need to find out what Kaleb was planning by way of a shouting match.

Feeling as though I'd just rationalized my way into selling off another piece of my soul, I gave Rachel my best smile.

"If you'll go wait in your room I promise that I'll come find you as soon as I'm done with

Mother and I'll tell you everything I know and everything I find out from Mother."

Rachel looked up at me and the eyes that met mine were far too old for her fifteen-year-old face.

"You promise?"

Mother gasped and I didn't need to look in her direction to know that she was desperately shaking her head at me, but I nodded.

"Yes, Rachel, I promise. There have been too many secrets around here for far too long."

Rachel took a deep breath and then stood and left the solarium. I watched her go until the door swung shut behind her and then turned back towards my mother.

"Thank you, Alec. To find out in that way would have destroyed her."

"I don't think that she's as weak as you think she is, but that's a different conversation entirely. I repeat my earlier statement. You've been lying to me."

She shook her head. "It's true that I've kept things from you, but I've never lied to you."

"A lie by omission is still a lie, Mother. You knew what Brandon and Vincent were up to down on the border and you never bothered to tell me. I could have easily been killed because of that hole in my education."

"I didn't *know* for sure, Alec. Jack, Donovan, none of us had been able to confirm the rumors and we were pretty sure that they were originating from Jaclyn Annikov. She's hardly the most dependable source given all of the axes she has to grind with the Coun'hij and your father."

"You should have at least told me of your suspicions. Unlike you and Donovan, I have to go out on the field and risk being killed by Brandon and Vincent in addition to the cats or vampires."

I'd only ever seen Mother look immaculate and calm. Her appearance and manner always seemed to say that she was in control of her situation, that anything that happened was at least partially by her design, but now I realized just how far her usual composure had cracked. She'd obviously been crying a lot over the last twenty-four hours and now she was the angriest I'd ever seen her.

"No, Alec, telling you our suspicions would have just resulted in you doing something brave and foolish in an effort to confirm those rumors. If I'd told you about what I thought was going on down in Arizona you would have probably gotten yourself killed months ago. You have incredible potential, but I've known for years that it would be all that I could do to keep you alive long enough for you to realize it."

"And you were willing to do whatever you had to do in order to make sure that happened."

"Yes, Alec, my morality is flexible where you are concerned. I will lie, cheat and steal to keep you safe and give you the chance to realize the destiny that is just beyond your grasp right now."

"What about murder, Mother? Will you commit murder on my behalf?"

She reached up to slap me, but I easily grabbed her arm, stopping her from hitting me.

"How dare you! I've never done any such thing. You have no idea of the hell that I've gone through for you."

"Haven't you, Mother? If you know of murder being carried out and you do nothing to stop it, doesn't that make you complicit in those deaths?"

She was shaking now. "I didn't know for sure what was happening down there. You can't hold me responsible for every rumor that flows through this place. I don't even begin to have the power around here to verify every crazy thing that crosses the lips of some of the gossipmongers in the pack."

"Not all rumors are created equal and you know it, Mother, but that's not even the only reason that I'm angry at you. How long have you known that Kaleb was going to give Rachel to Vincent to be his slave?"

"I was afraid he would tell you."

Her voice was so faint that I wasn't sure that I'd have been able to hear it if I'd had merely human ears.

"Yes, he told me. Does that disappoint you? Did you hope that I'd be taken by surprise so that I wouldn't have a chance to *do* anything about what is about to happen?"

Mother shook her head, the action almost violent in her desire to deny my words. "No, I begged Kaleb to tell you what was going on. I was worried that if it came at you without any warning that you would do something that would get you killed. I can't save Rachel, but I can at least try to make sure that you make it through this alive."

"How long, Mother? How long have you known that he was going to give her to Vincent like a piece of property?"

"Your father told me last night. I tried to convince him otherwise, but nothing I did swayed him in the least."

"Don't call him that. He's done nothing to deserve that title."

She reached out to me, but I shook her arm off.

"I'm sorry, Alec. I don't know what else to do. Kaleb can usually be convinced to moderate the worst of his inclinations, but lately he's been even worse than normal."

I looked at her for several seconds and she wilted under my gaze. I kept thinking that I should be feeling something, but the stillness inside of me hadn't shattered yet. Everything I'd felt for the woman before me had been swept away in one short afternoon. She'd made decisions that had undermined our relationship and the respect that I'd once had for her. From the outside things had still looked stable, but it had taken only a tiny nudge to bring everything crashing down.

Actually I did feel something, something that I wasn't sure I'd ever felt before in my entire life. Remote. I finally had enough distance from her and Kaleb to look at what was going on around me with a degree of perspective.

Her eyes seemed to beg me to speak, to say something that would make things better, but for long minutes I didn't open my mouth. When I finally did, my voice came out smooth and uncaring.

"The only other question I have for you is why you've stayed so long. You've told me for years that Kaleb was irredeemable, but you've stayed despite knowing that associating with him couldn't help but eventually drag you down to his level. Don't tell me that it was because you wanted to moderate his influence, that you stayed because of the good that you could do. All of the good you might have accomplished is washed away by the fact that you're ready to let him take Rachel away when you could have gotten her to safety years ago."

Her lips were trembling and I could see the tears forming in her eyes, but she refused to meet my gaze directly.

"I always thought that I was staying because of the good I was doing. I really have stopped Kaleb from doing some terrible things, but you're right in your accusations that I haven't stopped everything. It wasn't until last night that I realized just how much I've been hoping that I was wrong, that there was some little piece of Kaleb that was redeemable."

I stood to go, but she grabbed my arm again and this time there was such desperate strength to her grip that I didn't shrug her off immediately.

"Where are you going?"

"I've heard what I needed to hear. There's no reason for me to stay here any longer."

"He doesn't want to do this, Alec. I could see it in his eyes when he came to tell me last night. He would do almost anything to stop from having to give Rachel to that monster, but he's too scared to choose any other course. There is still good in him."

I pulled her hand off of my arm, but I tried not to physically hurt her as I did so.

"I don't have the luxury of worrying about whether or not Kaleb means well. He's said a lot of things lately that I don't agree with, but he's right about one thing. I have to deal with reality, not some make-believe version of it. Good intentions are nice, but they'll never outweigh terrible actions."

I turned and walked towards the door, but she called out to me one last time just before my hand touched the doorknob.

"What are you going to do?"

"I'm going to go tell Rachel everything I know just like I promised her I would."

"No, I mean after that. Please don't throw away your life."

"I'm not going to let Vincent have her without a fight, Mother. All of the potential that everyone talks about isn't worth a damn thing if I have to sacrifice Rachel to realize it. I don't believe that is what will be required to save our people, but even if it was I'd still do everything I could to save her. If it's really come to that then maybe our people don't deserve to be saved anymore."

Chapter 20

Alec Graves
Graves Estate
Sanctuary, Utah

Rachel was waiting for me in her room exactly as she'd promised. At her invitation, I walked inside and then closed the door behind me.

It had been an incredibly long time since I'd seen Rachel's room. We usually talked in the solarium. Actually, the last time that I'd been here it had been decorated in pinks with cartoon posters scattered over almost every inch of the walls.

It looked like a different room altogether now. The walls had been redone in whites and the furniture had been replaced with simple but elegant pieces made out of rosewood. The wood was fragrant enough that I was pretty sure that it was noticeable even to Rachel, but for me it was like stepping into a candy shop.

I took a deep breath of the sweet scent and then opened my eyes and took in the rest of the room. She'd had it remodeled so that the closets were bigger, which was hardly a surprise, but what did catch me off guard was the sewing mannequin just visible in the mirrors that took up the entire far end of the room.

"I didn't know that you liked to sew, Rachel."

"I don't, I mean not exactly. I like to design. Sewing is just kind of a necessary evil. Everyone thinks that the shopping trips are because I'm a spoiled little girl who likes to spend Kaleb's money, but mostly I just like to go see all those different clothes. Most of what Mom wears lately is stuff that I designed and made."

"How have we lived together all of these years without me realizing that?"

Rachel's smile was sad, but there wasn't any resentment to it. "Because we don't really live together. You live in one world and I live in a different one. You live in the middle of all of the constant machinations that define this place even though you don't realize it. I, on the other hand, just try to keep a low profile and hope that nobody notices me, because I can't protect myself and I hate the price it takes out of you and Mother when you're forced to protect me."

I shook my head. "I've never once begrudged anything I had to do to keep you safe, Rachel.

That bit about us living in two different realities is crap. I should have thought to ask you about your hobbies. I should have made more time for the two of us to be together without worrying about all of the craziness inherent in living here."

Rachel walked over and gave me a hug. "You never thought to ask because you've never had any hobbies of your own, Alec. Every time you started to develop an interest in anything other than fighting, Kaleb has done his very best to run you to the ground until you forgot about whatever it was that had caught your interest."

I opened my mouth to disagree with her, but she was right. I'd never seen it before, but Kaleb had stopped me from dabbling in anything that might have interfered with his vision of me as a weapon to be pulled out whenever he needed it and then safely locked back up once he was done with me.

"You're a pretty smart kid, Rach. Maybe we would have all been better off if you'd been born a shape shifter rather than me."

Rachel shook her head and tapped my chest over my heart. "I couldn't have done some of the things you've done already, Alec. There's something about you that draws people to you almost despite themselves. I think it's because you have such a good heart. That's your greatest asset—don't let anyone take it away from you."

"Kaleb thinks it's a weakness. He thinks people who are drawn to me out of loyalty are useless and that I should be creating a coalition out of people who bind themselves to me out of fear or greed."

"That's because Dad lost his heart a long time ago. I've spent a lot of time talking to Donovan about what things used to be like, and I think that Dad used to draw people the same way that you do, but somewhere along the way he let that be taken away and now he doesn't view it as a legitimate tool because it's not one that he can use anymore."

Regret filled me at the prospect of taking away the last little bit of innocence that Rachel had maintained despite having spent her life in this cesspool. The emotion seemed to rise up through my chest and neck bringing the threat of tears with it.

"Rachel, he can't be redeemed."

"I know that you and Mom say that a lot, Alec, but you didn't get to see the same side of him that I did. Maybe it was because I was a daughter instead of a son, or maybe it was because he always suspected that I wouldn't ever manifest a second shape, but he's shown incredible kindness to me at different points of my life."

I guided Rachel over to her bed and pulled her down so that she was sitting next to me.

"He's having Brandon and Vincent kill innocent people and framing the cats for it. He's hoping to create enough outrage among all of the other packs to keep his operations down there staffed with other people so that he can pull our pack out without negatively impacting his war."

Rachel looked like she was going to be sick.

"You're sure?"

"I saw Vincent and his guys kill dozens of people with my own eyes. They didn't know I was there or they would have killed me too to keep their secret, but I know that Brandon ordered them to do it and this whole war with the cats has always been Kaleb's idea."

"You didn't hear Dad order it though? That means that it's possible that he doesn't know about it."

"Mother is convinced that he's the one behind it. That's what she was hiding from us. She'd heard rumors that some of the deaths down on the border weren't actually the result of the cats, but she didn't know for sure until I confirmed it just now."

Rachel stood up like she was going to go find Kaleb and confront him, but I grabbed her hand and refused to let her go.

"Rach, you can't do that. Kaleb will know that you had to have heard it from Mother or me. He'll kill you to keep the word from getting out. This is the kind of thing that could ignite a spark of rebellion in all of the independent packs."

Rachel dropped back down onto her bed, but she was still shaking her head. "There has to be another way, Alec. I know it looks bad, but you don't know for sure. It's still possible that he isn't behind those deaths."

She looked like she was about to burst into tears, which made what I was going to have to say next all the harder. I put my hands on either side of her face and gently forced her to look at me.

"Rach, I just talked to Kaleb and he told me that he's giving you to Vincent. Brandon demanded you as part of continuing to support him and Kaleb agreed. Brandon and Vincent are flying up from Arizona this evening."

It was like I'd just cut the strings that moved Rachel around. She was still sitting upright on the bed next to me, but the liveliness and energy that I'd always associated with her had vanished in the instant that I'd told her the full range of her father's betrayal. When she did finally speak the words came out sounding cold and dead.

"Vincent caught me off by myself a few months ago. He said things, made threats, but I told him if he touched me that Kaleb would kill him. It made him back off, but he said that I wouldn't always have you and Kaleb to hide behind. I thought he was threatening Kaleb. I didn't realize that he was capable of making Dad just hand me over to him without a fight."

"You should have told me when it happened, Rach. I would have killed Vincent back then and none of this would have happened."

She shook her head, but the motion was too listless for the person I was looking at to be my little sister.

"No, Alec. If I'd told you then you would have tried to kill him. Even if you'd have won, you still would have paid too high a price. Everyone thinks that Kaleb goes easy on you, but he doesn't, not when it actually matters. He would have hurt you really, really bad. I couldn't have that on my conscience."

Rachel looked around her room and the first tears finally trickled down her cheeks. Someone else might have thought that she was crying over the things that she was going to be leaving behind, but I knew better. She wasn't crying for the things she would be losing but rather the dreams that she now knew would never be realized. She was mourning a world of possibility that had just been ripped away from her and replaced with one of the darkest futures imaginable.

I could see that she was already starting to retreat inside of herself, leaving behind everything that she could possibly sacrifice in an effort to preserve the most important bits of her identity for as long as possible. I left the bed and kneeled down in front of her so that she had to look at me.

"I'm not letting this happen, Rach. I have a plan, the beginnings of one at least. I'm going to get you out of here and we're going to go somewhere better than this. We'll find a place where we won't always be in danger of surrendering our humanity just to survive."

"No, Alec. I can't let you do that. It's just too dangerous."

"You don't have a choice, Rachel. I'm going to do whatever I have to do to stop this. You can go along and make it easier on me or you can refuse to help and stack the odds even further against me than they already are, but I'm going to do this."

"You'll die, Alec."

"Maybe, but I'd rather be dead than continue to live knowing that I've become just as guilty in my own way as Kaleb, Brandon and Vincent."

"I won't fight you, but if you change your mind and back out before Vincent comes to collect me I won't hold it against you."

"Okay, wear some sturdy clothes, some good shoes and pack light—really, really light. We'll buy whatever we need once we make it someplace safe."

Chapter 21

James Wright
Graves Estate
Sanctuary, Utah

Alec had called a meeting of the Fab Four, as Jasmin sometimes called us, but even just talking to him on the phone I'd been able to tell that this wasn't a normal meeting. I knew it probably had something to do with Brandon and Vincent flying up from the border, but beyond that I had no idea other than to hope that he'd come up with some way to break the story about the murders along the border without getting us and everyone we cared about killed.

I'd been home for three days and I'd spent all of four hours with my mom. There wasn't any way to hide the fact that I'd been ducking her, but I couldn't afford to have her figure out what I'd seen with Alec in Naco. Mom has had a mouth on her for as long as I can remember, but that doesn't change the fact that she's submissive to practically everyone else in the pack, it just means that she gets into more trouble than she should.

I could trust her not to spill the beans if I told her what was going on and asked her not to say anything, but it was just a whole lot safer for her if she didn't know anything about what we'd seen down there.

There wasn't any way for me to un-see what Vincent and the others had done to those people, and I wasn't sure I'd choose to un-see it even if it was a possibility, but I was going to try very hard not to take down my mom as a result of the stuff that Alec and I were tangled up in.

We were meeting in a cave that we'd found years ago on the extreme west end of the estate. It creeped Jess out a little, so it wasn't somewhere that we came often, but it was a good place to go if you didn't want anyone to overhear you. All we had to do was go in a hundred yards or so to the end of the cave and then put up three privacy boxes twenty yards before we got to our destination. The cave was straight enough that we could keep an eye on the boxes and it was narrow enough that the white noise generators completely masked the sound of us talking. The fact that we could sit a little ways away from the noise generators meant that the conversations were less strained than what you otherwise got when you crammed two or more shape shifters inside of a small room and made them talk to each other while listening to the constant hiss and pop of privacy boxes. We could still hear the background hum, but it was much less overpowering with some distance between us and the boxes, which meant that everyone tended to be much less on edge.

We'd all staked out rocks that were more or less comfortable over the years, so once everyone was seated, Alec cleared his throat and then got right to it.

"Kaleb has agreed to give Rachel to Vincent in return for Brandon's continued support. Brandon and Vincent will be here tonight to collect her and take her back down to Arizona."

I wasn't sure how many more shocks I could take without some serious time in between them. First Naco and now this. It defied belief. I'd always known that Kaleb wasn't a very nice guy, but unlike Alec I wasn't in line to inherit any money, and according to Mallory I wasn't ever going to develop any kind of power either. That meant that worrying about the fact that Kaleb was a real jerk didn't really do any good. It was like worrying about the weather. You could spend a lot of time thinking and fretting about it, but at the end of the day nothing you did was going to actually change anything.

That had bothered me for as long as I could remember, but I'd kind of grown resigned to it.

This was different. Rachel was too nice and good to deserve this kind of treatment.

"What's your plan, Alec?"

He looked surprised, but he shouldn't have been. I knew him well enough to know that he wouldn't just sit by and let Rachel be turned into some kind of sex slave.

"I'm going to try and get her out. I have a couple of different plans depending on how involved you guys are willing to get. There are risks obviously and I can respect the fact that you might not be willing to go all the way on this thing with me."

Jessica looked like she was scared out of her mind, but her voice came out remarkably even given how much her submissive instincts must be screaming at her to stay out of any kind of showdown between Alec and his dad.

"I'm in, Alec. We submissives take a lot of crap, but this is a whole new level of terrible. As scary as whatever you have planned is probably going to turn out to be, I'm in all the way. I'd rather be in a tiny pack with you at the helm than stay here."

Jasmin nodded. "Me too. I'd rather be one of the dispossessed like Isaac than end up in Brandon or Vincent's bed."

All three of them were looking at me now, but they were in a completely different position than I was in. Jasmin and Jess hadn't had any family for years. The pack had been in enough fights that a lot of people had died a little while after we all were born, and then even more had died over the last couple of years with Kaleb's two-front war against the cats and the vampires.

Alec had a family, or at least half of a family, but he could afford to burn all of his bridges. He would be taking Rachel with him and his mother would be fine no matter what else happened. The relationship between her and Kaleb was downright weird, but Kaleb let her get away with stuff that nobody else in the pack would have been able to do.

Jasmin, Jess and Alec could all walk away tomorrow without worrying what would happen to anyone they were leaving behind, but I couldn't do that. There was a chance that Alec's mom could keep my mom safe like she had before I'd finally shifted for the first time, but it was a long shot. Even back then there hadn't been a lot that Samantha had been able to do, and her efforts would be even less effective if Kaleb decided that he needed someone to make an example out of.

"I want to help out, Alec. I really do, but I'm worried about my mother."

Alec nodded. "I understand, James. I would be lying if I said that I wasn't at least a little worried about mine as well, but unlike yours, mine probably deserves whatever happens to her."

It was the harshest thing I'd ever heard him say about the woman who'd given birth to him.

Jess and I actually gasped in shock, but there was no apology in his eyes. I'd known that Jack and Juan had told him things that had shaken his confidence in her, but I hadn't expected him to turn so far against her so quickly.

"Are you sure about that, Alec? I'm not saying that we shouldn't do everything we can to save Rachel, but are you sure you want to abandon your mother like that? I'd hate for you to make a rash decision in anger and then regret it later on."

"She was prepared to let Rachel be taken away without doing a single thing to try and stop it, James. How can I ever trust a woman who would give up one of her children like that? She won't be coming with us. I didn't even make the offer."

Alec pulled two thick rolls of hundred-dollar bills from his pocket and then tossed me one of the wads.

"That's for your mom, whether you're willing to help or not. It's entirely her decision whether she stays or goes, but I think that it's past time for everyone who can to get out of Sanctuary. There's enough cash there for her to book a pair of charter flights, one west and one east. If she's careful about her scent trail and she gets one of them to lie and say that he has a passenger, nobody will know for sure which direction she went. With all of the craziness that is bound to ensue when I try to get Rachel out, she should have hours before anyone even realizes she's gone. She can buy a car once she lands and disappear into a suburb somewhere."

I shook my head in astonishment. There had to be at least twenty thousand dollars in the tightly rolled cylinder he'd just casually given me.

"I'll have to talk to her first, Alec. If it was just me then I'd say yes in a heartbeat, but I can't make that kind of decision without at least asking her whether or not she's willing to leave."

"I understand, James, I really do. If you promise not to let my plan slip even if you decide not to help me, then I'd like to bring you up to speed on what I'm going to do. We're not going to have a chance to all meet someplace private like this again."

"I won't be able to lie to Kaleb. I wish I could, but he'll see through me in a second."

Alec gave me a tired, almost resigned smile, and I suddenly realized that he didn't expect to survive this escape attempt. The knowledge should have had him in a panic, but he was strangely calm. It was like knowing what was going to happen had somehow freed him from worry.

"You're right, which is why you're going to have to trust me when it comes to how the plan unfolds. You're only going to know a tiny part of what is going down, not because I don't trust you guys to keep your mouths shut, but because if everything goes badly I want you to have the absolute most deniability possible."

Alec sighed and then tossed the other roll of bills to Jasmin. "If I'm going to be totally honest with you all, the smartest thing for you to do would be just to head for the hills rather than helping me. Jess, Jas, if the two of you stick together you'll have a much better chance in case you end up running into a vampire or something a couple of years down the road, but either way there's enough cash there to give you a start. I've got some more money back in a safe in my room. It's not an infinite supply and I'll need some of it in case Rachel and I actually make it out somehow, but if you need another hundred thousand dollars or so before you'd feel like you could do what you really want, which is to just make a break for it, then it's yours. Don't get yourselves killed because you don't think you can make it very far with the cash you've got there. Same for you, James."

Jasmin was the first to speak up. "If you had access to this kind of money why didn't you leave a long time ago, Alec?"

"Because I never felt like it was my money. It came at great sacrifice from others, but I've realized in the last little while that I'm not sure that they were really sacrificing for me. I think they were sacrificing to set themselves up, and that they just gave me a portion of it to salve their own consciences. Besides, even if their motives were completely pure it wouldn't change the obligation I have to use every resource at my disposal in an attempt to do the right thing."

Jess cleared her throat. "I'm still in. I'll take whatever you want to give me in case you don't make it, but if you do make it out, then it's yours again."

Jasmin nodded. "Same here. I'm in. I couldn't live with myself if I bailed on you and Rachel and then the two of you didn't make it."

Alec gave me an understanding look that seemed to say he knew he already had my answer, inasmuch as I was able to give it to him without talking to my mom, and then he pulled out a fistful of what turned out to be sim cards.

"I've been buying a couple of sim cards every month for the last few years. They are all prepaid and they were all bought with cash. The ones packaged in green were purchased in St. Louis and the red ones were purchased down in Arizona. They are the ones that will be least likely to be traceable, so use the others while you're still in this area. Once we all get together we'll ditch the ones I bought here and then once we're clear we'll put in a clean set of sim cards. Remember, Kaleb is using the Brain Box to hack into all kinds of government and corporate networks. Once he realizes what we've done he's almost certain to use them to try and track us down. If your phone is powered on and he knows the phone number associated with the sim card in your phone, then there is a chance that he can find you."

"So we don't swap out sim cards without turning off our phones and then traveling for a ways before swapping and then turning our phones on."

It was more of a statement than a question, but Alec nodded in response to what Jasmin had just said. "I have your first two sets of sim cards programmed into my phone. We should only be separated from each other for an hour or two. I'll call you with instructions once I have Rachel. If I don't have her, or if she sounds unnerved when I put her on the phone then you'll know I was captured and Kaleb is trying to lure you into a trap."

I nodded. "Okay, Alec, that all makes sense, but what do you actually want us to do?"

"I just need you to give Rachel and me a ride—a very short, harmless ride—and then you'll just need to drive north for a little while."

Chapter 22

Alec Graves
Graves Estate
Sanctuary, Utah

Sunset was less than an hour away and I'd just watched Kaleb leave the estate in a motorized cavalcade that was headed to the airport.

Two months ago Kaleb would have never considered meeting Brandon at the airport. It smacked of weakness, but now apparently Kaleb needed Brandon badly enough that he could no longer just snap his fingers and expect Brandon to come running to the estate without a proper greeting.

I must have done a better job convincing Kaleb that I was a changed man than I'd thought I had. I'd half expected for him to assign me a minder or two to make sure that I didn't get into any trouble, but his people all seemed busy with a combination of keeping the estate running and preparing for Brandon's visit.

I'd never paid much attention to just how many people it took to provide security for the house and the grounds, but it looked like Kaleb had scraped the bottom of the barrel when he'd sent reinforcements down to Arizona to support Brandon. Now that he'd left the estate, and taken along a suitable escort to show that he was still the one in charge, the house was practically deserted.

It was an opportunity that I hadn't anticipated, but it was one that I wasn't about to let slip by without capitalizing on it. I walked calmly through the halls and turned into Kaleb's office. I'd been prepared to find a single guard standing just inside of the suite to ensure that nobody came in to snoop around in his office. I'd mentally run through the idea that I was going to have to fight, and possibly kill, that guard in order to get what I'd come for. Somehow I hadn't ever considered the possibility that it would be Donovan that I would find there waiting for me.

"I see your mother's warning was correct, Master Alec."

"I won't let them have Rachel without a fight, Donovan. I don't want to hurt you though. Stand aside and I'll let you be out of respect for everything you've done for me over the years."

Donovan's smile was sad. "No words of recrimination for me, Master Alec? Your mother told me what you said to her. I fully expected that I would receive at least as scathing a rebuke as what you delivered to her."

"I don't have any energy left for anger, Donovan. I have a very narrow window in which I might be able to save Rachel. Anything that doesn't help me get her somewhere safe isn't worth the effort involved."

Donovan took a deep breath. "I understand your position entirely, but honesty compels me to tell you that while I did not know all of your mother's secrets, I was party to some of them and I too had a hand in keeping important information from you. I would not have you leave your home with a false understanding of the part that I played."

I suddenly felt as though I had the weight of the world settling on me. "Why, Donovan? Why didn't you just tell me what you knew?"

"In the final analysis it doesn't truly matter, Master Alec. Your mother was, I think, quite honest with me in her recounting of your conversation with her from a few hours ago. I would not offer you another set of excuses. Ultimately you are right, the reasons matter less than the outcome. I didn't come here to stop you, but to help you, to begin to regain some small measure of the trust that I've betrayed."

"You can't help me, Donovan. Kaleb would kill you when he found out."

"I believe you are wrong there, Master Alec. There will be a price to pay for my help, but if we are very careful about how we proceed then there is no reason to believe that your father will ever know of my part in what you're about to do."

Donovan didn't wait for me to respond, he simply walked into Kaleb's office and pointed to one of the wood panels behind the desk.

"Do you notice anything odd about this panel, Master Alec?"

I shook my head which caused Donovan to take a deep breath as though testing the air. I got closer to the panel in question and sampled the scents coming off of it. Walnut, lacquer and a host of other scents that one would expect, but there were three scents that were fine at first blush, but which I realized were the key to what Donovan was trying to tell me.

I could smell Kaleb, which was to be expected, but not as strongly as this. More importantly, I could smell both Donovan and Sam as well. I pushed the corner of the panel where their scent was the strongest and was rewarded with a click as the panel swung open to reveal a safe that had a biometric lock on it.

I looked back up to find Donovan holding his hand out. "You must do it, Master Alec, so that I may say with complete truth that you grabbed my hand and used it to unlock the safe. I will resist you, but you will have no problem overpowering me."

"You're walking a very fine line there, Donovan."

"Indeed, Master Alec, but Kaleb will not think to ask what form my resistance took. I will resist you with all my strength and therefore my response to his questions will be entirely truthful."

I took ahold of Donovan's wrist and pulled it toward the safe and he resisted just as he'd said he would, but he was right. He was entering his third century of life and spent most of his time behind a desk or managing the house. His best efforts were no match for mine and it took only a second for me to run his index finger across the sensor.

The safe beeped once and the LED light on the front turned green. There was cash in the safe, another fifty thousand dollars, but that was nothing compared to the rest of what was inside.

There was a stack of bearer bonds that looked like they were worth somewhere between ten and twenty million dollars along with a small tablet complete with an attached keyboard and a wireless card. Further back there was a paperbound ledger that, as I flipped through it, proved to contain accounts and amounts along with passwords and usernames for the online portal of each of the accounts.

"That is your father's insurance policy. It won't give you access to all of your family's assets as a large percentage of the Graves holdings is in real estate and private companies that aren't very liquid, but if you move quickly you should be able to move several billion at least out of the accounts you see there and into your own account."

My head was spinning. I'd known that Donovan and Mother had set aside several million dollars for Rachel and me, but this was something else entirely. Donovan had just given me the power to wage a small war if I was so inclined. Rachel and I would still be fugitives, but we would be fugitives with almost unlimited options.

"Thank you, Donovan. This will make all the difference for us."

"I fear that it will make less of a difference than you think, but I'm glad that I was able to help in some small way. I would suggest that in a moment you rip the hard drive out of your father's computer. It's encrypted, so it won't actually do you any good, but it will help hide the fact that you have that ledger and the records on the tablet for a precious few extra hours."

"I don't have an account to move all of this into, Donovan."

Donovan stepped forward and held out a slip of paper, a driver's license and a passport.

"I took the liberty of setting up an offshore account under a pseudonym with your physical description many years ago. I picked the country with the most favorable banking laws I could find at the time, but you'll still want to physically move the money to another bank the first chance you get. If there's no electronic trail then they won't have anything further to go on even if they do manage to get the bank in question to give up any kind of transactional detail."

I accepted the identification from Donovan and then reached inside to load everything into the small backpack that was in one corner of the safe, but Donovan grabbed my arm before I could get started.

"I must ask that you now do a convincing job of overpowering me. I'm a frail old man, but I'm still a shape shifter. You're going to have to provide a very believable set of wounds if I'm to avoid suspicion for my part in this."

I felt like my mind had stripped its gears. Donovan was right, and it defied belief that I hadn't come to the same conclusion myself. The only explanation was that I hadn't realized what was going to be required of Donovan because I hadn't *wanted* to see it.

"I was thinking that there should be quite a lot of blood. If you can manage something that will provide a convincing amount of blood loss without killing me that would be ideal. You could finish off by knocking me unconscious, which would explain my inability to summon help."

I shook my head. "Donovan, don't do this. Come with us. There's no reason for you to stay here."

"There is the most important reason in the world, Alec. Your mother is going to need my support more than ever once you and Rachel are gone."

"I can't guarantee that whatever wound I give you won't kill you before we get far enough away for me to call back and have someone come help you. You're risking death for her."

There was an oddly compelling serenity to Donovan's nod.

"Indeed, I am. I understand entirely why you feel that to be a fool's bargain right now, but there is tremendous good in your mother despite some of the mistakes that she's made during the course of her life. I hope that someday you'll have a chance to see some of the redeeming qualities that she possesses."

My voice cracked slightly as I addressed the man who'd been more of a father to me than my biological father. Out of all three of my parents, adopted or otherwise, Donovan was the only one that seemed willing to pay the price for redemption. I was younger, stronger and faster. I could easily knock Donovan out and then carry him away from the estate, but I knew it would be wrong to stop him from paying the price he was willing to pay. It wasn't my place to interfere with his efforts at atonement.

"You're sure, Donovan? Absolutely sure?"

"Indeed, Master Alec. I've never been surer of anything. May I just say before you proceed that I'm incredibly pleased at your reaction to all of this. You're becoming the man I always hoped that you would become. I never doubted for a moment but that you would move heaven and earth to save Rachel."

"Thank you, Donovan. That means more coming from you than it possibly could from anyone else."

At another nod from Donovan I let some of the rage that had been dancing at the edge of my self-control into the bubble of calm that had been the perfect protection from what was going on around me. A shaft of white-hot power raced down my arm and my right hand shifted into a clawed weapon that entered the right side of Donovan's chest like it was going into warm butter.

Donovan gasped as I pulled my hand out of his body and then I backhanded him with just a fraction of my strength and watched as he crumpled to the floor. I ripped Kaleb's computer open and pried the hard drive out of it before I let my hand shift back to its normal shape. Shifting form took care of some of the blood, but not all, so I wiped most of the rest it off on the heavy drapes that were only a few steps away.

It took only seconds to pack the hard drive and everything from the safe into the backpack. I was careful not to get blood on the money or the bonds but make sure to leave some on the inside of the safe before I closed everything back up and slipped my arms through the straps of the backpack.

After everything else that had happened, I nearly forgot my original reason for coming, but just before I turned to go I saw the ancient sword that had watched over Kaleb's shoulder as he'd put his own interests above those of the pack again and again over the years.

I lifted it out of its stand and left Donovan there in a pool of his own blood. Even more now than ever, I was working against the clock.

Chapter 23

James Wright
Graves Estate
Sanctuary, Utah

My mom was on her way to the airport. We'd had a short, but very heated discussion before she'd agreed to leave. I was pretty sure that if it wasn't for me she would have chosen to stay and help out Samantha even knowing that the two of them were playing a losing hand and that it was only a matter of time before Samantha couldn't protect her anymore.

Me being in the picture changed all of that though because she knew that if she refused to go, and I stayed out of the middle of Alec's plan to save Rachel as a result, I'd still more than likely pay a terrible price in the aftermath of Alec, Rachel and the others leaving.

She didn't like it, but she'd taken all of the money that Alec had given me and one of the prepaid sim cards and she'd gone. Her part in all of this was actually the safest. Even if someone happened to be watching the trackers on the vehicle she was using they still wouldn't think anything of it. The cars from the estate motor pool went back and forth to the airport a dozen times a day most days.

As long as she could avoid being seen by Kaleb and the others at the airport then she'd be fine. I'd told her to park on the north side of the airport because from there she'd be able to safely watch until Kaleb and the rest of the convoy headed back here. We were running late, but even according to Alec's original timetable she wouldn't have had to wait for very long. As it was now, there was even a decent chance that she'd pass them on the road as they were coming back to the estate.

Jasmin was nervously tapping on the steering wheel. It hadn't been particularly hard to find someone who was scheduled to leave the estate on official pack business, but we all knew that convincing Cassie to let us make the run into town to buy six gallons of ice cream that somebody had forgotten on the last shopping trip was a very slender shield.

Alec was trying to give us enough deniability that we wouldn't be killed if he failed to get Rachel out, but Jasmin, Jess and I had talked on the way back from the cave and we'd decided that if that happened we weren't going to just go back to Sanctuary and hope that Kaleb was feeling lenient. We'd make a run for it and deal with being fugitives for the rest of our lives.

In a lot of ways it simplified the plan, or rather it would have if we'd had a good way to get ahold of Alec and tell him about our consensus. Since we didn't even know where he was right now, we couldn't do that, and Jasmin wasn't the only one who was getting antsy about the fact that Alec was running late. What we needed right now was a good head start and every second that passed by while we waited for Alec was another second we weren't on the road speeding away from this place.

Jasmin's tapping had speeded up to the point where it sounded like one long roll of miniature thunder, and then Alec walked out of the house with Rachel at his side. Alec still seemed mostly to be surrounded by the odd bubble of calm that I'd noticed earlier in the cave, but Rachel was obviously holding herself together by nothing more than sheer will.

I didn't notice the long, sheet-wrapped object that Alec was carrying in his hand until he was almost to the SUV and I didn't realize it was his dad's sword until he and Rachel were climbing inside with us.

"Thank you so much, everyone. I'll never be able to repay any of you enough for what you're doing."

Rachel's voice cracked there at the end, but Jess reached up and patted her on the shoulder.

"You deserve a lot better than this, Rachel."

"Let's go."

Alec's order came out abrupt and harsh, but I was pretty sure it wasn't intentional, it was just the first signs that maybe the wall of space he'd put up to protect himself from the knowledge of what was coming had started to crack a little.

"You do realize that thing is going to do nothing but bring you trouble, right?"

Alec looked down at the sword and then shrugged. "I've already pretty much declared war against Kaleb, which means the rest of the Coun'hij will be blacklisting me as well. This isn't going to make any of that worse and it just might come in useful at some point. Besides, it's a symbol of a better time and place. It doesn't belong with Kaleb."

I looked up and my heart sank. Someone was manning the front gate. Most of the time the small guard post at the entry to the estate was empty, but I should have realized that Kaleb would have someone there to put on a good show for when Brandon arrived. If Kaleb had left orders that Rachel wasn't to leave the estate then we were sunk before we even really got started. I looked back at Alec, but he didn't seem particularly worried.

"Turn the radio on and set it to be louder back here than up front. We'll just have to hope that's enough to disguise Rachel's uneasiness."

He was putting it kindly. Rachel actually looked like she was going to throw up at any moment. I was sure it wasn't going to work, but I turned on some music and adjusted the fade as he'd requested. A second later we were to the gate and Jasmin was rolling down her window.

"Jasmin, James, everyone. Where are you all headed?"

Scott was exactly the kind of guy that you'd stick on guard duty. He was conscientious and followed orders exactly. If Kaleb had told him to stop everyone on their way out and find out what their plans were then he'd do it and never wonder why Kaleb wanted the estate turned into a prison.

"The cook needs more ice cream for dinner tonight. Cassie was supposed to go, but we all were feeling like getting off of the estate and stretching our legs a little so we volunteered to go instead."

Scott made a show of making a note on his clipboard. "Can you please roll the rest of the windows down, Jasmin? I need to log everyone in the vehicle. Sorry, but it's procedure."

I willed my heartbeat not to speed up as the windows came down and Scott looked back at Jessica, Alec and Rachel. Scott's eyes stayed on Rachel for an extra second and I knew we were in trouble. There wasn't any way to know for sure if he'd been specifically instructed regarding Rachel or if he'd just noticed how nervous she was, but he could obviously tell that something was up.

"How long did you say you were going to be gone?"

I heard Alec shift forward in his seat. "We're only going to be gone for a few minutes, Scott. We'll be back before you even know it."

It was the most egregious lie I'd ever heard, and I knew for a fact that Alec wasn't a very good liar, but everything pointed towards the idea that Alec had just told Scott the absolute truth. Alec's heart didn't speed up in the slightest, he wasn't sweating, his voice didn't even change.

Scott was a great guard, but he was a terrible actor. I could see him relax as he realized that he didn't have some kind of prison break on his hands. Any question as to whether or not he'd been told to keep Rachel at the estate was answered as he reached for his radio.

"I can understand getting a little stir crazy. I just need to make a quick radio call and then you can all be on your way."

Scott stepped back into the guard shack, which had been soundproofed well enough that I couldn't hear what he was saying, but I could see that he was nodding a lot and seemed pretty emphatic about whatever he was telling Kaleb.

It was the longest two minutes of my life, but then he came out with a smile.

"You're just going to town then? No need to go further than that for your errands?"

I looked back at Alec, which probably wasn't the smartest thing to do, but he was the dominant, so it wasn't entirely unusual. Alec's smile was the most natural thing I'd ever seen cross his face.

"You don't have anything to worry about, Scott. Given the way that Rachel is feeling, we might not even make it to town before we have to come back home."

Scott nodded. It was obvious that he knew at least something bad was in store for Rachel because he gave her a bracing smile and then waved us on through.

Jasmin rolled the windows back up as she waited for the gate to finish opening. As soon as we were moving and there was no way that Scott could overhear us, I turned back to Alec.

"How did you manage to pull off a lie like that?"

Alec shook his head. "I didn't lie. As soon as we pull onto the main road so that we're not visible from the house I want you to slow down and then Rachel and I are going to jump out and go back to the house. Everything I told Scott was true, I just didn't tell him that we'd be leaving again as soon as we got back home."

Alec had just blown my mind. I couldn't even begin to imagine how hard it had been for him to think on his feet so well that he'd been able to outsmart Scott like that, but it was all worthless if it meant that he had to go back to the estate.

"Alec, don't go back there. We can't circle back around and get you, we're already pretty much out of time. Kaleb could come driving back from the airport any minute. You pulled the wool over their eyes, and I know that you meant it when you were back there, but now is no time to be deviating from the plan."

Some of the calm seemed to be back, or maybe it hadn't ever really left and I'd just mistaken his earlier briskness for something that it wasn't.

"We're still on plan, James. The plan was never for Rachel and me to go more than a few yards down the road with you guys. I'm sorry to put you three in this position, but you're the bait. Go to town and shop for the ice cream just like you said you would. If someone comes out to get you tell them that we went back to the estate. It's the truth, and it's all that you know. Either way, regardless of whether Vincent shows up looking for Rachel or not, you need to be back on the road headed north no later than an hour from now. If Rachel and I survive we'll give you a call and I'll tell you how to get out of the state without Kaleb being able to track you down."

"And if you guys don't make it out?"

"Then you should head to a big city. Stop somewhere along the way and steal some plates to throw the cops off, but either way you don't want to drive for very long before you bail out and find some other mode of transportation."

My throat was tight. Somehow I'd never expected for this to affect me like this. Alec and I had been through a lot, and I was fonder of Rachel than I'd ever realized. It was hard to say goodbye.

Jasmin was completely focused on the road, but she was blinking more than normal, and Jess looked like she was about ready to break into tears. Alec grabbed my arm and then patted Jasmin on the shoulder before turning back and giving Jess a smile.

"I'm sorry that we didn't have more time to say our goodbyes properly, you guys, but I really do appreciate everything. Not just you all being willing to do this for Rachel and me, but everything you've done over the years."

"It's mutual, man."

I hadn't imagined it this time, Alec's cool had cracked just the slightest bit, but I could see him gathering it back around him like a blanket and then Jasmin was slowing down and Alec threw the door of the SUV open. Before I could say anything else he grabbed his father's sword and threw himself out of the car. He hit the ground with more force and less control than usual because of the sword and for a second I worried that he'd seriously hurt himself.

A second later Alec came up bloody but not seriously injured and sprinted alongside of the SUV for the couple of seconds it took for Rachel to make her way over to the open door and jump. It wasn't the most graceful exit from a vehicle that I'd ever seen, but she was only human and it did the trick. She got just enough hang time for Alec to grab her out of the air before she hit the ground.

They were both off balance and they hit the ground again and went tumbling, but I saw the two of them get up and dust themselves off as we drove off towards town.

Chapter 24

James Wright
Graves Estate
Sanctuary, Utah

We'd been driving less than five minutes before we saw Kaleb's caravan come down the road towards us. The lead car flashed its lights at us as though trying to tell us to pull over, but Jasmin just flashed hers back as if in a friendly hello and pretended like she didn't understand the signal as we went past them at exactly the speed limit.

"Make sure your phones are all off. We need to be able to play dumb as long as possible."

I double-checked that my phone was powered off and then checked the speedometer.

"Don't speed, Jas. We don't want to tell them that we know the jig is up. With any luck Vincent and Brandon are both riding with Kaleb and he'll refuse to come after us."

"I know, I'm just adding up numbers in my head. We dropped Alec off five minutes ago which means that he's got roughly ten minutes between when he gets back to the house and when Kaleb and the others arrive. What can he possibly do in ten minutes?"

"I don't know, but I hope that whatever he's got planned works."

We'd only been driving for a couple more minutes before I looked up and saw a single black SUV overtaking us from behind. Jasmin waited as long as possible before pulling over, but once they were within a few feet of us they started flashing their lights at her again, so she slowed down and pulled off to the side of the road.

Vincent was out of the other car and up to Jasmin's window before I even managed to unbuckle my seatbelt.

"Where are they?"

"Where are who?"

I tried for confused, but I was pretty sure that my tone came out sounding smug. Vincent came around the SUV as I opened my door and got out.

"Alec and Rachel, you idiot. Scott saw them leave with you. What did you do with them?"

"We didn't do anything with them."

He hit me with a left jab to the side of my head. My beast awoke with a flare of power as it tried to force a transformation. I managed to stop myself from losing my shape, but it was a close thing.

Vincent tried to hit me again, but I blocked his swing this time and hit him with an elbow to the jaw. He stumbled backwards and I saw his shape expand and then contract slightly as he overrode his beast's natural instinct to shift and take the fight to me with everything he had.

"News flash, Vincent, but you aren't dominant to me so I don't have to tell you crap."

"Brave words from a guy who's submissive to someone I almost killed the last time we fought. You're lucky that there's nowhere around here where we can transform without being seen. If we were back at the estate I would have ripped your heart out of your chest by now."

I needed to buy Alec more time so I did the only thing I could think of. I stepped forward and hit Vincent in the nose with everything I had.

"You talk big, but the fact that you may be able to kill me when we're fighting as hybrids isn't going to save you if I beat you to death with my bare hands out here."

Vincent's response was a wordless howl that was accompanied by such a burst of energy that I almost thought he was going to ignore the rules and transform. He stayed in his primary form though and hit me in the stomach with an uppercut that rocked me backwards.

I didn't actually expect to win. Alec had studied three or four different kinds of unarmed combat over the years in an effort to find something that he could adapt to fights between hybrids, but I'd never been interested in that kind of stuff. I'd always figured that all learning martial arts would do was wire the wrong set of reflexes and get me killed in a hybrid fight.

It looked like I was about regret my lack of interest in anything over and above basic boxing.

Vincent came in again with a blow to the body but I managed to absorb most of the force of the strike against my arm rather than my stomach. I threw a wild haymaker that he ducked and then he hit me with another jab to the nose.

I heard a crack as my nose broke, but although I hadn't been able to dodge his attack it had given me time to set up a response of my own. I saw stars from the force of his blow, but I managed to get a knee into his crotch and I had the distinct pleasure of watching him hit the ground as he curled up in pain.

I stepped forward to kick him in the ribs, but someone hit me from behind in the kidney before I could reach Vincent. I tried to turn around so that I could deal with my new attacker, but all I ended up doing was turning into the hardest punch anyone had ever hit me with.

I lost a couple of seconds because the next thing I knew I was on the ground and two of Vincent's guys were kicking me in the stomach and ribs. One of the kicks landed hard enough to puncture my lung and I blacked out again. When I regained consciousness it was hard to breathe and someone had propped me up against a rock on the side of the road.

"I hope you enjoyed that as much as I did, James. I'm only going to ask you this one more time before I just kill you and start in on the girls. Where are Alec and Rachel?"

It was incredibly tempting to smart off again, but I could see it in Vincent's eyes. He was actually hoping that I would give him a reason to kill me.

"I don't know. They jumped out of the car as soon as we were out of sight of the house. He said he was going back to the house and that we should just go get ice cream like we'd told Cassie we were going to."

Vincent stepped on my hand and another wave of pain threatened to tear me away from reality. I had a moment to be amazed at how much more everything hurt when I didn't have the weaker pain receptors of my hybrid body and then Vincent pulled my face up so that I had to meet his eyes.

"What else do you know?"

"Nothing that will help you catch them, you child-raping monster. By the time you make it back to the estate Alec will be long gone."

Vincent kicked me in the stomach and for several seconds I couldn't focus on anything other than a desperate need to get oxygen into my lungs as my diaphragm went into spasms. Vincent had only hit me with a fraction of the force he could have used, but it still was nearly more than I could withstand. When I finally sucked enough air into my chest to be able to notice anything other than the pain, I saw that Vincent was on his phone.

"…jumped from the car a little ways out from the house. You should be able to scent track them if you hurry. Oh, that's even better news than I expected."

Vincent dropped his phone back in his pocket with a satisfied look on his face.

"Congratulations, loser. You just got the crap kicked out of you for no reason. I called back to the house to get them looking for Alec and Rachel, but it turns out that Brandon took off after them nearly ten minutes ago."

Vincent turned back to the two bruisers standing behind him and pointed at me. "Keep him and the girls here. I'd say bring them back to the house but I want to leave our options open. It might work out best just to kill them out here and say it was an accident. Don't kill James without orders from Brandon or me, but if he happens to bleed out that's fine. I never have liked him."

Vincent started back towards his SUV with a smile on his face. "Tonight is actually turning out much better even than I expected it to. James is as good as dead, and Brandon will run Alec down and kill him too. By sundown my two biggest rivals will be dead and Alec will get the satisfaction of knowing that he didn't manage to save his sister from me. It's only a matter of time now."

Chapter 25

Alec Graves
Graves Estate
Sanctuary, Utah

I messed up catching Rachel and she hit harder than I meant for her to. She managed to avoid yelling and potentially alerting Scott to the fact that we hadn't stayed in the car with everyone else, but she let out a hiss of pain when she tried to put weight on her ankle.

"I think it's just sprained, Alec."

"I'm sorry, Rach. I'll carry you back to the garage. Once we get there you won't have to do much of any walking."

As I handed her the backpack that I'd stolen from Kaleb's office, I had a brief moment to hope that I hadn't broken the tablet when I'd exited the car, and then I lifted her up onto my back with one hand and picked the sword back up with the other.

We had to go the long way around in order to make sure that Scott couldn't see us, and I was in my primary form, but we still managed to cover the distance to the garage in a little less than three minutes. I set Rachel carefully down and then went and backed up the 450cc dirt bike that had taken up one corner of the smaller garage where Kaleb stored his toys.

I was pretty sure that Kaleb had forgotten about the bike years ago. There wasn't much reason to keep a motorcycle around when you could just shift to four legs and cover most uneven ground even more quickly than most dirt bikes, but the bike was one half of a matching pair that Kaleb had purchased back before things had gotten so bad between him and Mother.

They'd only ridden the bikes together a few times and Mother's had been scrapped a long time ago, but I happened to know that Donovan had seen to the care of this particular machine and that it was in perfect working order.

I checked to make sure it still had a full tank of gas and then wheeled it out through the side door before going back for Rachel. A few seconds later the bike roared to life and we set off towards a shallow wash that I figured would let us cover the first five or six miles while remaining safely out of sight of the house.

The noise was a concern, but we occasionally had people from Sanctuary come joyriding along the outer edges of the estate on similar bikes. I was hoping that, along with the fact that the bike had been stored in the smaller garage on the far side of the house from the main motor pool, would let us get away cleanly, but I knew it wasn't much more than a hope and a prayer. The fact of the matter was that I hadn't been able to come up with a better plan, at least not one that dealt with all of the other problems that became more important once we were a little ways away from the house.

I'd never spent any time on a motorcycle before now, but I'd spent a few minutes reading up on the relevant concepts before I went to Kaleb's office. I'd come away feeling fairly comfortable with the mechanics involved, but I still tried to start out cautiously. It was a good thing I did because I leaned too far to one side as I brought it around a corner and the back tire spun out.

I managed to get my foot down and stop from laying the bike down, but with Rachel's added weight on the back it was a close thing and I suspected that if I'd had merely human reflexes that I wouldn't have been able to save us.

We dropped down into the wash and I opened the throttle up a little more. I could feel the minutes ticking away and I knew that Kaleb and Brandon wouldn't be fooled by my sleight of hand with James and the others for very long.

As the bike hit forty-five miles per hour the wind started to become an issue. I squinted my eyes and cursed myself for not thinking to bring some sunglasses at least. A helmet would have been better, but I'd had no idea whether or not Kaleb had even purchased any safety gear with the bike let alone where he might have it stored away.

I tried to speed up a little more, but between the wind and my lack of skill I was already at the ragged edge of what could be considered safe when driving over terrain that I'd only ever crossed on four legs. I could probably survive any conceivable crash I might get into as long as I transformed into a hybrid quickly enough, but Rachel didn't have my inborn advantages and she probably wouldn't escape serious hurt if I were to lose control of the bike.

Kaleb's sword slapped against the tank as I came up out of the wash and we started across country. For a second I worried that the sword was going to drop away from the bike, but the bungees that I'd used to strap it down held, which meant that I could return my attention to driving.

It was slower going now that we were out of the wash and dealing with more broken ground than we'd been driving on. My shoulders tensed up as I realized that we'd slowed to the point where we were only a couple of miles an hour faster than a wolf could run. We'd gained a little ground on any potential pursuit up until now, but I somehow knew that it wasn't enough.

I pushed a little harder and squeezed a couple of miles per hour more out of the bike despite the risk that we'd crash, but it was unlikely to make much difference. The bike was inferior in almost every way to my normal mode of travel. The exhaust whipped away behind us, but not before filling the air with a burning, artificial scent that ruined my sense of smell. As bad as that was, even worse was the way that the drone of the engine drowned out my ability to hear anything else.

Despite all of the things that were working against me, something prompted me to look back just in time to see Brandon jump. I goosed the bike and it leaped forward just before Brandon would have hit us.

I had a split second of satisfaction as Brandon's lean, wolf body hit our back tire and then flew away in a yelp of pain. The impact nearly threw the bike over. The back tire broke loose from the ground and spun out in a spray of dirt and rock, but I threw my weight to the side which kept us from crashing and then I leaned forward and pushed the bike even harder.

We only had a few hundred more yards until we'd reach the road and I'd be able to safely speed back up, but Brandon was apparently faster in wolf form than I'd given him credit for. It was starting to look very doubtful that we'd make it.

We were riding on the very edge of ruin. I was driving too fast for the terrain and my skill level, and I was having to constantly look from side to side in an effort to keep tabs on where Brandon was. It took him only a couple of seconds to regain his feet and give chase and he was quickly gaining on us.

The road was less than fifty yards away, but we weren't going to make it. Brandon could have made another try for us at any time during the last ten seconds, but he hadn't which meant that he'd spotted a better opportunity and was just waiting for us to reach the right spot.

I looked ahead of us and saw a couple of likely spots. The sandy ground had robbed him of the extra edge of speed that he would have needed to bring us down last time despite my best efforts. There was a rock on the left that looked like it was big enough to solve that problem, but it still didn't seem quite right.

Desperation started to take me over and then I realized that I'd been thinking in terms of what would help Brandon rather than what would hinder us. We weren't going to just be able to drive up onto the road, we were going to have to turn left and then go up a slight slope first. There was no way to be positive that was when Brandon was planning on striking, but it felt like the right answer and I didn't have time to second-guess myself.

I floored the bike again as we came up to the rock I'd identified. It was a pitiful attempt, but all that I could manage in the way of evasion that wouldn't leave us sitting ducks if indeed Brandon was biding his time until just before the road like I thought he was.

BOUND

We flew past the rock and then there was only a couple of seconds before we'd be to the road. Knowing that Brandon would probably go with hundreds of thousands of years of instincts and aim for my neck, I leaned further forward on the bike and then we were to the turning point.

I grabbed the front brake with my right hand and mashed down on it hard enough that the back tire came up off of the ground and only then did I look over to see if my timing had been right.

Brandon was hurtling towards us, but he'd been aiming for where we were supposed to be which meant his aim was off by nearly half a foot. My right hand was still clamped on the brake in an effort to slow us enough to gain a few more inches of clearance, but it wasn't going to be enough. I leaned back, sandwiching Rachel between the back of the bike and me.

Rachel screamed in fear, but I didn't have time to reassure her, not when I was still trying to figure out whether I was a dead man.

It still wasn't enough. I could see the trajectories and although Brandon would miss us with the bulk of his body his jaws were still going to fasten around my neck. My analysis took only the tiniest fraction of a second, and then I threw my left arm forward. It was crazy. Given the relative velocities and the sheer inertia of something Brandon's size it couldn't possibly work, but I was out of other options. I shot my left arm towards thin air and by the time it had moved just a couple of inches the space I hit wasn't empty. I managed to time things just right and I made contact with Brandon's shoulder and shifted him just far enough that his teeth snapped shut two inches from my throat instead of ripping it out.

Shoving Brandon had imparted a sideways motion to us that I hadn't been prepared for and the back wheel of the bike crashed into the rock that we'd been turning to avoid. Brandon hit that same rock several feet ahead of us, but I was too busy trying not to lose complete control of the motorcycle to enjoy my victory.

I got the rear tire back on the ground and twisted my wrist to send us jetting away from Brandon, but although the bike did shoot forward I could tell that something was wrong. The back wheel had picked up a worrisome vibration and it got worse the faster we went.

We made it up onto the road and I took us up to sixty miles per hour, but between the vibration and the fact that we didn't have road tires, that was as fast as I could go without risking that something would go wrong and we'd end up miles still from our destination with Brandon stalking us.

I checked back to confirm that Brandon wasn't able to keep up, and then just focused on keeping the bike from snaking off of the road.

Five minutes later we were within sight of our destination. Getting the schedule for the high-speed passenger train that crossed through the extreme edge of the pack's territory hadn't been difficult, but finding a spot where the train slowed down enough that it was possible for even someone as fast as me to get on was a whole different proposition.

I'd superimposed the train's route over a topological map and finally found a two-hundred-yard stretch where the elevation change was steep enough that I figured I at least had a chance of getting on the train. Either way, as long as the bike held up for another couple of minutes then Rachel would be getting on the train.

As hard as it was to believe after the craziness and terror of the last few minutes, we were actually ahead of schedule slightly—that or the train was running late. As we finally pulled even with the tracks, I looked down the rails and was able to see the train racing towards us. I crossed over to the other side of the tracks and then started the bike slowly towards the train.

Once we were even with the train, I spun us around and started back the other direction. The ground wasn't particularly even, and the vibrations from the back wheel made it even harder to keep the bike steady, but I managed to match speeds well enough for Rachel to let go of me with one hand and reach for the ladder on the back of one of the cars.

"I'm scared, Alec!"

"I know, Rach, but if you don't grab the ladder with both hands then all of this was just a huge waste. Brandon is getting closer all of the time. We may only have a minute or two before he arrives!"

She was shaking so violently that I could feel it even over the road vibrations, but she let go of me with her right hand and started pulling herself up.

"I can't do it!"

I turned my head just enough to see that her fingers were starting to slip, but it was too late to try and get her back on the bike. I'd never convince her to try a second time. I rotated my torso and grabbed ahold of her leg so that I could push her up and off of the bike.

She screamed as she came free of the bike and for a heartbeat was supported by nothing but her hands and my grip on her leg, and then I pushed as hard as I could and her left foot made it onto the very bottom rung.

The motorcycle started to go down even as I saw that Rachel had made it to safety, but everything happened too quickly. I didn't have a chance to change forms, even if I'd been willing to do so where there were so many potential witnesses.

I hit the ground harder even than I expected to. I bit my tongue hard enough that I tasted blood and my elbow was driven into my side hard enough to produce the sharp pain of cracked ribs. For an instant I was tempted to just stay there. Rachel was safe. I'd achieved more than I'd expected to, but I knew that safety in the world that I lived in was a transitory thing. Rachel might be safe for the moment, but sooner or later she'd make a mistake and then Kaleb or Brandon would find her.

I levered myself up off of the ground and checked to make sure that nothing other than my ribs were broken. I was even more bruised and bloody than I'd been a few minutes before, but it looked like I could still run, which was good since the bike looked like it was totaled.

I jogged over to double-check and confirmed that the right handlebar had been snapped entirely off. Luckily Kaleb's sword had been strapped to the left side of the motorcycle and was undamaged. I pulled the weapon free of the wreckage and started running towards the train. I'd lost a lot of ground in the crash, but we were only halfway through the slow stretch.

In human form I could sustain speeds in the low twenties and even sprint up into the high twenties or low thirties for a very short period of time. The heavily-loaded train was only moving at a little over twenty miles per hour, so it took less than a minute for me to make it to the caboose and jump onboard.

The door was predictably locked so I started up the side of the car, thinking once again how grateful I was that the sword wasn't even heavier than it was. I could climb with thirty pounds in one hand, but I never would have been able to climb with a hundred pounds dangling from my right hand. I'd somehow expected given the incredible strength that hybrids possessed that the sword would be massively heavy, but it actually made sense that the ancient shape shifters would have wanted a sword that could be carried while they were in human form as well.

I made it to the top of the caboose without any problems and then started working my way up along the train as the engines in the front made it to the top of the grade and the train started picking up speed. It felt like we were doing nearly thirty-five miles per hour now and a sense of relief washed through me as I realized we were safe.

I turned back to check for Brandon and saw him arrowing towards us through the failing light, but he'd been just a minute or two too slow. At our current speed he could keep up as a wolf but not as a human.

A slightly juvenile part of me thought about taunting him, but I squashed the impulse and merely watched as he closed the distance between us until he was running just behind the car I was currently standing on.

I wondered if he was planning on pacing us for the next two hundred miles until the train slowed down again, and then without any warning Brandon planted all four feet and threw himself at the ladder on the back of my car.

I had a split second to hope that he'd miscalculated somehow and would be crushed underneath the train, but then he shifted in midair back to his human form and grabbed the ladder that should have remained safely out of reach.

I'd never seen such a smooth transformation, and frankly I wasn't sure that anyone else could have jumped hard enough to compensate for the sudden increase in air resistance as he changed forms, but Brandon had done it.

I shook the sheet off of Kaleb's sword and charged back in an effort to stab Brandon before he could make it to the top of the car and face me on equal ground, but he dodged my attack by throwing himself backwards, once again shifting in midair so that his hybrid claws buried themselves in the metal of the next car.

Brandon looked up at me with feral yellow eyes and a menacing grin on his face for several seconds before pulling himself up to the top of the car. I faced Brandon across a gap of four feet and even as I let my own beast trigger a transformation to our hybrid shape, I knew that Brandon was going to kill me.

Peripheral concerns tried to demand my attention. Fighting on the top of a train in our hybrid forms was a clear violation of every rule the Coun'hij had ever set down to keep our existence a secret, but that hardly mattered in comparison to the fact that I was about to fight one of the most deadly hybrids who'd ever lived.

I had Kaleb's sword, but I didn't really know how to use it, and even if I had, all of the stories I'd ever heard had agreed that a single hybrid, even with a sword, wasn't a match for the strongest of the jaguars.

Brandon was capable of killing a jaguar with nothing more than his claws and fangs. I had no chance whatsoever. I knew resisting him was pointless, but something inside of me refused to go down without a fight. The sense of exhaustion I'd felt after wrecking the bike hadn't gone anywhere, but my sense of calm had started to settle back over me.

I'd accomplished things that I would have said only hours ago were impossible. All I would have needed was a bit more luck. If Brandon had arrived a few minutes later the train would have been moving too fast for even him to board. I was proud of my efforts.

I backed up a few steps and then took a few practice swings with Kaleb's sword, *my* sword. It was incredibly light to my hybrid muscles and it fit my giant hands surprisingly well. Even the long, semi-retractable claws on the end of each finger didn't get in the way of cutting and thrusting with the ancient weapon.

Under other circumstances it might have been easy to lose myself in delight at just how responsive my sword was, but in between one practice slash and the next Brandon rushed me. It was just a feint, just something to allow him to begin getting a feel for how fast and dangerous I was with a weapon in my hand, but I still nearly scored on him.

The next few seconds were more of the same. Brandon probably could have overwhelmed me right at the start with his superior strength and speed, but he was obviously uneasy about fighting someone with a sword.

By the third or fourth exchange he had a pretty good idea of just how much faster he was than me, and I'd started to realize just how much of a benefit six extra feet of reach really was. Brandon was having a hard time compensating for any kind of lunging attack while I quite simply couldn't match his blinding speed.

If we'd been fighting on other terrain my best efforts wouldn't have kept me alive for more than a couple of seconds, but fighting on the top of the train car like we were limited the amount of mobility in the fight. Brandon could only move a few feet side to side, which meant that most of the motion in the battle was either advancing or retreating, which favored me more heavily than I could have ever hoped.

Brandon blurred forward in another attack and I stabbed where I thought he would end up, but he wasn't where I expected him to be. He'd come up along the right side of the car and dodged just far enough to the side that my stab had missed, if only by inches.

His claws raked across my right side, but I dropped the hilt of the sword and hit him as hard as I could on the shoulder with the pointed pommel as I backpedalled away from him. Something cracked as the sword hit him, but he'd already jumped backwards so that my follow-up slash missed him.

Physically he was still far and away my better, but I was realizing that in some ways he'd grown too dependent on outmatching anyone he came up against. He was making mistakes that wouldn't have even been noticeable in a normal fight, but which were keeping me alive longer than I'd ever anticipated lasting.

I charged forward, being careful not to overcommit as I tried to sink the point of my sword into his chest. He should have pressed forward on that last exchange rather than retreating. Once he was up close most of my advantages were negated and he would be able to overwhelm me quickly. I wasn't sure if he'd realized his error yet, but I now knew that I had to keep the offensive or I risked letting him close again.

Brandon sidestepped my lunge and darted forward, but I'd already anticipated the fact that I'd miss and I retreated with a slash that once again hit nothing but air. I was missing, but I was coming close and I got the feeling that Brandon didn't like how close I was coming. Fighting with a sword was a completely new experience for me, but it was proving to be an adjustment for Brandon as well.

As my blade sailed over his head Brandon sprang at me again, at which point I caught my next break of the night. He sank his talons into the metal roof of the rail car, but when he threw himself forward he did so with such force that the thin metal tore and gave way rather than letting him apply all of his strength to powering his movements.

Brandon's attack came up a few inches too short because of his lost momentum, and I let my left hand come off of the hilt of my sword and instead used it to rake him across the shoulder just before I backed out of range and brought my weapon around in an attack designed more to make him back off than to actually hurt him.

I'd actually been aiming for the side of his neck with my claws, and if I'd landed my attack the fight would have been over right then, but Brandon had thrown himself to the side at the last second, using his claws as well as his talons so that he could be sure of having enough traction to get his vitals out of the line of fire.

I was disappointed that I'd missed my true target, but I was starting to realize that I couldn't have picked a better arena for our fight if I'd tried. I'd used my full strength for the last several dodges and although the metal had creaked and groaned at the abuse I was putting it through, it had held. It was the football equivalent to me wearing cleats while Brandon wasn't. He was enough faster than me that he could still match my speed, but he wasn't going to be nearly as fast as he otherwise would have been.

I stepped forward and lunged almost to full extension and this time I caught him in the stomach, but he slashed the outside of my arm before I managed to pull the sword out of his body and back away again.

"Did you figure out yet that I was playing with you there at the start of the fight?"

I nodded. "Yeah, that wasn't hard to notice, but it's kind of irrelevant. What matters is that you're not playing around now, but you haven't managed to kill me yet."

"That's what I love about you, Graves. You're so damn overconfident. Of course I'm still playing around with you. Now that I know more or less what you're capable of I can pause and tell you all of the news that I've had saved up for you since I started chasing you across this sandbox of a desert."

I slashed twice in quick succession, but Brandon had assumed a low stance. It gave up some of his mobility, but it let him use his hands to help propel him back and forth at incredible speeds. Neither of my attacks landed and when I tried to follow up with another lunge he simply swatted the point of my sword away with his claws.

"Before I kill you, I wanted to make sure that you knew that Vincent was chasing down James and your girls. He'll probably kill them, but even if he doesn't I can guarantee you that I'll kill them when I get back. I suspect that you had some fancy plan that you thought would shield them if this all went badly, but Kaleb is dancing to my tune now. I'll demand all three of their heads and he won't be able to say no to me."

I swung my sword again, putting more effort into it in the hopes that it would give me enough speed to land a blow on him, but Brandon knocked the blade away again and this time he slashed the inside of my arm.

I recovered before he could get any closer and this time I clipped his shoulder, but mine was the more serious wound and we both knew it. There was a chance that he'd missed the bigger arteries that ran along the inside of my arm, but just judging by the amount of blood pouring out of my arm he'd at least gotten one or two of the smaller ones.

"You were always the one I knew I needed to beat. I'm young enough that I can always just outlast fossils like Kaleb if that's the only way to power, but you were a whole different problem. Mallory must have told me a dozen times a year just how much potential power you had. I think she hoped it would scare me away, but it just made you a bigger target. If I would have known that you'd be stupid enough to throw your future away over your sister, I would have made this happen years ago."

My beast had been strangely quiet since before the fight started, but mention of Rachel brought a roar of power out of me and this time when I stabbed at Brandon I had that little extra bit of speed that I'd been lacking and the sword went into the right side of his chest. I'd been aiming for his heart, but he'd twisted to the side at the last second.

I pulled back, but Brandon moved with me. I tried to use the sword to keep him back but he simply let the blade sink further into him in his quest to reach me. I let go of the sword with my left hand and managed to grab ahold of one of his arms, but his other arm savaged my right leg.

Brandon backed away, pulling himself off of the sword rather than pressing his advantage, but we both knew that the fight was over. I used the sword to help get me back to my feet, but my leg was just too damaged to provide the kind of mobility I needed in order to take advantage of the superior reach my sword gave me.

"In some ways I almost can't blame you, Alec. I've seen what happens to the girls that Vincent takes an interest in and it's not pretty. The shape shifter girls last a little longer, but even they can't take more than a few weeks before they just don't have anything left to bring them back from the edge when he takes them there. Still, you would have been better off just waiting and avenging her once you finally came into your full power. As it is she's still going to become his pet and you're going to be dead."

Brandon liked to gloat, I'd known that for years, but there was something else there this time. As my sword started to shake in hands that were becoming too weak to hold it upright, I tried to figure out what angle he was trying to work.

My mind reached blindly for any explanation and then suddenly I knew why he was stalling. I'd spent nearly half an hour pouring over maps, satellite and otherwise, in an attempt to find the absolute best spot to board the train. My realization almost came too late. I had nothing but instinct and a slight change in the sound of the air hissing around the train to go on, but I was dead either way, so I threw myself forward, stabbing with my sword as I shifted back down to human form.

Unlike me, Brandon had been facing forward and had been able to see the metal girder we were quickly approaching. He'd no doubt been planning on ducking down underneath it just like I'd done, but he hadn't been counting on my sword slicing through the exact volume of space where he'd been planning on taking shelter.

Any other hybrid probably would have been impaled. Brandon had already started moving forward and there was only so much the laws of physics would let you do to change direction once you had that much weight committed to a course of action, but he somehow twisted up just enough that my sword missed him.

It was as though everything was happening in slow motion. I saw Brandon sink his claws in the sheet metal below us and begin pulling himself back down in an effort to dodge the girder that crossed over the tracks, but even he wasn't fast enough to drop the last couple of inches before the train swept him into the beam and he was knocked from the train accompanied by the crunch of broken bones.

Chapter 26

James Wright
Three miles outside of town
Sanctuary, Utah

We all watched Vincent vanish down the road leaving Jess, Jasmin and me with two of Vincent's bruisers. Doug and Randy would have outclassed all three of us even if I hadn't been broken and two hard kicks away from death.

It shouldn't have surprised me that the two of them were well-versed in cheap tricks, or that they were completely unthreatened by Jasmin and Jessica. They'd spent their entire adult lives bullying people. It didn't particularly matter whether you matched them up against the girls as hybrids versus wolves or if you left all four in their primary forms. Either way the girls didn't stand a chance.

I was the dominant here, it was my job to put myself between jerks like this and submissives like Jessica and Jasmin, but I just didn't have anything left to give. I tried to move and nearly passed out from the pain.

I looked up to tell Jasmin that I was sorry and when our eyes met I could see her plan in her eyes. We'd been through a lot together, but I never would have guessed that we'd be able to communicate so much without using words. I looked over at Jess and she seemed to be on the same page, so I took a deep breath and tried not to cough.

"You know, it really is too bad."

"What's that, Wright? Are you talking about the fact that you chose to back the wrong horse or that you were dumb enough to think Vincent would honor a challenge match when there weren't any witnesses around?"

I shook my head slowly. "No, it's too bad that we didn't have this conversation before you killed all of those people in Naco."

I could see the wheels turning in their head for the split second I gave them before I shifted into my hybrid form in the biggest, noisiest show of power I'd ever managed.

The two of them had been standing so that they could watch the girls over by the SUV and me off on the side of the road. Even though they were both a half beat slow from trying to solve the riddle of how I knew that they'd been responsible for Naco, they still turned towards me to honor the threat of a fellow hybrid.

It was exactly the kind of thing that you'd expect them to do, exactly the kind of thing that their beasts would demand of them, and it was exactly the wrong response.

They never even saw the girls shift and spring towards them. Jasmin and Jessica timed their jumps perfectly and they ripped out both of the guys' throats a split second before either of them managed to shift to their hybrid forms.

Shifting into a hybrid had healed some of the worst of the damage to my body, but it was still more than I could do to pull myself to my feet. After a couple of seconds, the girls shifted back to their human forms and cleaned the blood off of their mouths.

"Just shift back and we'll carry you, James. It's time to get back on the road or we're going to miss Alec's timetable."

"All right, but I was kind of looking forward to freaking out the next people to drive by here. As long as we're going to be outlaws we really ought to get the full enjoyment out of the experience."

Chapter 27

Alec Graves
The Express Rail Line
Southern Utah

It had turned out that Brandon had in fact missed the big arteries in my arm, and the small ones had mostly healed when I'd shifted back to human form. It had been too dark to see what happened to Brandon after the girder scraped him off of the top of the train, but I had a feeling that he'd survived somehow.

One thing that the fight had convinced me of was that Brandon had been hiding the full extent of his ability for years. It was terrifying to think of a hybrid durable enough to survive colliding head-on with something at more than seventy miles per hour like that, but I was pretty sure I hadn't seen the last of him.

As the train continued on into the night I slowly made my way up to where Rachel was huddled between two of the cars. We then found a cargo car and I used my hybrid claws to punch through the lock and let us in.

Reception for my cell phone had been much spottier than I'd counted on, but I still managed to get a series of texts through. The first one was to Mother asking her to go get Donovan if nobody else had found him yet and then I sent a couple to Jasmin with instructions on how we were going to meet back up. Once that was done I turned my phone back off and swapped sim cards again.

Rachel and I passed a quiet hour or so huddled on a couple of cardboard boxes before it was time for me to go back outside again. The best use of the lull would have been to start working through the accounts from Kaleb's safe and get as much money transferred away as possible, but I just couldn't bring myself to pull the tablet out after having come so close to dying.

The air was colder when I finally opened the door to the cargo car and worked my way to the top of the car Rachel was in. It took only a few minutes before Jasmin and the others were visible. They were strung out in a line almost a hundred yards apart from each other just as I'd instructed.

There was a bit of a grade on this section of the track, but nothing like the one that Rachel and I had used to get on the train. By my best estimate we were still doing in excess of forty miles an hour, but that was okay, James and the girls had their instructions and everything should work.

I climbed back down so that my feet were on the bottom rung of the ladder and then wrapped my right arm around another rung. Even after such a short time my arm was mostly healed, but I decided not to risk opening the wound back up. I'd already lost a lot of blood today.

I swung around so that I was looking down the track towards Jasmin and then waved until she saw me and waved back. She started a slow jog as soon as she saw me, and then sped up to an all-out sprint as I reached her.

"Jump on three!"

The count went smoothly and Jasmin jumped right on schedule. I grabbed her arms, plucking her out of the air and then pulling her over to the ladder so that she could get her feet under her.

"Rachel is in this car. Go ahead and go in so that there is room for the others."

Jasmin shook her head and anchored herself similarly to what I'd done.

"You're going to need help with James. Vincent beat the crap out of him. He's standing there, but you're not going to get any kind of speed or life out of him, it's pretty much going to be lifting dead weight."

I grunted in response and then it was time to pick Jess up. Things went even more smoothly then they had with Jasmin and as soon as I got ahold of her wrist Jasmin helped me lift her up onto the ladder.

Jessica climbed over the top of me so that I was sandwiched between the two of them. I took a deep, preparatory breath and had a second to revel in Jasmin and Jessica's scent. It was like being home again, but not the home I actually remembered from my childhood—a home where people I loved would take incredible risks to protect me and my sister.

An instant later we'd caught up with James and it was every bit as bad as I was afraid it would be. James tried to jump, I saw him go white from the effort, but he barely got his feet off of the ground.

I grabbed his outstretched hand and both of my arms nearly ripped out of their sockets. I think James screamed, but it was hard to tell over my own cry of pain, and then the girls had ahold of his arm and they were helping me pull him up to the ladder.

A few minutes later we were all inside of the cargo car with Rachel. Rachel hugged everyone and then gave them all a big, tearful thank you. We made James as comfortable as possible on a makeshift bed of boxes and then once he was asleep and Jessica was talking to Rachel, Jasmin turned to me.

"So what next, oh criminal mastermind?"

I fished the tablet and the ledger out of the backpack and then tossed the rest to her. She let out a low whistle as I hit the power button on the tablet and found that it did indeed still work.

"That's a lot of cash."

"A fifth of it belongs to you; don't go spending it all in one place."

She shook her head. "This wasn't about the money for any of us."

"I know it wasn't, but I need to know that you guys are all taken care of in case something happens to me."

I fired up the wireless connection and started looking for the login information for the first bank before I realized that I hadn't answered her question.

"We'll ride the train for another few hours and then we'll get off somewhere around Salt Lake City. I haven't had a chance to scout a spot yet, but if we jump off the same way that we got out of that helicopter we can afford to exit at a higher rate of speed than we got on at. Some of it will depend on how James is feeling by then."

Jasmin nodded, but she didn't seem satisfied with my answer.

"What about after that?"

"Well, we're going to spend some time consolidating all of the Graves resources that I can get my hands on, and then we're going to start a war. I'm going to do whatever it takes to bring down Kaleb and the Coun'hij."

Author's Note

This is one of those books that I probably shouldn't have written. I have a bad habit of doing that, unfortunately. From an income perspective, I should just write Alec and Adri books for as long as I can, but that's not the way I think.

As much as I love Alec and Adri, the Reflections series is more than that. There is a much larger story that needs to be told, and Dark Reflections is part of telling that. Bound is a great story in and of itself, but it also has let me start paving the road for even greater things to come. I couldn't do justice to Alec and Adri's story without writing the Dark Reflections books.

I hope you enjoyed Bound; Hunted will be out soon and will show us what was happening with Adri during this same block of time. If you haven't read the Reflections books yet please go pick up Broken, Torn and The Greater Darkness. There are some great stories in those books.

Acknowledgements

As always, there have been a lot of people who have helped make this book a reality. My editors, RJ Locksley and Amy Jirsa-Smith did stellar work just like they always do. My advance readers continue to provide much-needed feedback. Larry, Loa, Mark, Mimi, Matthew, Shalese and Kim have been joined by Chris—thank you one and all!

There isn't any getting around the fact that Katie is the glue that holds all of this together. Not only is she my first reader, she also puts in countless hours working on covers. All while keeping our daughters from starting the house on fire. Thanks, Katie, you're the best!

For Bound, the cover was actually done by Elle Casey, another indie writer who is a much bigger deal than I am, who was kind enough to give Katie and me a hand simply because she's an incredible person. You may want to check out her writing at www.ElleCasey.com. Thank you, Elle, for being so awesome.

Lastly, I want to say thanks to the many great fans out there who do so much to help spread the word about my books. Without all of you I'd be back working a day job by now and many of these stories probably wouldn't ever be written.

About the Author

Dean Murray is a prolific author with more than thirty titles across multiple pen names and more than half a million copies of his work currently in circulation.

Dean started reading seriously in the second grade due to a competition and has spent most of the subsequent three decades lost in other people's worlds.

Things worsened, or improved depending on your point of view, when he first started experimenting with writing while finishing up his accounting degree.

These days Dean has a wonderful wife and two lovely daughters to keep him rather more grounded, but the idea of bringing others along with him as he meets interesting new people in universes nobody else has ever seen tends to drag him back to his computer on a fairly regular basis.

Keep up to speed on Dean's latest projects at www.DeanWrites.com.

Torn

Shape shifter Alec Graves has spent nearly a decade trying to keep his family from being drawn into open warfare with a larger pack. The new girl at school shouldn't matter, but the more he gets to know her, the more mysterious she becomes. Worse, she seems to know things she shouldn't about his shadowy world.

Is she an unfortunate victim or bait designed to draw him into a fatal misstep? If she's a victim, then he's running out of time to save her. If she's bait, then his attraction to her will pull him into a fight that'll cost him everything.

The Greater Darkenss

Dean writing as Eldon Murphy

Something powerful is stirring in the darkness. Something so ancient that even creatures who've been alive for hundreds of years have long since discounted this new threat as nothing more than myth.

Normal humans will be caught in the crossfire, but then that's always the way of things. Geoffrey has no memory of his past life or any idea how to survive in the violent, dangerous world in which he's trapped. Despite his best efforts, he's about to find himself in the middle of a conflict that threatens to sweep away everything, and everyone he's been fighting so hard to protect.